Also by Bonnie Glover

The Middle Sister

Going Down South

One World

Ballantine Books

New York

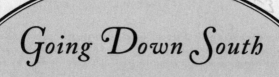

Going Down South

A NOVEL

Bonnie J. Glover

Bonnie J. Glover
2009

A One World Books Trade Paperback Original

Copyright © 2008 by Bonnie Glover
Reading group guide copyright © 2008 by Random House, Inc.

Published in the United States by One World, an imprint of The Random House Publishing Group, a division of Random House, Inc., New York.

ONE WORLD is a registered trademark and the One World colophon is a trademark of Random House, Inc.

READER'S CIRCLE and colophon are trademarks of Random House, Inc.

Library of Congress Cataloging-in-Publication Data

Glover, Bonnie J.
Going down south : a novel / Bonnie Glover.
p. cm.
ISBN 978-0-345-48091-0 (pbk.)
1. Teenage pregnancy—Fiction. 2. Mothers and daughters—Fiction.
3. Grandparent and child—Fiction. 4. Intergenerational relations—Fiction.
5. Alabama—Fiction. 6. Domestic fiction. I. Title.
PS3607.L68G65 2008
813'.6—dc22
2008005956

Printed in the United States of America

www.thereaderscircle.net

2 4 6 8 9 7 5 3

Book design by Karin Batten

This book is dedicated to four women whom I have loved and admired. They aren't with me on this physical plane any longer, but I carry them in my heart, and for now, that has to be enough.

Dorothy M. James, my mother
Lydia O. Laughinghouse, my aunt
Kathleen C. Freeble, my dear friend
Olga V. Glover, my mother-in-law

I miss you all, every day!

Some are kissing mothers and some are scolding mothers,
but it is love just the same.

—PEARL S. BUCK
(1892–1973)

PART ONE

Olivia Jean

Her father, Turk, went down first, holding his work boots by the strings with his overnight kit tucked under one arm. He walked on his toes, taking the seventh step down with a side maneuver because he knew it creaked. He had learned his lesson the hard way from her mother, Daisy, waiting at the top of the stairs one night about five years ago. His foot strayed and pressed ahead when he should have gone to the left or the right. He might have made it past her if it hadn't been for that step. She had dozed off, and there were ways to get around Daisy when she was asleep. But he was in no state to remember all of the things he should have remembered. And besides, Daisy was sitting with her legs flung across the top of the landing just so she could catch him. Clutched in her right hand was a broom leaning forward at a cockeyed slant, straw bottom down and ready to do damage.

That night in March, Olivia Jean had just passed her tenth birthday and should have been asleep when he touched lucky stair number seven and it whined loud enough to wake her mother. Daisy grunted, choking on a snore, and was on her feet lightning quick without even rubbing her eyes or wiping the thin line of drool at the corner of her mouth. She gripped the broom in both hands, turned it upside down, and swung it at Turk's copper-skinned head. He leaned away in time but she started at him again. Her robe fell open, and Olivia Jean saw long, thick legs under a nightgown that stopped near her coochie, and then one of her titties fell out as she lifted her arm and aimed again. Olivia Jean was crouched at the keyhole of her bedroom door, jaw wide, the scene surprising her so much that she banged her head against the doorknob as she tried to get a better view.

Daisy kept swinging as if she were trying to get at a spider in the corner or a big, fat cockroach that always appeared out of nowhere when company came to visit. There was rage in her swinging, rage reserved for bugs, bad impressions, and drunken husbands. Then her other titty bounced free, and Turk fell back, clutching the railing. It seemed as though he was as surprised as Olivia Jean was. In all her days Olivia Jean had never seen Daisy's girl parts, and seeing them then, when her mother was in the middle of trying to kill her daddy, was enough to freeze Olivia Jean right where she was—on her knees, peeking into the dim hallway when she should have been curled up asleep with her Raggedy Ann tucked under her arm.

That was when Olivia Jean took a deep breath, stood up, opened the door, and ran out of her bedroom. Turk wasn't grabbing the broom or telling Daisy to stop or trying to move away or anything. He had leaned back, dropped his arms, and let

Daisy continue to hit him with the broom across his shoulders, moving him backward as if she were going to push him down the stairs. Olivia Jean knew someone was going to call the police if they didn't stop. At four in the morning people should be in bed, going to bed, or at least thinking about going to bed, not on a rampage like Daisy was, beating Turk with the straw end of a broom while she danced around the hallway half-naked.

So when Daisy raised her broomstick higher, above her shoulders, aiming for the top of his head, Olivia Jean jumped in front of her father. No one moved. The only sound had been the swish of the broom as it waved through the air and its connection with Turk's body—a muffled *whack, whack, whack*—and, too, the sound of Daisy's heavy breathing from all the work she was doing beating Turk.

Now things were still except for Daisy's heaving shoulders and breasts. Olivia Jean felt her heart pounding so hard that she thought it might thud out of her chest.

Then Daisy smiled—one of those low-down smiles she used when she punished Olivia Jean—aimed the broom, and almost hit her daughter; the straw brushed the air, tickling the end of Olivia Jean's nose. Olivia Jean had felt the panic rising in the pit of her stomach as the broom swept toward her. Daisy laughed when Olivia Jean flinched. Daisy's breathing was hard, and Olivia Jean smelled the last cigarette Daisy had smoked and the Pond's face cream her mother rubbed into her elbows every night. She dropped the broom as Olivia Jean tried to shield Turk, her arms thrown out so that she covered a fraction of his belly. Daisy was giving him the evil eye the whole time, but he was busy ducking behind Olivia Jean as though Daisy were still hitting him, his hands in the air trying to block the broom she was no longer swinging at him. He didn't know Daisy had stopped. All of his moving almost made Olivia Jean fall off the landing; his daughter had to plant herself in front of him, solidly, and not move. Olivia Jean was close enough to smell his body, which reeked of underarm musk and day-old pee. She wrinkled her nose and tried not breathing for seconds at a time.

Olivia Jean moved away once the broom rested at Daisy's side. But she stayed near, trying not to glance at her mother's face, since it was frightening when the older woman tightened her lips, raised her eyebrows, and sucked in her cheeks. Olivia Jean was scared of what would come next, but she wasn't going to let Turk stand up to Daisy all by himself. He was her daddy, and even if Daisy did turn the broom on her, Olivia Jean was determined to take the beating. At ten years old, she loved Turk Stone with every ounce of heart she had in her thin body. And hated her mother with equal passion.

Daisy moved in close to Turk. She pointed a long finger at his chest. He had stopped twitching, but the eye he was able to keep open was streaked with red and the other was half-closed. He fell back against the wall.

"Damn, girl, stop slingin' them things around. I can't think straight watchin' 'em titties jumpin' at me all over the place. Close your robe," Turk said.

"Turk, I ain't playing with you, coming up in this house all hours of the night. You better stop this tomcatting around or I'ma stop you." Her voice never rose. It whispered slick across the hallway. The righteousness of it made Olivia Jean tremble. Daisy turned with the broom and swished back into the apartment. The girl heard the dead bolt turn with a sharp click, and then Turk and Olivia Jean were alone in the hallway.

"Don't worry, baby," he said as he sank to the floor on the second step. Olivia Jean sat down by him. He laid his head on her lap. Again she held her breath, because he smelled. As soon as he fell asleep, so that his head became heavy on her lap and his mouth opened with one long inhale that became a gasp for air, he woke himself up. "She ain't gonna stay mad. She let us in by day." Olivia Jean counted to 3,563 before the door opened.

Now Daisy was in flannel pajamas buttoned up to the top.

"Next time, don't get in the middle of grown-folk business." Daisy didn't meet Olivia Jean's gaze. She held a half-smoked cigarette in one hand along with her favorite ashtray, the one she swore was good crystal given to them by a Mr. Shorty Long when she and Turk married. This was the same ashtray she would sometimes throw at him when he came home from work too late.

"This ashtray," Daisy would say after each bout of throwing it at Turk, "is a testament to good, quality workmanship. The kind you don't get these days." There were dents in the wall and chipped linoleum on the floor from where Mr. Shorty Long's present had landed, but never even a hairline fracture in the crystal itself. Olivia Jean didn't know if it was a testament to good workmanship or just plain dumb luck that nothing had happened to it. She did know enough to stay out of the way when Daisy aimed at Turk, since Daisy didn't have a good aim.

Holding the ashtray in one hand and the cigarette in the other, she twisted a thumb in Olivia Jean's direction, her signal for Olivia Jean to hit the road, go to bed. It wasn't easy moving Turk's head from her lap. Daisy didn't help, but Olivia Jean didn't expect help from her.

When the girl crept out of bed the next morning and peeped

in the stairwell, Turk was still there, a blanket thrown over him, now using Daisy for a pillow. Olivia went back into her bedroom, slammed the door, and got ready for school.

*T*hat night in late August as they slipped out of their apartment and down the stairs, Daisy made Turk carry his shoes so his footsteps were barely heard, but there were other noises coming from his body. Because he was so big and uncoordinated, when he walked down the stairs his shoulders bumped against the wall, and his breathing was loud, like a fish gasping for air.

Olivia followed him with her traveling bag, but not too close. She owned one suitcase, a pink one with a poodle on the front that had real hair and two glued-on pink barrettes. The suitcase kept bumping her legs as she walked down the narrow flight of stairs.

Daisy shored up the rear, and every few steps she told the other two to "hush up" as though Turk, a grown man, and Olivia Jean, a teenager, were children on a field trip. Daisy was dressed especially for sneaking out of their apartment; she wore a tan A-line dress cinched at the waist with a wide belt, a camel-colored scarf over her head, and big rhinestone-studded sunglasses. In the middle of the night. Olivia Jean wanted to ask about the sunglasses, but she already knew what her mother would say: "Olivia Jean, the first thing people notice about you is your clothes. You've got to learn how to make a good impression."

Daisy toted a powder blue overnight case, and the color was too bad. Olivia Jean covered a smile when Daisy took it out of the closet and packed a nightgown, two changes of clothes, and makeup. What Daisy wore and the suitcase clashed. Olivia Jean knew it must have hurt her mother. But Daisy hadn't been able to let go of the dress or the high-heeled pumps that she carried. She looked like a movie star creeping down the stairs, except for the overnight case that shouted Pitkin Avenue all the way. Olivia Jean leaned forward to whisper to her daddy about wearing sunglasses in the dark. He would have, under other circumstances, turned and smiled with her, but she stopped short. Things were different, and Olivia Jean would have to get used to the way they were between her and her father now. She'd learned that a woman had to let loose of the past and concentrate on the present and the future.

Daisy's pumps echoed a snatch of color in her scarf, but they were run-over and scuffed from being worn every day but Sunday. She was careful to carry them in her hands like Turk carried his work boots. And really, there was something about both of them, acting the way they were, clutching their shoes tight to their chests so as to not make any noise, instead of having them on their feet, and sandwiching Olivia Jean in closer than she wanted to be, that made Olivia Jean ashamed. It was all for Olivia Jean and all because of her.

It was the middle of the night, about two a.m., and Daisy had said that they should leave like this, skulking down the dimly lit stairs like thieves in the night. They reached the bottom of the steps, and Turk swung open the first hallway door. There was a sharp squeal of rusty hinges, and Olivia Jean sighed. Turk had proved once more that he didn't have the ability to sneak and not be caught. Before he could put his foot over the threshold, the basement door opened and their neighbor Miss Chessman appeared. Her hair was done up in large pink rollers, but in the front was one curl that was plastered to her forehead with Dippity-

Do. She clutched a pink bathrobe against her skinny bones, the air being cool in the hallway and Miss Chessman being a mostly modest woman.

"Y'all going somewhere?"

"Ah, Miss Chessman. Sorry we woke you. We sure didn't mean to wake anybody up at this hour." Turk smiled at her and bent to put his shoes on, still smiling while he tied the laces. She tightened her robe and held it closed, and as he stood she eased back toward the entryway of her apartment, her hands on the doorknob, her face confused with sleep.

Turk acted charming to all women. Charm oozed out of him like Karo syrup, heavy, smooth, and sweet on a plate of buckwheat pancakes. But that night, in front of their neighbor Miss Chessman, he was the best ever. Olivia Jean would have laughed, except she liked Miss Chessman and knew that Miss Chessman liked Turk and the way he spoke to her and looked her in the eyes as if she were a very important person to him.

"We got word Daisy's mama ain't doing so good, so we headed down south to see about her."

"I'm sorry to hear that, Mrs. Stone. You take care of your mama now. You only get one."

Miss Chessman looked over Turk's shoulder to talk to Daisy and nodded. Miss Chessman and Daisy had had words. They generally did not speak.

"Y'all be careful on the road, now. You call me if you can't get home by the first and I'll be sure to let Mr. Willie Boyd know." Mr. Willie Boyd was the landlord and he lived on the first floor, as opposed to Mr. Jerry Boyd, his brother, who lived on the third floor. Olivia Jean knew Mr. Willie hadn't heard them creeping down the stairs or else Turk's fast-talking wouldn't have gotten them anywhere. Turk's sweet ways didn't work as well with men as they did with women.

"Um, you gonna stay with your mama, Mrs. Stone? Mr. Stone, you comin' back?" Olivia Jean was standing on Daisy's side and saw her mother's face as Miss Chessman held the doorknob to her apartment with fingers that reminded her of a bird's feet, skinny, long fingers, nervously moving from the door to her robe. Restless fingers.

Daisy stopped in front of Miss Chessman, boldly throwing back her shoulders and shaking her hair. She flipped her sunglasses up to her forehead and studied the smaller, leaner woman.

"We'll be back soon. Mr. Stone and I will, that is. Olivia Jean is gonna stay with her grandma. So don't you worry about us. We'll be back before the first."

Daisy was impatient to leave after she finished speaking, and she reached to push Olivia Jean out of the door. Olivia Jean had been staring at Miss Chessman's face, looking at her jaw, the tightness around her mouth that meant she was uncomfortable. Then Miss Chessman caught Olivia Jean's gaze and looked at her, at her stomach area; then her eyes darted back to the girl's face, but that made Olivia Jean know that she knew, and she began staring at Miss Chessman's neck instead of in her eyes. It was a reed-thin neck, corded and strong.

Daisy pushed again, so that Turk, who was waiting for them across the threshold, had to catch Olivia Jean to keep her from falling. As soon as she was steady his hands fell from around her waist and he picked up his overnight kit. He walked on to the car.

"Didn't mean to be so rough. You better hurry on so we can

get on the road. Good thing your daddy caught you like he did," said Daisy.

Turk opened the trunk of the Chrysler, threw his kit in, and waited for Daisy to hand him her overnight bag. While Daisy slipped on her shoes, he opened the passenger door for her and she slid in. Olivia Jean climbed into the backseat with her poodle suitcase, because Turk hadn't asked for it and had slammed the trunk down before she could give it to him. As they pulled away from the curb, Olivia Jean turned to get a last glimpse of the only place she'd ever lived in. She waved to the house and to the little woman in the doorway, Miss Adele Chessman, who had been her friend.

There was the neighborhood to drive through first, Brooklyn streets, narrow, lined with aged trees and even older buildings. On successive blocks they saw trees spaced to sit in between every other house. Families shared them; children carved their initials in them and played ring-around-the-rosy, holding hands and running around the dark gray bark with their sturdy brown legs; adults put chairs to sit underneath them when the afternoon sun began to sink and the rustle of the leaves announced the beginnings of cool Friday evenings. Those were Olivia Jean's favorite times, lazy summer nights spent on the sidewalk; Daisy sending her around the corner to get cigarettes, a can of beer, and a scoop of ice cream—butter pecan or vanilla, enough for a double-dip cone.

In the back of the car, enfolded in the darkness, Olivia Jean cried, one hand over her mouth, a soiled tissue balled in the other. They had told her only yesterday that she had to leave. One of the neighbors had asked Daisy if Olivia Jean was picking up weight. The way Daisy told it, there was knowledge in that question, with a sly look on the other woman's face and the way the woman's eyes darted without meeting hers. The neighbor, Mrs. Gloria Miles, was known for her mouth's ability to suck a person dry once she latched onto some juicy gossip. And Olivia Jean, a straight-A student and the daughter of Daisy and Turk Stone, was juicy, mainly because of her fall from grace, and secondarily because of Daisy, a well-disliked woman in the neighborhood. Daisy was afraid that Olivia's secret was going to come spilling out and that her daughter would be laughed at and mocked, unable to go to normal school and graduate. And even though she didn't say it outright, Daisy was afraid Olivia Jean would become a "rotten egg" and start having baby after baby. Daisy told Olivia Jean that if she went down south she could have the baby, and then somehow they would manage her return home. When Olivia Jean told her mother that she didn't care, that she didn't want to leave New York, Daisy glared at her and told her that she wasn't old enough to understand. Turk had sat still, on the edge of his seat in the living room, and Olivia Jean couldn't tell if he was listening to the conversation or not. When Daisy got tired of Olivia Jean's arguing, she folded her arms and told her to "go start packing." Olivia Jean glanced her father's way, but Daisy had been there first, and Olivia Jean couldn't get him to see her anymore. Olivia gave up then. Without him she knew she was alone.

As Olivia Jean rode in the backseat, headed for Cold Water Springs, Alabama, and her mother's mother, memories of her life in New York swept by as the shadows unfolded and disappeared in the predawn light. She kept wondering why things had turned out so different from the way she pictured they would; she'd had big plans, dreams. Olivia Jean had wanted to be a

Nellie Bly and travel the world, or a Lena Horne and travel the world, even if she couldn't sing and wasn't nearly as beautiful. Now she was going to be a mother.

And, of course, Olivia Jean thought of her father and how bad it was to have disappointed him. He could barely look in her direction, and there were a hundred little things every day that showed her that he hated her. Olivia Jean sank into the backseat and gave herself over to thinking about her problems; her father was near the top of a long list.

Turk Stone was a singing man. Daisy had said many a time that she couldn't stay angry when he sang. He'd start low, and his chin fell into his chest as if there were something caught there, and for a minute he looked like a bullfrog, with a puffed-up neck and wide pop eyes. And then suddenly he raised his head and the song rolled out, rich and pure, sounding so proper, making a body want to sit down somewhere and listen. He sang songs he said he'd heard while watching old movies that starred a man named Mario Lanza. Olivia Jean heard him sing "Arrivederci Roma," and she cried because it was like he was singing goodbye to her. Sometimes he made songs up. They were mostly love songs to Daisy. One time he sang about how much he loved a sassy-tailed girl named Daisy, and Daisy reached into her pocketbook and gave Olivia Jean a dollar to go to the store and get some ice cream. She said that Olivia Jean could go over to the park to play, too. And there were other songs, too, Turk sang and moaned in the night as if Daisy had got him by the heart and was ripping it up piece by piece. He stood by their bedroom door once and sang these words:

Oh, why can't you love me like I want you to love me?
And why can't I love you like you want me to love you?
I guess we're just fooling ourselves,
Playing at love instead of being in love,
Always taking the love instead of giving it back.
And my heart is breaking, just like yours is
Because we're just fooling ourselves
Playing at love instead of being in love. . . .

And Olivia Jean watched him slide to the floor after he sang and fall asleep there. She was six years old then and still in love with him. Olivia Jean had gotten her pillow from her room and a blanket from the closet. She covered him so he wouldn't feel a draft and stuffed her pillow under his great bull neck. She went to sleep on the sofa, and the next morning, when she awoke, Turk was in the bedroom with Daisy and she was alone. Olivia Jean made a bowl of oatmeal, turned on the radio, and waited for the mattress springs to stop singing before she knocked.

Olivia Jean watched the Holland Tunnel as the off-white tile walls rushed by on either side of the car. The sound inside the tunnel with the windows down was a continuous roar of wind and metal, rubber tires thundering over concrete. She held her hands over her ears. They needed the car windows open because Daisy insisted on smoking as they ran away. Daisy's scarf kept flying back, and Olivia Jean had to keep batting at it to keep it from covering her face. They were on their way down south, and Olivia Jean was scared.

She leaned to the right to stop Daisy's scarf from tickling her nose and finally closed her eyes to the wind that whipped across her face and thought of Miss Chessman, the lone person to see them sneak out that morning. The trouble between Daisy and Miss Chessman had started when Olivia Jean was thirteen. Back then they didn't care for each other but they were civil, nodding as they passed in the hallway and asking about things like the weather and when the rent man was due to come and collect. Olivia Jean heard them laughing once because both of them hit the number at the same time. Old Mr. Charlie Brown was mad that he had to pay two times at one house.

But things started to heat up between the two of them when Olivia Jean stayed home from school one day because she was having trouble with her stomach. She'd noticed there were brown stains in her panties that she couldn't completely wash out, and she didn't know what to do. Crossing her legs tightly hadn't helped, neither had stuffing her underwear with toilet paper. She decided to stay home and see if there wasn't some way for her to fix things so that she would stop messing in her drawers. On the morning Olivia Jean slept in from school, when she got up to go pee, she screamed. There was blood in the toilet. She screamed and screamed and screamed. She knew she was dying.

There was a pounding at the door that she heard through her hollering. The noise surprised her so that she stopped midhowl. There was banging hard enough to pop the door off its hinges and yelling loud enough to match Olivia Jean's. "Olivia Jean, open this door. Let me in right now." Olivia Jean fell to the linoleum and crawled through the hallway to the door. She thought that if she stood, the bleeding might keep on and the life would pour right out from between her legs. She managed to pull herself up with the help of the doorknob, turn the dead bolt, and unhook the chain; all the while there was a steady thud against the door, and when Olivia Jean finally opened up, Miss Chessman fell in and knocked her down to the floor again. They were a mass of pink bathrobes and elbows.

"Baby, what is wrong? What's wrong with you?" Miss Chessman grabbed her by the arms when they both managed sitting positions on the floor. Olivia Jean noted that the woman's boniness didn't stop her from having strength and a firm grip.

"I'm bleeding," she managed to say as she wiped the tears from her face. "I'm bleeding to death"—and Olivia Jean pointed to the place between her thighs—"down there." She lifted her skirt and turned her head, afraid to look at the pool of blood that must have formed while she was on the floor.

The grip on her shoulder loosened and Miss Chessman was quiet—so quiet that Olivia Jean stopped crying and opened one eye to see what Miss Chessman was doing. Had she already started flying through the apartment to the phone, kicking things out of the way, calling for an ambulance? And then what about nursing her until help arrived? But Miss Chessman's little mouth and dirt-brown face didn't look concerned. In fact, she was trying not to smile. Her lips were pulled together in a pout as though she was getting ready to laugh. And there Olivia Jean was, dying.

"Miss Chessman, did you hear me? I'm bleeding." The girl leaned forward to whisper and point once more. "Down there."

"Baby, didn't your mama teach you anything?" asked Miss Chessman.

She took Olivia Jean by the shoulders, hugged her, and led her to the bathroom. When they got there, Miss Chessman explained about having a monthly cycle: that it wasn't a matter of controlling herself, and that what Olivia Jean saw in the toilet was not some new variety of shit or blood that came from a deep wound, and that she would be all right. Olivia Jean began crying again and threw up on Miss Chessman: on the front of her robe, on her slippers, on the floor. Miss Chessman still smiled and held her hand and kept telling her that things would be fine and that she was now a young lady, a woman.

After she helped Olivia Jean clean up, Miss Chessman left a note for Daisy telling her where to find her daughter, and they went downstairs to the basement apartment. She fed Olivia Jean little sandwiches with cheese and tea with honey to ease her stomach. And she told Olivia Jean some more about being a woman and that she should expect to bleed every month. The girl rubbed her belly and put her hand to her mouth, getting ready to throw up again, so Miss Chessman stopped. Olivia Jean decided that she was not looking forward to being a woman, and by then she'd figured out what the Bible meant when it said that God cursed Eve.

Olivia Jean fell asleep waiting for Daisy to come home from work. Her mother was employed as a seamstress in a department store in downtown Brooklyn called Abraham & Straus. Daisy said that what she did was to make fat women look skinnier and skinny women look normal.

As they waited for Daisy, Miss Chessman opened the window to let in some air. Olivia Jean wondered why she had ever thought that the basement apartment was gloomy. The sofa was under the window, and Olivia Jean listened to the sounds— women walking in high-heeled shoes, scraping the sidewalk, children running in the streets and yelling with pleasure as they played freeze tag or double Dutch or handball against the solid stone wall of the monument factory at the end of the block. Olivia Jean was a caterpillar in a cocoon waiting patiently for her mother. She awoke to Daisy shaking her shoulder, hard.

"Get up. It's time to go home. Thank Miss Chessman now for her hospitality so we can leave." There was no smile on her mother's face. Her eyes were narrow and cold, as though she had seen something she disliked. She jerked the blanket off Olivia Jean, grabbed her arm, and pulled her from the sofa.

"Now, Mrs. Stone, there's no need for you to be so hard on the girl. She had a scare was all, and I was happy to let her stay with me until you got home." Sometimes Daisy looked so hard at Olivia Jean that she wanted to curl into a ball and hide. That was the kind of look Daisy leveled on Miss Chessman.

"Miss Chessman, I told you already how much I am beholden to you for helping Olivia Jean out today. But I would appreciate it if you would stay out of our business from now on."

Olivia Jean got angry then, the heat rising from her stomach to suffuse her face. She snatched her arm from Daisy and returned a cold look to her mother. She smoothed down her dress and walked over to Miss Chessman, knowing that when she and her mother got upstairs Daisy was going to beat her with her tongue.

"Thank you, Miss Chessman, for helping me today." Olivia Jean put her arm around Miss Chessman and kissed her on the cheek. Olivia Jean never kissed Daisy. Daisy had told her once that she didn't like people slobbering all over her and that she was glad Olivia Jean was not the type of child who needed to be kissed or held all the time. Since that conversation, Olivia Jean had kept her distance and reserved her hugs and pecks for Turk.

Upstairs, Daisy slammed the door so hard a small piece of wood splintered off and landed on the floor between them.

"Don't you ever do that to me again," said Daisy.

"Do what?"

"Embarrass me like that. How you not know about your monthly? Ain't I been telling you?" Daisy's face was tight.

"Mama, I was scared and I didn't know what was happening. I must have forgot what you told me. All I knew was that I was bleeding."

Daisy stopped circling her daughter. She sighed, and Olivia Jean knew she'd somehow let her mother down, not knowing what she should have known.

"Let me get you some rags. You need to start a drawer for 'em. I'll get you a belt tomorrow. And now you got to remember—don't go letting no boys put their hands under your dress." When Daisy said that Olivia Jean was confused. Why would she let a boy put a hand under her dress?

Daisy's fingers massaged the place between her eyebrows, and Olivia Jean thought she looked old and tired. But nothing would make her forgive her mother for how she had spoken to Miss Chessman, or the way her mother's hands had so roughly touched her in the little woman's basement apartment.

"And don't you go to that woman for help no more. She ain't nuthin' but a bitch in heat an' I don' want her near my family."

Turk came in late, but Olivia Jean didn't wait up for him. She didn't want to hug him and didn't want him to know about her monthly curses. When he opened her bedroom door and stepped inside she pretended to be asleep. He left after a few minutes.

When Olivia Jean finally drifted off she dreamed of bleeding, rags, and barking dogs in heat separated when buckets of water were thrown on them. But it was Daisy's face she saw instead of a snout. Daisy was the bitch in heat. When Olivia Jean woke up in the morning, there was a bundle of old cloths on her dresser, and she got ready for school, fixing herself up as best she could like Miss Chessman showed her so that she wouldn't spot through her clothes.

Night faded, and there was a chill in the morning air even though it was summer. They called it an Indian summer because it was to last longer and the leaves were to stay on the trees and gust down later, right after the cusp of September and October. Now the windows were up in the car and the radio was turned down low, but Olivia couldn't make out the music except that she knew that it was not any of the new songs from groups she liked because Daddy didn't like them. When she had asked him once about trying something different, he claimed that the new lyrics were flimsy and didn't speak to his heart.

Daisy was talking to him, her voice as low as the radio. Olivia Jean could only barely make out what she was saying.

"Turk, you can't keep on treatin' her like this. We gonna be leavin' her down there, and you gotta speak to her before we drop her off. It ain't right that you treat your own flesh an' blood like she don't matter no more."

All of Olivia Jean strained to hear his reply. But there wasn't one. Nothing except louder music. She saw him turn up the volume. The Platters were singing "Smoke Gets in Your Eyes," and she guessed that he didn't think their lyrics were too flimsy. He kept the station on.

• • •

*T*urk named his Chrysler Sally. He said she looked like a Sally, bright red and hot. Daisy had thumped him on the head for that remark, a loud plunking sound that made him howl and bend over, but Olivia Jean knew better than to think it hurt. Daisy had thumped her on the head a couple of times, and she didn't have the fingers to do much damage. Olivia Jean's hurts lingered when Daisy had grabbed something to use or laid her five fingers on her behind. Those were the times that she had learned to get out of the way.

Olivia Jean was almost thirteen the Sunday Turk brought Sally home, a 1958 Chrysler Saratoga hardtop. A dream car. A car that Daisy, Olivia Jean, and Turk saw on television commercials. A car, Turk explained, with 325 horsepower under its hood, enough to make any man proud.

That evening Olivia Jean and Daisy were in the kitchen. Daisy had fried up some whiting and made a batch of potato salad, and they had a couple of slices each of light bread from the corner store. Olivia Jean had a cup of milk, and Daisy had pulled the tab on a can of beer when they heard Turk's voice booming upstairs.

"Daisy, Daisy Stone, get your butt down here." Daisy didn't pause in the pouring of her beer, glass tilted to the side so that the foam wouldn't run over and spill on the Formica table. Turk was quiet for a minute, but then he started yelling upstairs again.

"Did you hear me, woman? Don't make me climb up these stairs. Both y'all get down here right now. Come on down, Olivia Jean."

Olivia Jean was sitting on the edge of her seat, ready to fly down the stairs. She eyed her mother. Daisy didn't seem to understand that it was Turk calling them.

"Finish your plate, Olivia Jean. We having Sunday dinner. If your father cares to join us, he can come on. But we finishing our food."

Daisy's mouth, generally full and red with lipstick, was thin, pursed, and there were no dimples showing on either side of her cheeks. Olivia Jean was trapped at the dinner table imagining running downstairs to her father. She picked at the fish, poking it with a fork. When Daisy cleared her throat, Olivia Jean looked up, hoping that she had changed her mind. After all, they hadn't seen Turk since he left for work on Friday.

There were three doors off the main hallway that led into their apartment. There was Olivia Jean's bedroom door, the living room door, and the kitchen, closest to the second-floor landing. They were hardly ever locked. While Olivia Jean sat and chewed on her whiting and tried to make sure a bone didn't get stuck in her throat, Daisy rose and headed to the kitchen door. Turk climbed the steps, his breathing loud, his feet falling heavy on the way up. He paused to rest after he hit step number seven. Daisy turned the lock on the kitchen door and was heading for the living room when Olivia Jean spoke.

"Mama, your food getting cold."

"Don't you worry about my food. Just make sure you clean your plate. That's what you got to do for me. And don't be getting up from no seat until you do. You hear me?" When she came back to the kitchen table there was almost a smile on her face. She had managed to lock all of the doors before Turk could get through one. Daisy was a mean one when you got her fired-up angry, thought Olivia Jean. Turk should never have stayed away two days in a row.

He pounded on the door. He yelled. And with her eyes alone Daisy kept Olivia Jean sitting, pushing the fish around and spearing eggs from the potato salad. When he finally burst through the kitchen door, Olivia Jean choked. Daisy used her knife and fork to cut a piece of fish and held it to her mouth.

"Turk, we just having us some dinner. Care to join your wife and your daughter? That you ain't seen in two days?" She had been calm until she hit the part about the two days. She turned to him with the fork in her hand.

Turk laughed. "Daisy, you is the craziest woman I do know. Put that down and come on and see what I done brought you."

She threw the fork at him and turned back in her seat to face Olivia Jean and folded her arms against her chest. Daisy started to cry, and Olivia Jean was amazed at how quickly her mother became ugly. Her face turned red and blotchy. Her nose was runny, and as she wiped her eyes streaks of mascara smudged and sat on her cheekbones.

"Oh, Daisy, baby, ain't no need to cry. You know I ain't never gonna leave you and Olivia Jean. Never. I just had to take care of some business. A man gotta get away from y'all women sometimes, you know. I can't stay up under you like you want. I ain't no housebroke man. You been knowing that."

He put one of his hands on her neck and rubbed it until her sobs stopped. Olivia Jean could not look at either of them. The wallpaper in the kitchen was faded, but near the stove it was discolored from the grease popping out of the skillet Daisy used to fry chicken and fish. The wallpaper was buckled where Daisy had tried to use a sponge to wipe it off, and the color ran so that there was no design in some spots. In other places the wall showed bald. Olivia Jean wondered how it had looked years ago, when they first moved in. She had never lived anyplace else.

Daisy took a good bit of time before she spoke. She reached for her beer and gulped down some as Turk's hands continued to travel on her neck and shoulders. Olivia Jean was ready to excuse herself. Turk's bloodshot eyes did not see her. He was busy with Daisy.

"Where were you, Turk?"

He spun her chair around to him and bent down close to her face, almost nose-to-nose. Olivia Jean wondered what he smelled of. Old Spice and whiskey? Cigarettes? Denial?

"I was busy winning you"—and he glanced up to catch his daughter's eye and nod—"and you a new car." He grabbed Daisy and pulled her out of her seat. "Come on; that's what I was try-ing to get you shiftless women to come on downstairs and see. I got a little present for y'all."

Olivia Jean could see her mother. The woman was trembling. Turk had to steady her to get her walking to the door, but Olivia Jean couldn't wait and cut in front of them and was down the stairs, jumping when she got to the last three steps. Olivia Jean was singing inside with excitement. *Daddy got us a car! Daddy got us a car!*

And she was beautiful. Fiery red with sleek whitewalled tires and fins. There was already a crowd around her, kids up close and leaning inside because Turk had left the windows down. An old man from up the block pursed his lips together and whistled. It was more beautiful than a preacher's car. It could have been a preacher's car. Silver and red. Olivia Jean's fingers touched the beige interior, and she turned to ask Turk if the car was really theirs, but he was too busy with Daisy, who was crying again.

"See, Daisy, I caught me a number an' used that to stake me in this game with Junnie Lee King. I won big and then went over to the car lot an' got us this beauty. She all paid for, too. I wanted my redbone woman to have a red car."

And just like that the joy flat-out left Olivia Jean, and she stepped back from the car. It was one thing to know that she was second to Daisy, but she was tired of hearing it and being it. And that part about her mother being redbone. That had hurt. Olivia Jean couldn't help it if she wasn't light-skinned. She was dark to the bone. Nothing about her was like Daisy.

Olivia Jean watched as Daisy got in the driver's seat and raised her arms, letting her fingers trail over the back of the headrest while she stuck her chest out. The men in the crowd drew closer. A woman with an ugly mouth pretended to spit in the car. Daisy didn't notice, but Olivia Jean did and gave the woman a look so dirty that the woman lost herself in the crowd and melted away. Daisy continued to touch the seats and *ahh*ed at the softness of the leather under her fingers. A few men wondered aloud how much the Chrysler had set Turk back, and Olivia Jean wondered how soon Daisy would be finished showing off.

"Baby girl, you can get in, too. Go on, get in next to your mama." Turk nudged Olivia Jean to the car but his eyes were on Daisy and the fun she was having running her hands over everything and playing with all the buttons on the dashboard. Olivia Jean hesitated and dragged her feet when approaching the passenger side. That last remark about getting a red car for his redbone woman had made her uncomfortable; this was a car for Daisy, and Olivia Jean was incidental.

"C'mon, baby. Get in here with me." Daisy was grinning now, the light back in her eyes, her skin flushed from excitement. There were still mascara marks on her cheeks, but it didn't make a difference. She was still beautiful. Olivia Jean forgave the red-bone comment. The car was too pretty for her to stay away from. When she settled into the passenger side, Daisy became Batman and Olivia Jean imagined herself as the old butler, Alfred Penny-worth. But at least she was in the story again. She consoled herself with the fact that being in the story was better than being left out.

Despite the fact that Daisy's hands had roamed the entire dashboard and all the buttons, Olivia Jean was hesitant, afraid to touch anything. Daisy put the key in the ignition, turned the engine over, and started the windshield wipers. The new-car smell surrounded Olivia Jean; she breathed deeply. Her fingers dipped out of the side to touch the paint. She leaned over, through the window that was down, and kissed it. A man laughed, and Olivia Jean had to smile at him. Getting Sally had to be the most exciting thing that had happened to her in all of her thirteen years. The Stone family had a car. Hardly anybody on the block had a car, and no one had a red car with fins and gleaming silver rims.

"Humph. Coulda put a down payment on a house 'stead of wastin' money like that on a car. Probably that Daisy's fault; you know how she act. Like she too good to take the train like every-body else." Daisy had been chatting to someone, but she stopped as Miss Chessman's voice rose to almost a shout above the neighbors' din outside of their apartment building. And the crowd, taking its signal from Daisy, stopped talking and moved aside so that they could all get a clear view of Adele Chessman and her meager figure. Olivia Jean could feel a blazing streak of bad feeling cross between the two women. She couldn't understand why Miss Chessman had something bad to say in public.

"Miss Chessman, my husband does think I'm too good to catch a train. That's why I married him. He takes good care of me. Bought me a beautiful car and everything. You need to get yourself one." Mama opened the door and walked around the back of the car, her fingers trailing over the fin, her behind shaking, little slow jiggles. She stopped in front of Miss Chessman and leaned forward. "A man, I mean. Of your own. Maybe then you could get yourself a car, too, like I did."

The men laughed because it was absurd to think Miss Chessman could ever be like Daisy. They were night and day, one a dry piece of bread, the other a thick pork chop with dripping gravy. And Olivia Jean thought that Daisy was where she loved to be, in the spotlight. She was best with men around her, laughing. No one could tell a body where to step off better than Daisy, no one could poke fun better than her, and no one looked better than her, with her light-skinned golden body, thick legs, and high butt. Despite the things that gnawed on her about Daisy, Olivia Jean was proud of her mother's looks. Hadn't her daddy always said that Daisy was a prize he'd won unexpectedly? Like getting Sally or hitting the numbers on a day when all you had in your pockets was a little bit of lint and an old peppermint candy?

Miss Chessman turned and ran up the steps of the apartment building. And even though Olivia Jean thought she was mean for starting things up, she felt sorry for the little woman, too. Daisy always held up better compared to less beautiful women. And for where they were, in a thicket of men, Daisy would always win, even if she didn't open her mouth to say a word.

At the door Miss Chessman hesitated and turned back to Daisy, who stood at the bottom with her hands on her hips.

"Ain't nobody mean no harm. I was just making a comment, is all. About what you could do with a good piece of money."

"Sister, you could do with a good piece of something, that's for sure."

That made the men in the crowd roar, and Miss Chessman ran into the house.

Daisy turned back to the car and stroked it once, lovingly, as perhaps she might have stroked Turk's bald head. He was standing next to her. She grabbed him by the face and kissed him full on the mouth until Olivia Jean heard a sigh from someone in the crowd.

"Baby, you deserve that and a whole lot more. See you soon, huh?" she said to him. Her hand trailed along the side of his face.

"I'll be upstairs in a minute," he said.

Everyone held their breath, watching Daisy twist herself up the stairs, deliberate and slow enough to keep the men staring. She didn't call to Olivia Jean to follow; in fact, she didn't look for her daughter at all. So Olivia Jean hung back and watched the men clap Turk on the back for having Sally and Daisy.

She heard one man say, "Brother, you is one lucky son o' bitch," and Turk laughed, loud and deep, and made his way to the same steps that Daisy had sashayed up a few minutes before.

"Friends"—he turned to the crowd—"I would tell you that I'll see you later, but God knows what Daisy's got planned for me."

"Go on and do your job, Turk. For alls us that can't," said Mr. Willie Boyd, a short man with a flowered shirt, and their landlord for years.

"Or don't want to," shouted Mr. Perry Harry, whose wife was tall and mean and was thought to beat him when she got a good taste of applejack on Friday nights.

Olivia Jean waited until the crowd dispersed, then ran her hands along the car, just as her mother had, and headed for the library, wondering if her copy of *Peyton Place* was still where she'd left it hidden in the nonfiction stacks. The librarian had screwed up her face when she went to check it out and wouldn't stamp the book, telling her that she'd have to find something "more appropriate to borrow." That was when Olivia Jean smiled at the woman behind the desk and went and hid it. She couldn't think of another book in the world that would beat out her mother and father for the drama they put on every day.

Their first stop was less than three hours into the drive. They had been on the highway, and Daisy began to complain that she needed some cigarettes. While Turk stopped in Pennsylvania and bought her a carton, she managed to change into blue pedal pushers and a top that fell off one shoulder. She said her tan dress was too hot and uncomfortable. Olivia watched while she wriggled her butt into the high-water pants and wondered if her mother would be embarrassed if someone came along and got a peek at her undressing and dressing again. But she could imagine Daisy if she had gotten caught:

"Oh, ain't this your lucky day. Guess I better hurry up and cover up. It's a little chilly out here." And then she'd give the man a big honey smile, and he'd have to smile right back, because few men frowned at Daisy for long. If she got caught, it needed to be by a woman, Olivia Jean thought. Daisy wouldn't know what to say to a woman.

Turk's window was open in the car as they made their way down the highway faster than he had ever driven them in New York. Daisy was smoking Pall Malls and flicking the ashes out of the window. One time the ash came straight back at Olivia Jean and landed in her mouth. Her mouth had been open, tasting the air, as she wondered if there was any difference between this air outside of New York and the air in New York. She gagged when the cigarette ashes blew into her mouth, the saltiness melting on her tongue quickly, even though she tried to spit. Her imagination was vivid, and she pictured Daisy in a movie, starring as the mama bird, and herself as the baby bird, Daisy feeding her ashes instead of nourishing worms. Then the picture shifted and Olivia Jean became the mama bird, feeding her own baby. Olivia Jean had a bottle, and little droplets of milk poured from it down the tiny baby bird's throat. She was not going to feed her baby ashes or worms. She was going to have milk, the very best thing in the world for a growing baby. Olivia Jean rubbed her stomach.

"How long do I have to stay down to Grandma Birdie's?" Olivia Jean yelled over the noise of the highway.

"Until the baby comes, maybe a little longer. We need some time to figure out what we gonna do," said Daisy.

Daisy turned in her seat and their eyes met, but Olivia Jean knew how to discourage her mother from speaking. She was angry with Daisy. Not for the same reasons she was angry with Turk. Olivia Jean was upset because Turk wasn't talking to her or forgiving her for getting in the family way. No, Olivia Jean was angry with Daisy for deciding that she had to leave New York, and for being the one Turk loved no matter what. Brooms across his body didn't matter; ashtrays thrown at his head didn't matter. All the things that Daisy had ever done to him could be forgiven, but not Olivia Jean's mistake. The fact that she had always done her best to protect her father weighed down on top of her chest, and Olivia Jean sighed as Sally raced through the countryside.

Night was gone. They passed open fields, animals. Cows flicked their tails; horses bent to nibble at the grass. With the window down she smelled the greenness, felt the wind against her skin as she held her hand out of the window. She saw the beauty in pastureland, land not filled with houses or paved with concrete. Turk did not slow, his foot pressed steadily on the gas pedal, and Daisy did not seem to notice the beauty either, her mouth belching smoke like a chimney.

"Honey, you don't need to tell nobody in Cold Water Springs about you being in the family way." They were at a Phillips 66 Station near the border of West Virginia when Daisy spoke. Olivia Jean's eyes were on the gasoline pump, the white numbers rolling up and up, stopping finally with a little ping so they knew when the tank was full. She wondered how they did that, made numbers that rolled and rolled on the pump like the speedometer in the car. But Olivia Jean couldn't figure how the machine worked and finally gave up, deciding instead to focus on what Daisy was telling her.

Olivia Jean knew that she would stay in the country with Grandma Birdie and then they would tell her if or when she could return home. But what if no one ever said anything? She was panicked at the prospect of never seeing her room again or playing her record player to listen to Smokey or Gladys Knight and the Pips. And then there was a big problem, the one she couldn't bring herself to think about for too long. What were they planning for this baby? Was she going to be able to keep her? The baby knotted in her stomach as if Olivia Jean's thoughts made her curl into a ball.

"What happens when the people in Cold Water Springs notice? I'm gonna get bigger soon, right?"

Daisy had a cigarette dangling from the side of her mouth, and her hair moved with the summer breeze behind her. The rhinestone sunglasses she wore shielded her eyes, but her voice was tough, scratchy. She moved closer and clutched Olivia Jean's shoulders for a moment, staring her daughter deep in the eyes, but Olivia Jean couldn't see what her mother was trying to say because of the glasses. Daisy turned away to take a puff and spewed it back out.

"Okay, look, I have an idea; take this." She threw her cigarette to the ground and put it out with the tip of her shoe. Then she opened her purse and began to hunt. Small papers fluttered away while she was digging, and all the while she was saying little curse words under her breath like *damn* and *hell*. When she finally had what she was looking for, she paused before handing it to Olivia Jean.

"Wear this," she said, laying a plain gold wedding ring on the palm of her daughter's hand. "I bought it special for you before we left. Thought it might help things a little if you and Grandma Birdie tell folks you married, just come down to visit and all. And wear them big dresses I got you from downtown. Ain't no need for folks to know your business."

Olivia Jean turned back to the car. Turk had a foot on the front whitewall tire and was drinking a Nehi orange soda. A few weeks ago Olivia Jean would have teased him out of the last swallow and he would have laughed. Now she got in the car and slammed the door, taking advantage of the fact that he was not speaking to her, because otherwise Turk would have said something about the way the door was handled. She heard him call to Daisy to hurry up so that they could get on the road again.

In the backseat, Olivia Jean slid the ring onto her finger, the fourth finger of her left hand, where Daisy wore hers, and felt some better, as if having the ring had somehow changed things. Maybe she'd ask Daisy to pick out a new last name, too, since she needed one. Was her husband a Mr. Cleveland or a Mr. Green? Or could she have an exotic name like Ludwig, a principal at her old grade school? She'd ask Daisy. And even though Olivia Jean was angry with her, she thought that when she was older she wanted to be as smart as Daisy. She wanted to be smart enough to protect her child if she needed to, but she didn't want to have to send the child away. Help, Olivia Jean decided, should be given at home. And people should not have to be shamed until they couldn't lift themselves up because of a mistake. Didn't most people make mistakes?

While they rode down south on the highway, Olivia Jean thought about being in the family way and how she felt about the baby moving around inside of her. Only it didn't feel like it was a baby. It felt more like the bad time before her monthly when her breasts hurt and everything that came in contact with them made them hurt more, her blanket, her bra, a careless brush against a wall. Nothing was the same with her body.

And there were other changes. Her parents' attitudes were different. Suddenly Olivia Jean was the center of attention, when she had always felt as if she played a bit part in her family. She never thought of herself as the lead, that part went to Daisy hands down. She was Tonto, the Lone Ranger's sidekick, always assisting in the adventure but never the lead. Now she was the star and she didn't like it. She was being moved down south, where she didn't want to go, to live with a grandmother she'd never met and had hardly spoken to over the phone, with no knowledge of what was going to happen after her baby came into the world. Was life all about these changes and unknowns, or was it because she was going to be a mother at fifteen that made everything so complicated? There was no one to ask, and she couldn't even guess at the answer.

Olivia Jean gazed out of the window as Sally tore up the highway, and maybe there were tears in her eyes as tree followed tree on the side of the road, but she couldn't linger over tears or trees. She picked up the paper bag that Daisy had thrown in the backseat at the last rest stop and threw up in it. Bile rose from the pit of her stomach, and she silently thanked her mother for remembering that she could no longer travel in the backseat with ease.

Turk stopped the car at Daisy's urging, and her mother came to the backseat, felt her forehead, and murmured something in her ear. Then Turk pulled Sally back on the highway without a word. Olivia Jean laid her head against the cool glass of the car window. And the faster Sally flew, the more she remembered.

Olivia Jean drifted back to an early April morning, and it seemed that she could smell the promise of rain and feel the heavy moistness surrounding her, how the air tickled the end of her nose. Turk had not come home the night before, and Daisy was out the door before Olivia Jean woke fully, reminding her to go around to the butcher's after school and get three steaks.

Olivia Jean knew Turk was expected home. Daisy woke up without an alarm clock. Her forehead was already wrinkled from frowning, and her eyes were bloodshot from beer. On days that Daisy rolled out of bed wreathed in cigarette smoke and without a word to Olivia Jean other than about what to start for dinner, Olivia Jean made sure to listen carefully and keep her mouth shut.

The clouds hung low, and the wind blew cool enough for Olivia Jean to pull an old cardigan out of the drawer and wrap it around her shoulders as she leaned out of her bedroom window to get a taste of what was to come for the day. She put on a deep gold saddle skirt and brown penny loafers with brand-new pennies in each slot. Right before leaving she bumped her bangs with the curling iron and used her fingers to fluff them out. She dipped her finger into the Vaseline jar, caught a small dollop of grease, and skimmed it over her lips.

Olivia Jean walked to school with her girlfriends Dora and Ernestine. The trio had long ago shortened Ernestine to Ernie. While they walked, the girls argued over who was cuter, Smokey Robinson—who to Olivia Jean's mind was good-looking, but to hear Dora carry on he was a gift that God sent for all womankind to worship, mainly because of his light-colored eyes and skin—or Preston Douglass, a dark-skinned boy at their school who was rumored to date only senior girls who put out. They giggled, shoved one another, and had fun arguing back and forth.

Olivia Jean spoke her mind, telling them that Preston Douglass could not be put in the same category as Smokey Robinson. After all, Preston Douglass was a flesh-and-blood person, whereas Smokey Robinson was a big-time recording star.

"But," Olivia Jean concluded, "Preston gets my vote as the

handsomest boy in the school." Dora punched Ernie and they both started giggling. Olivia Jean glanced over her shoulder. Preston Douglass was walking behind her, and he was smiling, one of those big, true-life grins that made her heart stop, start, and then beat as though it were an African drum. She walked faster. They were less than a block away from school, and suddenly Olivia Jean was in a hurry.

"Glad you think I'm handsome. I been watching you, too. You ain't bad for a little short girl." Dora and Ernie tittered and dropped behind the pair. Preston kept up with her, easily matching her frantic stride. He even reached for her books, but she held them tight to her body and wouldn't let them go. He shrugged and continued to walk. They didn't talk. Then, without warning, he grabbed her arm, only it wasn't so much of a grab but a light touching that let Olivia Jean know that he wanted her to slow down, that he had something to say. They stopped. He was taller than her by almost a head, and although Olivia Jean felt shy, she found herself staring up at him. Dora and Ernie passed them within seconds, Ernie dragging Dora, who seemed reluctant to leave them alone.

Preston leaned in close. His face was clear and brown and sweet, making Olivia Jean want to reach out and lick him, to taste chocolate skin. Her tongue brushed against her teeth, and she had an urge to lean in even closer and let it graze his cheek, perhaps his full lips also. But she knew better. Nice girls didn't lick boys just because they were near or because they looked and smelled of chocolate.

"So, why don't we meet after school today. By the back closet. Let me buy you a soda and you can tell me some more about how much you like how I look."

Olivia Jean thought he might have been talking to someone else. She turned around, but turned back when he started laughing. He had a deep-in-the-throat laugh. Her shyness returned once he asked her out. She nodded with her books clutched to her chest, her head down. That was when she noticed his feet. He was wearing black-and-white Converse sneakers, the latest kind that only the very cool guys wore. She realized that she was talking to Preston Douglass, the most popular boy in school, and he was going to take her for a soda later. She had to take a deep breath in and let it out slowly before she gathered the nerve to look up again.

They were steps from the school. Ernie and Dora had already gone inside. Preston made a fake basketball move, dribbling air and running the last few feet up the steps to the school. He paused at the door and gave her the Douglass one-dimple smile and the wink that made girls sigh, and Olivia Jean was transfixed, knowing the fake dribble and the smile were all for her benefit.

"See you later."

She waited by the closet every day for the next three days, but he never showed. He'd stop her in the hall, and the excuses rolled off his tongue while the dimple cluttered her thinking. There was basketball practice, math homework, a friend he needed to help. All those excuses and all those secret caresses he offered: holding her hand, touching her cheek, bending close so that she could smell and breathe in his scent, in return for the forgiveness she gave freely.

At the same time Turk still had not made it home and he didn't call either for three days. Olivia Jean watched Daisy fix his plate each night: a T-bone steak on Monday, meat loaf with mashed potatoes on Tuesday, and fried chicken on Wednesday. At nine o'clock each night, right before bedtime, Daisy stood by the garbage and managed to catch Olivia Jean's eye and hold it while she scraped off every last bit of food. Olivia Jean got through the evenings by concentrating on schoolwork and mooning about Preston. On Monday she was busy thinking of Preston and why he didn't show at the closet; on Tuesday she was afraid of the look Daisy sent her way as she held the garbage pail open with her foot and threw the meat loaf in; and on Wednesday Olivia Jean was angry with Daisy and Turk, but also with Preston for not showing for the third day in a row.

And then, too, on Wednesday, Daisy took to drink. She didn't drink the usual Pabst Blue Ribbon or Miller High Life from the icebox. She reached into a kitchen cabinet and pulled out a bottle and started pouring a dark amber liquid into a cup after she scraped Turk's plate into the garbage. Olivia Jean helped her to bed that night and put out her mother's last cigarette in the ashtray that Mr. Shorty Long gave her long ago. Olivia Jean pulled off her mother's socks and pulled the covers over her. Daisy mumbled Turk's name before she turned over.

On Thursday morning Olivia Jean spotted Preston in the hallway next to his locker. But it was not an accidental spotting at all. She knew his schedule and knew where his locker was. He was contrite. He asked if they could meet after school, and he promised to be there. He said that he had something special to give her. He caught her hand in his and held it as they walked in the crowded corridor. She noticed that other girls moved out of the way for them, and a few had unhappy looks on their faces.

"Some people take things too serious," he said as they continued to hold hands and tried to ignore their glances. He brought her fingers to his lips in the doorway of her geometry class. Someone sighed, and Olivia Jean thought it was because they were looking at Preston and her, thinking what a great couple they made.

During class, when Mrs. Randolph talked of angles and degrees, Olivia Jean saw Preston and his triple-dark skin merging with hers and hoped that he would meet her by the closet. She wanted to be close to him, to hear his voice near her ear, to have him touch her cheek again, and to hold hands as she stared at his skin and into his eyes. That was what she told herself, that she wanted to hold his hand and talk to him. Maybe she'd let him kiss her. She might lick his lips. But that was all she wanted. She'd go no further than the taste of his lips on her tongue.

She met him by the back door, near the coat closet, filled with hangers and the smell of old paper, dirt, and mothballs. As soon as she was close, Preston pulled her to him without a word of greeting. He was urgent in his demands, and she followed him, doing the things that he asked her with his mouth and with his body. Olivia Jean dropped her books to the floor. They were standing in dim light, bodies tightly wrapped together, lips and tongues dipping in and out of each other.

Olivia Jean had never had anyone touch her titties. She kept repeating to herself that it was Preston Douglass who was kissing her, Preston Douglass who was inching his hands where no one had ever inched his hands before. She didn't push him away. But somehow there was the knowledge that she should have. She could hear Daisy on the edge of what was real, talking to her about boys and not letting them put their hands where they shouldn't be. The problem was, his tongue tasted sweeter than the sweetest candy, and his hands felt good where they touched and tweaked. She pressed closer to him.

He hiked her dress up. She spread her legs. Daisy called her "hussy." He grunted. She grunted, grinding her hips against his. Olivia Jean could smell the smoke of Daisy's cigarette and see her looking down at her, shaking her head full of princess-pink rollers, hands on her hips. Preston pulled her into the closet and reached behind her to close the door. Their touching became faster, frenzied. He pushed her onto the floor and she was surprised to feel some type of material, perhaps a coat, already spread and waiting. She saw Daisy throw up her hands and walk away, and she was glad her mother had left. She wanted her gone.

It was over before Olivia Jean could wipe the dust from the front of her sweater, and Preston was zipping up his pants in a hurry and pushing her out of the closet, saying that the janitor was making rounds and that they had to leave.

*T*hat was what she remembered—the sound of his zipper traveling down and then up. And almost nothing in between about the sex except that Daisy kept cropping up. He'd thrust. And so had she. Olivia Jean was sore in her pocketbook, that secret place that she touched only to wash. But what happened between them lasted no more than a few minutes. How could minutes have changed her life, made it so that she had to leave her family, her friends, and her home? But she had to face up to the fact that the little time in the closet with Preston did change everything. And there was no going back to the road and trying to get things right by choosing the other way.

She wanted to tell Dora and Ernie, but she couldn't think about it without wanting to cry. Then she tried to forget Preston, because he stopped speaking to her. Acted like she didn't exist. Olivia Jean saw him use the same trick of kissing the hand of a girl who was taller than her and rounder in more desirable places. The girl had curly hair that she wore close to her scalp, and long legs that she showed off every chance she got. When Olivia Jean ran into them she'd nod and smile, the same stiff, hurt smile she had seen on other girls' faces. She felt stupid.

As she cried into her pillow at night, there were two things she promised herself. She wouldn't go into another coat closet with a boy again. Bad things happened in coat closets, even if they felt very good at the time. And she also decided that she was not going to use looks when making up her mind about a boyfriend. There had to be something more than looks for her, like kindness. Being handsome was in no way as important as being smart, and neither handsome nor smart was as important as being kind.

*Y*es, she needed kindness, she thought as she pressed her face to the cool glass inside the car. She didn't want Turk's quiet meanness or Daisy's guilty fussing. They were getting closer and closer to Grandma Birdie and Cold Water Springs, Alabama, and she didn't know what to expect. She told herself that her grandmother might not be a loving person. Look at how Daisy turned out. She might not even be kind. Grandma Birdie might be as angry as Turk was with her and refuse to speak. There was no one to ask. Everything was so confused.

Her final thought as she fell asleep was of Daisy and Turk. It was to wish that they would disappear as they were banishing her to the backwoods country of Alabama. That would bring her great satisfaction.

Sleep came easy in a car like Sally. Olivia Jean awoke only when Turk pulled over for gas. During their last stop Daisy had grabbed her up and hugged her. When Olivia Jean saw the tear in the corner of her mother's eye, she almost laughed. This new Daisy was not one she was used to, not even one she liked very much. She let her mother hold her and then slipped quickly from her grasp. She didn't want to be reminded that she was going to be dropped off and left, and the hug, nothing that she was used to, reminded her of the coming betrayal. When Olivia Jean got back in the car, she closed her eyes and thought of home and how things used to be before this trouble with Preston and the baby changed everything.

Every year before school started in September, Ashford Street had a block party. People got together and spoke as they cleaned the sidewalks in front of their apartments. Daisy and Olivia Jean did the sweeping for their building. The police came and set up barricades so drivers couldn't drive through the street. Tables were in front of each building, topped with white plastic table-cloths and food: hot dogs, hamburgers, ribs, beans, cakes, cookies, and even hand-churned ice cream. Any kid on the block could go to any table and ask for food and get it with a smile.

This year the block party was to be held on her fourteenth birthday, and Olivia Jean begged Turk to sing for her. She stood in front of his chair one night when he came home from work, and when she saw him struggling to get his work boots off, she got down on the floor and started to pull. He wiggled his feet and smiled down at her when his toes finally got free.

"Now, what did you want, baby girl?"

She loved him best when they were alone and he'd call her pet names, like *baby girl* or *lambkins,* or stupid names like *sweet pea.*

"Daddy, will you sing a song for my birthday at the block party?"

He rubbed his eyes, and she knew he was tired. He'd been gone since midnight and it was four o'clock in the afternoon. But she had a mission. She wanted him to sing, to let people see that there was something more than the double chin and wide belly that hung over his work belt. More than the man who dragged himself home so late at night that his wife and his daughter sometimes wondered if he would come home at all.

"Sure, I'll sing you a song, baby girl. Anything for you."

She got up early the morning of the block party, glad that it wasn't raining. It was a beautiful September morning, a breeze cooling things off from the high temperatures they'd had almost all summer long. She closed her eyes tight and prayed that Miss Chessman had made a coconut cake and a pitcher of lemonade. The table in front of their house was always popular, because everyone loved her cake. Last year Miss Chessman had made two and every last crumb was gone by the end of the night. Miss Chessman always made sure that Olivia Jean got a slice, and in turn Olivia Jean would make sure that Turk had a piece, too, even though she had to slip it by Daisy.

She threw on a pair of jeans and one of Turk's old shirts and went outside to begin cleaning. All she could hear was the sound of the broom crossing the sidewalk, a gentle scratching noise.

There were no kids running around playing marbles or stickball in the middle of the street, no one yelling for them to come inside, and no sudden squeal of car brakes when they darted from between parked cars without looking both ways.

Around nine a.m. other people came out and started to clean, too. When Olivia Jean finished she went back upstairs and watched from the window. Nothing was set to happen until later in the day, close to sunset. A few people sat outside with backgammon cases or tossing hot, slick cards around, declaring war. Upstairs, Olivia Jean and Daisy made deviled eggs and sucked on Popsicles. Neither of them wanted to eat anything else before the tables were set up downstairs and the party started. At sundown, mother and daughter headed downstairs, ready to join in the fun.

There was a group of men playing dominoes at the corner. Old Mr. Lem Waters sucked on a pipe; Mr. Charlie Brown kept on calling people out and telling their business about the numbers they were playing or should have played; Dirty Red was fooling with his hair, which was conked like in the old days, slicked back and straight. There was talk that Dirty Red had once been a singer in a band, and after he got old and gave up the singing he kept his hair because he loved it so much. Olivia Jean had heard that he paid to get his hair washed every week and that sometimes he didn't have money to pay the rent on his one corner room because of getting his hair done.

In between the talking they did, the men were slamming the dominoes down on the table and laughing. They held those little black pieces in their hands, cupping them tight so no one could see. When she walked by, Mr. Charlie Brown yelled after her, "You Turk's girl, ain't you?"

"Yes, sir."

"When your daddy comin' home?"

"Should be here in just a little while. He gets off work about six."

He nodded. Good girls didn't stay around old men, or "minor Negroes," as Daisy called them. Bad things happened to girls who got the curiosity so bad they had to be up under an old man. And since Olivia Jean had seen Dirty Red up-and-down her when she was standing there answering Mr. Charlie Brown, she knew Daisy was right. Dirty Red tried to be slick about his looking, but he wanted her to know. When he got back up to her face he stuck the tip of his tongue out the side of his mouth for one hot second. He did it so fast that Olivia Jean questioned whether she saw what she saw. But she knew she had.

When she walked away she heard Charlie Brown say, "Man, is you crazy? That's Turk baby girl. He'll kill you over stupid shit, but for sure he'll kill you over his baby. Better watch your step and keep that muthafuckin' tongue of yours in your mouth, where it belong."

The dancing started, and people were sweating by the time James Brown blasted out of the speakers begging, "Please, please, please." Some of the little ones stood and rocked to the music, and a few of the older kids were on the side, practicing new dance moves. Olivia Jean stood near her building's table, keeping an eye on the cake and waiting for Turk. Daisy was nearby, fanning herself with the latest Hollywood gossip magazine. No one was allowed to eat yet.

Mrs. Gloria Miles, who was the block president, party organizer, and PTA president, was also the mother of twin boys, Melvin and Myron, and in charge of everything on Ashford

Street. According to Daisy, she even directed the wind. The woman approached the middle of the block, where the stereo equipment sat near the boy who was spinning the records. Mrs. Miles made a sign for the boy to lower the music, and he did, nodding his head.

Mrs. Miles was dressed in mint green, which was a pretty color on her, Daisy said, but the front of her dress was too tight. Olivia Jean could see the glint of a small safety pin the woman had used to try to keep the gap in the front of her dress closed. Daisy shook her head.

"Remember, Olivia Jean, it's the small things people will eyeball you for. Don't ever let me see you stand up in front of people with your clothes fitting like that. Ain't no reason that woman trying to squeeze into a fourteen when she know good and well she a sixteen at least. Might be a twenty with all that shelf."

"Mama, please." Olivia Jean didn't want anyone to hear her talking about Mrs. Miles. Daisy could make people hoot and holler over the way she talked.

"You oughta relax, Olivia Jean. Ain't nobody listening to us."

When nobody paid Mrs. Miles the slightest attention, and people kept right on walking around and conversing as though no one were in front and trying to talk, she turned to the young man playing the record and made the *cut* sign under her neck. He almost fell over his equipment rushing to pull the needle up.

"Ladies and gentlemen, welcome to the eighth annual block party." She stopped as if expecting applause, then hurried up when none came. "It's a blessing and a privilege to be here today." Still no one said anything, but they all thought the same thing: She was trying too hard to sound like someone she wasn't. She wasn't white. She was Mrs. Miles from the block.

Olivia Jean spotted Turk as he turned the corner from the bus stop. His gait was slow but steady, and she was happy because he was on time. She watched as he raised his hat to all the ladies he met on the way to their home. With one lady he bowed at the waist and swept his hat off his head. The woman giggled, her hand over her mouth. Daddy was a charmer, even to old ladies with no teeth and no hair.

"Well, before you eat," Mrs. Miles said, and there was a groan that spilled out of the crowd, "we're going to have some singing. Mr. Turk Stone is gonna sing a song for his birthday girl, Olivia Jean. Y'all know Olivia Jean, right? She got straight A's last year in school. This girl is an achiever." Olivia Jean hung her head at that but Daisy took her hand and squeezed.

Turk walked up to Mrs. Miles, and she gave him the microphone. He reached in his pocket for his handkerchief to wipe his brow. He always started that way. The handkerchief was gleaming white because Daisy used Ivory Snow at the corner Laundromat every Saturday morning. He stood very straight in front of the crowd, and Olivia Jean found herself pushing forward. She wanted to be close when he sang. She wanted to be able to see him and wanted him to see her. She had changed into a blue dress that hugged her waist, with a hemline that hit midcalf, and Daisy was wearing pink and had a pink polka-dotted scarf around her neck. They were nearly touching when he began, dropping his chin, closing his eyes for a moment. He sang the song about the Indian princess and her father, the one where they were parted, far across a lonesome river. Tears welled up in Olivia Jean's eyes.

But he was not singing to her. He had turned his body, his sweet voice, in Daisy's direction, and every note, every arm gesture was for her. Turk was singing Olivia Jean's song to Daisy, and she was smiling at him as though they were always on the best of terms, as though he made it up the stairs every night at six p.m. on the dot and she had his beer cold and food on his plate.

People clapped when he was finished. He handed the microphone back to Mrs. Miles, searching the crowd for Olivia Jean and Daisy. When he found them, he gave Olivia Jean a kiss on her cheek but grabbed Daisy around the waist and gave her a wet one on the lips. Olivia Jean pretended that they were cute by pasting a smile on her face, but she felt cheated. Why couldn't she have him to herself sometimes? Daisy was all he saw, all he begged for, when Olivia Jean was the one who really loved him. She marched straight to the table where their building had food and got a piece of coconut cake. Then she plopped down on the step in front of the door and devoured it, licking her fingers and wishing she had nerve enough to ask for another slice.

Miss Chessman came and sat with her after a while. "My, my, your father sure has a beautiful singing voice." But Olivia Jean couldn't bring herself to talk. She wanted to cry. She said something about having a stomachache and was about to go upstairs when she realized that Daisy and Turk had made a beeline for their apartment. For the rest of the block party she sat on the stoop and listened to Miss Chessman and watched the neighbors enjoy themselves.

When it was time to go in, Miss Chessman said, "You're one lucky young girl," she said, "your daddy being as handsome as he is and singing to you like that. Must be nice." Olivia Jean was polite, and she nodded to Miss Chessman and said, "Yes, Miss Chessman," and left the woman by herself.

When Olivia Jean went upstairs, she turned on the living

room lights and sat at the window, listening to the sounds of the block party winding down. Some bigger kids had gotten hold of firecrackers and they were lighting them and throwing them into the street. Finally Mr. Charlie Brown walked up to one of the boys and pointed a finger in his chest to make them stop. And they did, shoving the rest in their pockets and heading across the street and down the block.

Everyone had disappeared. The music was off, and there were no more wooden tables sagging in the middle from all of the food. The litter from the party had been cleaned up. The little children had pitched in, dragging those big plastic bags around and filling them over and over with paper cups and plastic spoons and white paper plates, rib bones, chicken bones, and whatever else they found on the street. It was sad watching. The day had started with so much anticipation. Now it was over and there was nothing to remember of the event except bags and bags of garbage.

Ernie called and sang "Happy Birthday" over the telephone. She had wanted to come over, but Mrs. Miles and the block committee were very strict about outside people coming to the party. Daisy wanted to fight the issue, but Olivia Jean convinced her not to bother. "Mama, school starts soon. I'm gonna see Ernie every day then. No need to fuss now." Dora was away at her aunt's in North Carolina, but she had sent a card, and that was good enough for Olivia Jean. The card had a picture of a cat with pink whiskers, licking its paws. It was dressed in pink and white, too, and said something about friends and birthday greetings from the cat's meow to the cat's meow. Olivia Jean put it on top of her dresser.

She went back to the front window to peer at the stars in the late night sky. She closed her eyes and said a prayer:

"God, I'm gonna start the ninth grade this year. But school hasn't ever been a problem for me, and I don't think it will be. I just have to work hard. Daddy says that you can get anything you want through hard work. So I'm planning on doing that.

"But, God, I'm gonna need some help with Mama and Daddy. They get on my nerves too much. Every time I think something is gonna happen one way, they change things on me and it winds up another. I wish you would make them stop. And behave like they got some sense. And be nice to me all of the time and not every once in a blue moon."

When she opened her eyes there was a sharp cracking sound and then darkness across the sky. Her first thought was that God had heard her and was giving her some kind of personal response. Then she looked down into the street and saw Melvin and Myron slinking off near the side of a building and realized they had busted out a streetlight. Olivia Jean put down the window and got ready for bed.

When Olivia Jean's stomach growled so loud she thought the baby was singing, Turk pulled Sally over and they ate the cold fried chicken Daisy had packed, with a couple of boiled eggs each.

"How much longer we got, Turk?" Daisy asked as she peeled her egg.

" 'Bout six or seven hours more. Not too long," he answered. Olivia Jean thought he sounded tired.

"You gonna let me drive some? Look like you gettin' ready to keel over."

"I let you know when I need a break." There was no teasing in his voice. His tone was flat and discouraged conversation. Olivia Jean took a bite of the drumstick and glanced out of the window. When she finished the chicken she reached into one of the paper sacks her mother had packed. There she found pieces of home-made pound cake wrapped in wax paper. She opened her thermos and poured herself a cup of milk and ate the pound cake with gusto, wetting her fingers to pick up the crumbs that fell on her lap or back on the paper.

Afterward they collected all of the garbage and filled a sack. Turk let out a huge belch and didn't say, "Excuse me." He turned the ignition and drove Sally onto the road again, headed south. Olivia Jean sat in the back, covered by the dark and a blanket.

Olivia Jean knew better; she just didn't do better—something that Daisy talked to her about every once in a while on the stoop or in the apartment when Turk wasn't around. They talked about housework, homework, and boys, with boys being the subject Daisy was more prone to speak about as Olivia Jean grew older.

"Olivia Jean," her mother would start with a voice that she tried hard to make sound friendly but wasn't, "you have got to think better than what you're doing now or you gonna get yourself in big trouble."

Well, Olivia Jean thought, she should have listened good and thought two times, three times, and even four times before she let Preston with the curly hair and brown, brown eyes come up on her in school and pull her into the coat closet.

But she didn't know any better. Daisy had told her not to let "no boys put their hands up your dress," she hadn't said a word about their things. She hadn't said, "Don't let them put that up your dress or in you." Boys' things had never been a part of the conversation.

The air in Sally smelled of the Old Spice Olivia Jean had given Turk for Christmas last year. Now she hated the scent. But she couldn't figure out what was worse: his cologne or the stale smell of cigarettes coming from Daisy. Her stomach was queasy again, and she wondered how long she was going to have to go on smelling her parents. She rolled down the window an inch and pressed her nose to the opening.

Was there a certain length of time a father was supposed to be angry at a daughter because of a mistake? She'd been mad with Turk before, but her anger was not like his. Hers blew over with the first smile he aimed at her, the first pull on her arm or tug at her hair. Daisy, too, was a sucker for the dimple that poked into his cheek when he knew he'd been wrong. Why was it that she, Olivia Jean, could forgive him for all the times he'd hurt and let her down and chosen Daisy, and he would not, could not, seem to even look at her? He acted as though she were a stranger, as though they had never been father and daughter.

Endless. The questions without answers. Better, perhaps, to think of other things. She had been so certain her father loved her at least a little, but he didn't seem to at all now that she was in the family way, and her heart ached. And her head, too, from all the crying she was not doing.

Two weeks before they left home, Daisy had broken down and taken her to the free clinic on the other side of Brooklyn, far away, so that no one would recognize them. The nurse gave Olivia Jean a book that told her about what happened to a woman's body during that "special time." She read it two times from cover to cover, with the exception of the last two chapters. She peeked in the back, and it didn't seem to her that things turned out so well. She read about pain, bearing down and pushing hard. And then about feeding the baby from her breasts. She ran to the bathroom, threw up, returned, and closed the book, vowing not to read the rest of chapters ten or eleven until she absolutely had to.

Because of the book Olivia Jean understood that the flutters tickling her stomach belonged to her little girl. At night, while Daisy and Turk slept, she sat by the window in her bedroom, turned on a small lamp, and began to read aloud, one hand resting on her stomach. The baby knew things already. She'd heard the poetry of Langston Hughes, stretched to Zora Neale Hurston, twisted to her mother's laughter. Olivia Jean wanted her child to know about everyday colored people, not cardboard people painted brown. So she read each night with the knowledge that in the reading, she was teaching. From her womb would spring a wondrous child, fully formed with colored-folk knowledge, which, in essence, was everyday-folk knowledge.

Now, as the sun struggled to overcome night, she rummaged through the backseat and found her book, *The Street* by Ann Petry, opened it, and started to whisper the words to her baby. No time was better than the present to prepare for what was to become of them, husbandless and fatherless in a world that wanted women to have male protection. *But we'll make it,* she thought as she read. *I promise.* She stroked her belly and swallowed all thought of everything else as she read to and readied her baby.

•   •   •   •

*B*efore Daisy told Turk that Olivia Jean hadn't had her monthly in two months because she'd checked her rag drawer and panties for stains and found none, Daisy took her to a woman in a small house so that they could try to solve the problem themselves. It was an unremarkable house, painted so light a brown that it almost looked gray. The door blended in with the brick masonry, and the only brilliant color was the brass knocker. They climbed the stairs.

"Olivia Jean, you let me do the talking. Your place is to be quiet," said Daisy before knocking. The woman who opened the door was pretty, and she smiled at Olivia Jean first. Then she paused and turned to Daisy, who did nothing more than lift her lips at the corners in greeting. They stepped inside, and Daisy took off her hat and gloves and handed them to the woman as though she were a servant.

"We have an appointment with Madam St. James."

The woman smiled and said, "Yes, I know. Why don't you have a seat in the parlor, Mrs. Stone, and I'll be right with you both."

Olivia Jean could tell that Daisy was not happy that the woman was pretty and that she'd made a mistake about her being the maid. Her mother had had the same look on her face when they went to visit Miss Randolph, her ninth-grade algebra teacher, because of Olivia Jean's first B, and Turk had smiled a lot and made small jokes about Olivia Jean getting her math skill from him. Then Daisy acted as if she had put a sour grape in her mouth and chewed it to the skin when she only meant to swirl it around. Olivia Jean shook her head and rolled her eyes to the ceiling.

While they waited, seated together on the sofa, they did not speak. Daisy was fidgety and nervous and kept plucking nonexistent nits from Olivia Jean's sleeves and smoothing down the front of her own dress that was too short for her long legs. Olivia Jean stared at the pictures on the walls filled with colored people doing everything from dancing to chopping cotton in open fields, and she was fascinated. She had never seen such things before. Everything smelled good, too, like the first of the morning before the garbage trucks plowed through their block, or the laundry when it was pulled in from the backyard clothesline.

When the woman returned she carried a large tray with a teapot, and plates with small sandwiches and cookies. She told them she was just about to have a snack when they rang the bell and asked if they would care to join her. Daisy still tried not to show her embarrassment that she had mistaken the woman for a maid, but Olivia Jean was tickled, and she could see by the lady's smile that she was, too. Madam St. James put the tray down on a serving table of dark mahogany and took a seat directly across from Daisy. Olivia Jean noticed how her dress swirled around when she sat, and the sound it made, soft crunches as she smoothed it under her bottom. *I've seen ladies like her on television,* Olivia Jean thought. The woman gestured to the plates and told them to please help themselves. Daisy nodded yes to a cup of tea.

"What may I do for you today?" said Madam St. James.

"My daughter, Olivia, is in . . ." There was a pause, and Olivia Jean glanced out the window, because Daisy had started to cry before she could get the rest of her sentence out. Olivia Jean thought she would be sad, too, if her daughter had let her down and gotten in the family way, but it seemed to her that Daisy was carrying on too much about this matter. She promised herself that if such a catastrophe should ever hit her daughter she would not cry as though it were the end of the world, especially not in front of strangers. She would save her tears for real problems. It wasn't as if they didn't know of girls who got into trouble. She'd whispered about them and pointed at them with Dora and Ernie. Now it was going to be different. She was going to be the one people whispered about and pointed to.

Olivia Jean blinked away her tears. Madam St. James moved to where Daisy was sitting and put her arms around her. Daisy had started to cry more, hunching her shoulders to her neck and moaning deep down in her throat and rocking back and forth on the sofa as though someone had died. There was nothing for Olivia Jean to do except slide closer to the edge and make room for Madam St. James and Daisy, Daisy whose hands clutched at Madam St. James as though the woman were a lifeline, a savior on a sinking ship.

Olivia Jean looked down at her penny loafers and the shiny 1960 pennies that she kept in the slots. She examined the paintings on the wall again and at one point considered touching the rug on the floor, because it was so thick and she had never seen anything like it: springy threads that stood up and buried feet in softness. Finally Daisy's crying tapered off, and Olivia Jean looked up again. The white, initialed handkerchief that Daisy had held pressed to her face was now brown from makeup. Madam St. James remained on the sofa, seated between mother and daughter.

As Daisy picked up her cup of tea, her hands trembled and the cup rattled against the saucer. Olivia Jean told Madam, "No, thank you," very politely when she was offered a cup again. She shook her head no at the food, too. It was easier for her to keep in control of her feelings if there was nothing to do but sit and pretend that she wasn't in the room.

"Mrs. Stone, I'd like to be able to speak with Olivia alone, if you don't mind."

Daisy seemed surprised by the request, but she stood very slowly, setting her cup and saucer down with a soft clink, leaving Olivia Jean with Madam St. James.

"Your mother is very concerned about you and the baby you're carrying." *Shit*, Olivia Jean thought, *she's not the only person who's worried.* The woman moved closer. She took Olivia Jean's hands and held on to them tightly. Olivia Jean finally raised her face and stared into Madam's eyes.

"And so am I. This is not a good time for a fifteen-year-old to be a mother. You'll have to leave school, and people will label you. They will say that you are fast. Boys will not respect you."

Olivia Jean didn't know how to tell her that she knew these things already. Her throat was too full to talk, so she nodded.

"Do you want this baby? Your mother would be happy if it went away."

"I know she would be. But I won't be happy. Not ever again. I want to keep my baby." Her voice did not sound like her own. The frog had taken over, croaking in order to hold the tears back.

"Do you know how to be a mother?"

No, but I do know how not to be one. I've seen that firsthand. And I do know what I have to give this baby: patience. I have more than Mama does, lots more love, lots more time. But Olivia Jean only said, "No."

Madam St. James rose and crossed the room. Her shoes were

not run-down like Daisy's, and Olivia Jean wondered if they had ever left the house and taken the subway downtown.

"Do you know what I am?" Madam St. James walked back to stand in front of Olivia Jean, tall and unblinking. Her brow was creased but her back was as straight as a rod, unbending.

Olivia Jean shook her head and stood up, too. She did not like the feel of the woman standing over her.

Madam St. James nodded her head and let out a big sigh before she continued. "Some people call me an abortionist. Do you know what that is?"

Another head shake.

"I help young girls like you, and sometimes older women, married or unmarried, not to have babies they don't want."

In all her life Olivia Jean had never imagined such a person existed. Never imagined that there might be a need for getting rid of babies.

"Why would someone not want a baby?"

"Maybe they can't afford to have them. Maybe it's not the right time. Perhaps they're not married. There are many reasons why a woman might decide not to have a baby."

"How do you help them?"

"Now, that is a very complicated question. I will tell you that it depends upon the situation. If you decide that you don't want this baby, I can help you. If you decide that you want to keep it, there's only so much that I can do."

Olivia Jean was not hesitant. "Well, I do want this baby, so you're probably not going to be able to help me. I appreciate your time but you'd better call my mother back." Olivia Jean moved closer and glared at the woman. "I'm going to have this baby."

Madam St. James stared at her. She studied Olivia Jean up and down and sideways until she started to smile. And Olivia smiled, too. She could see the woman wasn't going to tell Daisy that she had been fresh. Finally, here was someone on her side—Olivia Jean could tell by the way her smile came through Madam St. James's eyes and lifted them at the corners. The lines around her mouth were dug in deep. She wondered what it would be like to be her daughter.

"There are many girls that come to me, and when they tell me they want to keep their babies, I tell them they are fools. I can't tell you that, Olivia Jean. You've got more sense than plenty."

Olivia Jean smiled again, trying not to think of her queasy stomach and the fact that the tips of her breasts hurt.

"Let's get your mother back in here so I can speak with her."

Madam asked Olivia Jean to wait in the hallway so that she and Daisy could talk. Olivia Jean glanced around the hallway, painted a pale sky blue with white chair-rail molding, to make sure no one else was around, and pressed her ear to the door. She heard the women faintly, her mother's voice rising with anger, Madam's low-pitched and even.

"I didn't pay you this money for you to tell me you won't help us."

"Mrs. Stone, I am helping Olivia Jean. I told you from the beginning that if she didn't agree, I wouldn't go forward. I'll give you some of your money back, but not all of it. You and your daughter took my time. I get paid for my time."

Olivia Jean hurried to her seat across the hall when she heard the sharp clicking of Daisy's heels on the wood floors. Even her feet were angry. When she came out Olivia Jean was sitting across the room, hands on her stomach, pretending that she had not moved.

Madam St. James followed Daisy and stood in the doorway, her face blank but alert, taking in the entire scene. Daisy took several deep breaths and finally turned to Olivia Jean.

"Come on, Olivia Jean. Let's go home."

When Olivia Jean turned to say good-bye, Daisy snatched at her arm. But Madam nodded, and Olivia Jean imagined she wanted to say that things would be fine, that Olivia Jean would make it and so would her little girl.

Olivia Jean thought it funny that her body knew she was in the family way before the voice in her head knew. Her voice thought she had the flu or ate something rotten when she started being sick to her stomach in the mornings before school. Suddenly she couldn't stand the smell of Turk, whose underarms reeked from a day of mopping hospital floors, dumping garbage, and moving hospital beds. The smoke from Daisy's cigarettes that curled through the air as she waited for Turk to come home made Olivia Jean's eyes tear and the saliva gather at the sides of her mouth.

She thought perhaps that this was what she'd heard called the wages of sin. She didn't know what else to do, so she prayed. Olivia Jean had been to church a few times in her life and remembered the rolling thunder voice of the preacher talking about heaven and hell and the best way to get to both. But what she remembered most was the man speaking about God's anger and how a person had to ask for forgiveness when they'd done wrong. On the third morning she threw up before school, she went into her bedroom and closed the door. She turned off the light and lowered the blinds in her room. Turk and Daisy had already left for work and she was alone. She took one look around and knelt by her bed, head down and hands clasped, as Daisy had taught her long ago. But this time she did not say, "Now I lay me down to sleep."

"Dear heavenly Father, I know you are angry with me. Going into that closet with Preston Douglass was not a good thing to do. I know that now. Especially since he's not with me anymore and won't pay me no mind. But, Father, please leave my stomach alone now. I promise not to go back to Preston again. I've learned my lesson. I will even listen to Mama from now on when she lectures me about men and boys. After all, she was right. They do just want one thing. But Lord, let me tell you—that one thing is not so bad, and if you were smart, you'd stop making it feel so good."

When she finished, she got up slowly, picked up her books, and headed for the door. But before she could cross the threshold she felt heat on the back of her neck, and the inside of her throat constricted. She dropped her books and ran to the bathroom. As she cried and retched into the toilet, she remembered that one of the preachers had said, "When you do not truly repent, God does not truly forgive."

𝒯wo days after visiting Madam St. James, Daisy and Olivia Jean sat down.

"Olivia Jean, we got to tell your daddy that you in a family way."

Olivia Jean appreciated the fact that her mother hadn't used the term *knocked up*.

"He's not gonna be happy, but we have to tell him. Let's see, you must be about two months now. You gonna be showing soon, and we got to decide what to do."

They were sitting at the kitchen table. As Olivia Jean drank a glass of chocolate milk, Daisy poured a Budweiser in a glass tilted sideways, waiting for the foam to gather before she set the bottle down. Everything else was quiet in the room, like things were waiting to begin. Daisy had been studying the bottle, peeling the label off, when she looked up and asked the question that Olivia Jean had been dreading.

"Who the daddy?"

Olivia Jean had finished her drink. Without thinking, she shrugged her shoulders.

"Girl, you telling me that you don't know who you was with?" Daisy grabbed her wrist and held it until Olivia Jean met her eyes.

"How many boys you done been with, Olivia Jean? How many?" Her voice was harsh, low and growly, as though she were speaking to Turk coming home late from work.

In all the time they had shared her secret, Daisy hadn't asked Olivia Jean anything about Preston. There had been her urgency when she figured out that her daughter hadn't had her monthly. Then there had been the meeting with Madam St. James. But now she was remembering what she forgot to ask and wanted to know to be prepared for Turk. Now it was important that she know everything, when before it was important only that they get rid of the baby. Olivia Jean thought about lying.

They heard Turk's footsteps at the same time, heavy steps with frequent pauses so that he could lean against the wall and catch his breath.

The kitchen door opened and Daisy jumped from the table. "Turk, we got to talk about something."

"And hello to the both of you, too." He grabbed Daisy around the waist and tried to plant a smacking kiss on her lips. She turned her head at the last minute so her cheek got wet instead. He bent down to kiss Olivia Jean on the forehead and stroke her hair. His breath stank from breathing through his mouth and the whiskey shots he must have downed before making it home. When Olivia Jean wrinkled her nose and tried to move away, Turk laughed.

"Girl, you ain't too young to know that a man gotta have a taste once in a while. A man gotta have his freedom and be able to go get a drink with no problem. I'm right, ain't I, Daisy? Tell the girl I'm right."

"Turk, you need to sit down. I gotta tell you something."

He sat in one of the kitchen chairs, the seat ripped and the foam cushion gaping out the sides. He took Daisy's hand, brought it to his lips, and began to hum. Olivia Jean hoped that Daisy wouldn't tell, that maybe her mother might break it to him some other time. He was happy, drunk and red-eyed. And getting ready to sing.

"Olivia Jean in the family way."

He seemed not to hear, still holding on to Daisy's hand and humming. Daisy said it again. There was a pause. He stood and took a step toward Olivia Jean, his eyebrows running together and his mouth moving but with no sound, no humming, and no words. He put his hand up against the green-blue of his uniform, near his heart, and turned around and around in a circle. Olivia Jean began to cry. She knew that she had broken something

within the big man and that things might never be the same between them again.

When he finally stopped and stood in front of Olivia Jean, she
waited. She thought he might slap her. "Get out of my sight," he
said. The words rumbled low in his chest. She knocked the chair
down and ran to her bedroom.

More than a week passed before Olivia Jean got up the
nerve to tell Preston she needed to speak with him in private. She was busy reeling from the fact that Preston had a new
girlfriend—Dora.

When they first started dating, Olivia Jean hadn't noticed. She
was too busy at home with problems because her father had
stopped speaking to her. When Turk came into a room and she
was there, he didn't look in her direction or acknowledge her
presence. He referred to her as "the girl." This brought on a sor-
row so deep she caught herself thinking of Madam St. James,
wondering how things would have been if she had made a different choice. But Olivia Jean knew that for her, there was only one
right decision. Her distress about her father not speaking would
not have been as deep a misery as getting rid of her child. She
was sure of it.

It was only when Ernie pointed to Dora one day and then to
Preston that Olivia Jean understood. Dora was wearing sweaters
with plunging necklines, gauzy scarves wrapped around her neck
hitting at the beginning of her cleavage, like a dart pointing to
where she wanted people's eyes to rest. Her penny loafers weren't
good enough anymore. She wore saddle oxfords with white

bobby socks stopping at her ankles. At the sock hop she didn't wait against the wall with Ernie and Olivia Jean; she was laughing and twisting and spinning her hips to the latest jive songs, making her little bit of a ponytail bounce, shaking like she was some kind of hoochie mama. But when the love songs played, when the music slowed and the lights dimmed, she and Preston managed to find each other and become one. Olivia Jean saw them pressed together like two buttermilk pancakes with only a lick of syrup between. They were the couple the chaperones pulled apart. It would be a lie to say Olivia Jean wasn't hurt.

"Aw, you just sore because the two of you didn't work out. You should be happy for Preston and me instead of jealous. We gonna get married someday." The Monday after the dance, Dora and Olivia Jean stood outside of their first-period science class.

"Yeah, I'm happy for you," was all Olivia Jean could manage as she walked off.

What she wanted to do was to reach out and slap her old friend. Dora and Olivia Jean knew the rule—friends did not deal with another friend's boyfriend, whether he was a current boyfriend or an ex-boyfriend, if they expected to stay friends. Ernie nodded in agreement. So they stopped walking with and talking to Dora, and that was okay with Dora because she had stopped before they stopped. Only Olivia Jean and Ernie hadn't known it.

Olivia Jean put a note in Preston's locker when she got the nerve and told him to meet her by the back door again. He passed her in the hall and winked after he got the note. She winked back and smiled, thinking about how Preston would respond to the news. Maybe he might want to get married. That would show Dora.

As soon as he got there he was trying to hold her hand to pull her into the closet. She made him stop and he leaned against the door, hands folded across his chest, while she stood in front of him. He seemed nervous and unsure, maybe waiting for Olivia Jean to yell at him about Dora. But she didn't yell. She told him she was in the family way and that her daddy was looking for the daddy of the baby in her stomach. Preston started shaking. She stared at his hair. Now she could see small dollops of Dixie Peach hair grease that he must have forgotten to rub all the way in. She noticed a hole in his sweater and the way one of his teeth turned a little to the side. She thought about her baby and shook her head. Olivia Jean was glad that she was carrying a girl and that half of the baby was hers. Her half might cancel out his half. That was what she had to hope.

"You know, I ain't gonna make no good father."

She considered his words. "Why you saying that?"

"I ain't the settling-down type. My daddy wasn't. His daddy wasn't, and I'm not gonna be either."

"Oh."

They were quiet for a while, finally sitting on the floor of the deserted school building. It was still light outside, and beads of sunshine flickered across the hall erratically. The floor was cool beneath her, but even with that she was content to sit and talk to Preston. That was what she should have done two months ago when they ended up in the closet. She should have taken the time to get to know him then so she wouldn't feel so out of time and in trouble now.

"Do you wanna go back in the closet with me? I can do you real slow this time and you'll like it. We don't have to rush. The janitor ain't coming back until about six."

She studied Preston. Up close this time, he was only a boy. But he was a handsome boy, even with the flaws of crooked teeth, greasy hair, and holey clothes. He was also the father of her baby, and Olivia Jean's telling him still didn't make him want to do anything other than spend time in the closet with her. He had not said that he would give up Dora or that he would marry Olivia Jean or even that he would face her daddy. She thought that Preston had some nerve.

And then she thought, *I'm already in the family way and can't get in more trouble, so why not?*

When she nodded yes she thought Preston would start jumping up and down and hollering. But he didn't. He helped her up from the floor and opened the closet up as if they were headed to their first prom together.

"Just one thing, though."

"Yes," he said, looking down at her and smiling.

"I'm going back in there with you. I ain't gonna tell my daddy your name. And I ain't gonna bother you about no money or getting married or anything. But when I come around with my baby girl, when you see me with her, I want you to come over and pick her up and kiss her. I want you to hold her tight, and for that minute I want you to love her so I can tell her that you did when she gets grown. I want you to be her daddy for a minute." Olivia Jean closed her eyes and waited, one hand behind her back, fingers crossed. She had thought about asking him this for a while, once she got over the shock of seeing him with Dora. Deep down she had known he wouldn't go with her to Turk and that he would not own up to this child he helped make. But she needed something besides the memory of the closet to keep her going. And she believed that his promise to do this one thing might sustain her through the laughter, the pointing, and the bad times to come.

Preston was still. She opened her eyes and searched his face. She couldn't read him and thought he might say no. She prepared herself.

"I can do that. I can do that."

He smiled and she thought there was something close to tenderness on his face. He pulled her into the closet and she closed her eyes again—to all that had gone before and to all that might happen once they came out. All she wanted was his slow, steady weight and the knowledge that they were together, maybe for the last time.

Olivia Jean rested her head on the cool glass of the window and knew it was time to sleep. They had just crossed into another state, maybe Georgia. She was not sick, and the air held a coolness of an early night. She overheard Turk telling Daisy that there were only a few more hours to go, and telling her that she would have to take the wheel soon. He turned the radio on again. Chubby Checker had been replaced and The Shirelles were singing "Will You Love Me Tomorrow?," and Olivia Jean almost laughed aloud. She thought, *Who is going to love me tomorrow? Nobody. I am damaged goods.*

She dreamed of leeches and fire and having Ernie twirl her around in the corner at the sock hop because they didn't have anyone else to dance with, until Preston drifted their way and smiled, holding his hand out to dance with Olivia Jean. But Dora was on his other arm, short, chic, and chewing gum with a big smile on her face. She hated them both. Yet, in the dream, she still drifted toward Preston, holding his arms open wide with the bonus of Dora on his other side. She was almost in his arms when Ernie shouted about being left alone. Her mouth was wide like a baby's and there were these big, oversize tears sliding down her face and sticking there, not moving down to her chin, just stuck on her cheek like empty, see-through pimples. Olivia Jean turned around. When she awoke, face pressed into the warm leather, she wondered if pregnancy caused her dreams to be so real. Could being in the family way make a person dream in Technicolor?

It seemed like the only relief Olivia Jean got was in her sleep, even if she was having nightmares. Things were worse than when they were at home, all together in the apartment. Turk still wasn't speaking to her, and Daisy tried to be the mother she had never been before—looking at Olivia Jean with eyes full of tears and patting her head at every rest stop, like Olivia Jean was dying instead of being in the family way and taken to live with an old woman who probably didn't want her.

"Baby, baby, you want some water? It's nice and cold from the ice chest."

"No, thank you, Mama."

"Baby, you gotta drink a lot of water and eat good. You gotta take care of yourself."

Daisy started to say the word "baby," but Olivia Jean saw her glance over at Turk and stop. Besides, how could Daisy say that when she had taken Olivia Jean to Madam St. James, the abortionist? Olivia Jean wondered how many people didn't want babies. Maybe a lot of them, because Madam's house was nice-sized and she looked like she had money. Not a scuff mark on her shoes. No smell of collard greens simmering on the stove or fish frying. There was only the smell of lavender through the house.

"Don't keep at the girl for drinkin' no water or nothing right now. I don't wanna have to stop again till we can get through Georgia." Georgia was hilly and full of trees that soared on both sides of the road. The green was deep, verdant. Olivia Jean wondered if Alabama could match the lushness of Georgia, if there would be hills rolling in green carpeting as far as the eye could see once Sally crossed the border between the two states. She would have to stay awake to see. She pushed herself up to a sitting position, determined to keep her eyes open for this last leg of their journey.

She was getting ready to ask for a drink when she looked up and saw Turk's eyes in the mirror. He saw her and turned away, but not before she saw the coolness and indifference. Turk regarded her as a stranger, someone off the street. There had always been a smile in his eyes for her, as if the two of them were sharing some kind of secret joke that even Daisy was not privy to. He'd wink at her or purse his lips as though her head or cheek were near. Now there was nothing for her in his eyes. Turk had stared straight at her, and it was as though he could have been staring at Mr. Charlie Brown, the numbers man, or anybody else in the world.

Olivia Jean sat back and let her book slide from her lap. She no longer wanted to read about Lutie from *The Street*. She wanted to think about how she would get even with Turk for treating her so poorly. She had already decided never to slip him another beer when Daisy had said no more and he looked at Olivia Jean from the corner of his eyes and she knew to meet him downstairs with one more cold one before bedtime. She would also stop hiding his six-pack of Budweiser that he kept in the very back of her clothes closet underneath her winter coat and sweaters. And if he got another hiding place, she would make sure that Daisy found it, accidentally on purpose. And the clincher, Olivia Jean decided, would be to tell him that he had lost his singing voice and that he should keep quiet from now on because she liked Smokey better.

That was the beginning of some good payback. But then she got sleepy and couldn't think of anything more to get his goat. She patted her belly and the baby fluttered. Olivia Jean yawned without making a sound and settled in for a short nap.

She was asleep when Daisy shook her awake. She felt the gravel crunch under the tires as Sally came to a stop. When Daisy opened her door it was not so much her voice as her smell that woke Olivia Jean. Today she wore White Shoulders and to-bacco.

"C'mon, girl. Go on over there in the bushes and make water. Then get up front with your daddy."

"Huh?"

"I said, time for a stop. Take some tissue, and when you fin-ished you get up front. I wanna stretch out and take a nap."

Olivia Jean almost fell getting out of the car, trying to get past Daisy with it being so dark. She couldn't see beyond her hand. They were far enough from the road that any other car coming their way wouldn't know that they were doing their business in the bushes. Olivia Jean clutched the tissues and wiped well, the way Daisy had taught, and hurried back to the car after hearing her name sung out. Daisy knew she was taking too long on pur-pose. As Olivia Jean touched the handle, she took a deep breath and let it out before opening the door. She was going to sit next to Turk.

PART TWO

Daisy

*D*aisy wanted to smoke so badly that her tongue itched, and she sucked on the first two fingers of her right hand, brushing her tongue around the raised nodule of her writing finger. She enjoyed the texture and feel of her fingers at the roof of her mouth, especially when she had decided to stop smoking for a spell because of Turk's coughing. Before turning on her side to take a nap, she strained to hear any conversation between Turk and Olivia. She had made Turk stop the car earlier by saying that she had to pee. The man had rolled his eyes in frustration; two women, one of them pregnant and one having to pee all the time, were too much for him to deal with on a road trip that was supposed to be a quick turnaround. The goal had been, as Daisy insisted, "Get Olivia Jean out of town and to Alabama quick. Then we hotfoot it on back so we can both be to work on time Monday morning."

So they had stopped, and she stretched her legs in the high grass behind some bushes and finally decided that maybe she did have to pee. After squatting, wiping, and strolling back to the car, Daisy realized that things had been way too quiet for the past few hundred miles. They were in the middle of the backcountry, and there were few radio stations that had anything other than Elvis Presley singing and asking women, "Are you lonesome tonight?" And Elvis Presley was not enough for Turk. He shut the radio off.

Daisy couldn't recall a time in the recent past when they had been cooped up for so long and Turk hadn't started singing and Olivia Jean had been so silent. The child hadn't even told one of her silly jokes. Instead, she sat in the back of the car, staring out of the window with her arms folded across her stomach.

Daisy knew she had helped cause the rift between Turk and Olivia Jean. She could have sent her daughter down south without Turk knowing about the baby. That had been a possibility, although a slim one. She hadn't been able to think of a good enough reason for Olivia Jean to go to Alabama and to stay. And then, too, Olivia Jean had the idea that she wanted to keep the baby. Daisy didn't know when she started to discount the idea of not telling Turk—most likely that night when he came through the door and she wanted to wipe the drunken grin off his face. In that moment she had hated him for being the kind of husband he was, hated that she felt stuck, and most of all hated that she still loved him. And after she told him, when she saw the wound that opened on Olivia Jean's face, her anger dissipated. She was sorry then, but there was nothing she could do to change the situation or the fact that Turk knew. Each time she thought of that day, she reminded herself that it all came down to Olivia

Jean being foolish, even though she had plenty book smarts. So, maybe Daisy caused the rift, but she didn't do the initial damage. Olivia Jean did that.

Daisy had slipped into the backseat after the break, taking that refuge from her daughter, forcing Turk and Olivia Jean to at least breathe the same air in the front seat. Before she fell asleep Daisy's last few thoughts were, *I'm too young to be a grandma,* and, *Why the hell couldn't she keep her legs closed?* And then, *Damn, why did I have to decide to cut down on cigarettes now?*

*D*aisy's size-nine booted feet scrunched through the streets of Brooklyn with the delicacy of a big hunter cat. She was used to dodging black ice, shit, and yellow patches of dog piss to get where she needed to go—whether it was in the city, with tall buildings and churches littering every street corner; or in the country, with back roads and woods tucked away, country places that no map had ever charted. Either country or city, nastiness had to be gotten around, and she was an expert at getting around and through nastiness.

Her dream self paused at the bottom of a short flight of stairs. She was no longer a pair of boots striding through snow. Her vision had progressed. Now she saw her hand gripping a banister, her ringed hand. A red scarf was tied at her neck, thin, gauzy material that didn't belong in the winter, not with snow. Her foot touched the stair.

Then she was at the door, her hand poised to knock. And there was no longer any doubt. The number took care of the doubt. Thirteen. An unlucky number, the apartment of her friend and adviser, a woman of mysterious talents, who wore a pink turban,

Charlene. The door opened without Daisy touching it. In the car she shifted. In her dream she walked forward.

"Ha, ha. I'm glad you could visit, Daisy flower. Glad you came to see me."

Daisy sat and said nothing to the pink head, all that she could see of the woman. The turban had hands without a face, and now those hands squeezed Daisy's and held on to them.

"Um, little sister, you got troubles. Many, many troubles."

"What troubles do you see?" Daisy leaned in closer to the pink turban.

"You not gonna catch the trotters for a long time. No luck with the horses. The luck has gone."

The relief moved from the pit of Daisy's stomach upward. She could deal with no luck with the horses, no luck with the numbers.

The blank face with the turban atop was directly in front of her. The hands holding hers were cold, becoming colder by the second. Daisy shifted again in her sleep.

"You gonna hafta choose. One or the other, the girl or the man. Make up your mind."

And Daisy heard the words floating through the open window in the backseat as Sally plowed forward on the highway. She curled her body tighter and in her sleep willed the dreaming to stop and it did.

But soon Daisy was sitting up again. The quietness bothered her, and even the rocking motion of the car as it sped through the countryside did nothing to keep her asleep. She was worried, mostly about Olivia Jean, some about Birdie, her mother, and a lot about Turk and what the situation was doing to him, to the family, to their couplehood.

She looked out of the car at the trees. She missed the street play of night in the city and the constant murmur of voices outside her window. Even a long, soothing ride in Sally could not lull her to sleep as the city did with its discordant lullabies. And now they were going to Cold Water Springs, Alabama, a place that in so many ways mirrored the journey in Sally: quietly gentle, interrupted only by nature—perhaps the wind gusting through an open window or rain pelting the roof. But deceptively so. There was still shit and piss to be gotten through under all that rich country living, just like there was in New York. She was going to have to tell Olivia Jean about watching out. She hoped her daughter listened more than she had in the past.

Up front, Olivia Jean sat far to the right side, her shoulders touching the door, her neck all but disappeared, like some small animal huddled in a corner.

"Olivia Jean, sit up. You gonna get a crick in your neck like that." There was no verbal response, but the child obeyed. She straightened. And Daisy cursed herself for having a voice that cut through the night like an angry trumpet, for her inability to do more than direct when she knew more was needed, for being unable to feel what that "more" was, other than that it was not something Olivia Jean was getting from her. Daisy sighed and began to contemplate the country night and the road that was carrying her back down south to her home, her mother, and long-buried secrets belonging to that time when she lived in Cold Water Springs, Alabama.

$\mathcal{B}$efore she knew anyone else, there was Mama Birdie and Mr. Shorty Long. Mama Birdie showed her the mysteries of nature and the meaning of color and fabric; Mr. Shorty Long sat in his big house on top of the hill and expected them all to break bread together on Sunday afternoons before the long shadows of twilight fell across the porch steps.

She loved the wild freedom of the woods, walking barefoot among the roots, letting her feet sink in the rich red clay dirt of Alabama. She stuck flowers in her hair and learned the name of each calling bird before she knew her alphabet. And then she learned the feel of color and cloth in her hands; the heaviness of velvet; the sweet air that floated through lace, making it a mystery. For how could something so light, so riddled with openings, so insubstantial, also be so beautiful?

She and Mama Birdie danced on the shore of the lake at midnight, rejoicing in the coolness of the air near the water, and sat in the little house at the foot of the hill on days when the sun shone so fiercely that it scorched the rocks and caused them to blanch. Then they sat with scissors and made cloth into clothes. As a child Daisy loved to press velvet against her face, and sometimes placed the remnants in her mouth to suck on. Birdie laughed at her and said that fabric was in her blood, and Daisy nodded. Everything Birdie said was the truth in those days.

Daisy learned stillness and patience trying to coax style from mounds of fabric. Often she and Birdie did not have patterns. An outfit might catch their eye from a magazine or store window. They would put their heads together and decide how to approach the project, estimating the length and width of material needed and the type of cloth that might make their outfit work. And Daisy also learned not to offer her opinions so freely. Birdie did not want to hear how red and green did not go together, how purple and blue did not work, or that certain shades of pink did not complement orange. Her mother was adamant. "All colors are created by God, and how can you or anyone else say they ain't meant to be together? You make God out to be a lie then. He put 'em all here for us to wear. And that what we gonna do— wear 'em all."

Every dress they created on those days when they waited out the sun were like Joseph's coat of many colors, pieced and hung together with love of color and love of fabric. Birdie claimed every creation as her own, and Daisy smiled a secret smile of contentment. She had no intention of going to school in purple, green, brown, and navy. Let Birdie parade. Daisy was happy with the act of piecing together and stitching. And this she did, assiduously, until she became a teenager with thoughts and ambitions of her own. But the early days she worked with Birdie set the foundation for what was to come. They made Birdie's clothes, using yards and yards of colorful fabric, and purchased Daisy's from the local dress shop or Sears catalog. Daisy wanted everything to match. If she had a dress, she wanted shoes and a purse to go with it. For church she asked for and received gloves. Daisy and Birdie were an unlikely pair; Birdie was flamboyant and colorful, while Daisy was carefully distinguished by her style and overall color coordination.

The only glitch in young Daisy's life was Sunday afternoons, when she was forced to eat dinner with Mr. Shorty Long, her mother's employer. She hated meals with Shorty Long because he expected her to recount all of her activities during the week. Had she learned her seven times table well enough to recite? How was her spelling? Did he hear right that she had punched Seth Hall in the nose for calling her a banana-skinned nigger?

After church, Mama Birdie and Daisy climbed the hill to the

big house and put on aprons. They generally made fried chicken with collards and mashed potatoes and sometimes a chocolate cake. Mr. Shorty Long rarely came into the kitchen. He sat on the porch rocking and nodding at cars as they passed by while they cooked. Daisy felt resentful that he didn't move, not even to help set the table. Setting the table was her job as soon as the biscuits came out of the oven, buttermilk biscuits that rose like small Towers of Babylon, with slick coatings of honey and butter on top. Then Mama Birdie allowed her to mix the lemonade. And that was a treat, to pour the sugar and stir with a big wooden spoon until the ice clinked on the side of the pitcher and Mama Birdie told her that that was enough.

At the table they said no grace. Mama Birdie had told her that Mr. Shorty Long did not believe in God. Daisy was supposed to say her grace silently. But most times she didn't. She figured that if God had not sent a thunderbolt in Mr. Shorty Long's direction for not saying grace when he should, God most likely wouldn't fool with Daisy either, especially with her being a child and Mr. Shorty Long being a stooped old man who only let loose of the bottle on Sunday when they came to eat with him.

At dinner they passed the dishes without so much as a rustle of the tablecloth. The only voice was Mr. Shorty Long's as he asked about what he had heard Daisy had done at school. He asked about who she had sassed, and who she might have fought, since Daisy was also known to roll up her sleeves and leave a few children crying. Each incident was discussed with a thoroughness that sometimes made her sick to her stomach. And then there was his question: "Well, why y'all do that, little girl?" Even into her teens, when she could find no reason to be with Mr. Shorty Long at the dinner table, Mama Birdie frowned up a blue

streak and pinched hard when Daisy spoke of skipping their routine. He never varied his conversations with her. He never shared
his week. Never discussed anyone else, and never made any comment on anything but what he had heard about Daisy and her
doings.

Mama Birdie prepared the food and sat with them. While she
rarely spoke, she did have to hide a grin behind her table napkin,
especially when the subject had to do with Daisy fighting.

One afternoon, when Daisy was ten, Mr. Shorty Long started
with his questions. He did that when the silences among the
three of them were punctuated by the clatter of forks and knives
and persistent chewing.

"I heard tell that you punched Lou Willie Neloms in the face
so bad she had to get a stitch under her eye. Why did you hit her
that hard?"

Daisy pushed the peas around on her plate. She never looked
at Mr. Long when she answered, and always remembered to say
"sir" and "thank you kindly." Mama Birdie told her that Mr.
Shorty Long was white, and that on no account was she to go
around looking white people directly in the eye. The best way
was to look down or away. That other way would get a body in
trouble, maybe hanging off one of the trees that sat as a dividing
line between the house on the hill and the one below. No, Birdie
had told her, Mr. Shorty Long would never hurt her, but there
were plenty of other people in the world that would, and Daisy
had to be prepared.

"Know your place, Daisy. That way nobody can fool wid you."
That was what Birdie told Daisy every day.

"Speak up, child. Why you punch Lou Willie? She's a good
girl, to my knowledge. She gets her work done and doesn't trou-

ble anyone. I asked the teacher myself." Mr. Shorty Long pressed for an answer. He put his fork down and stared at Daisy, who was surprised. Mr. Shorty Long had spoken to her teacher?

"She done told me something." The peas marched across her plate in a straight line, stopping at the gravy. The gravy was the muddy Mississippi.

Mr. Shorty Long waited.

"She said the only reason why that River Jordan boy like me 'cause I light-skinded. She say he'd like her, too, if she was my color. I just told her the truth. Ain't nobody gonna like her, 'cause she evil. Ain't no skin gonna make her nice. Then she pushed me, an' I had to punch her out."

Mama Birdie coughed and stood from the table. She said she had to get the extra butter for the biscuits from the kitchen.

"Well, why did you hit her? You couldn't walk away and let her be?" asked Mr. Shorty Long.

Daisy's head fell lower, and her nose almost touched the peas on her plate.

"No, sir. She was mean. And I ain't bothered her none. Plus, if I let her push me like that, them others gonna think they can push me, too. Mama Birdie done told me not to hold my licks, and I ain't. They can't be hittin' on me and get away with it."

Her voice was louder than she had intended, and she expected Mama Birdie to come back into the room and thump her on her forehead. But she didn't. Instead, Daisy's mother sat, put her napkin in her lap again, and started to cut her meat. Mr. Shorty Long remained quiet for the rest of the meal, not asking another question or saying anything else about Lou Willie. When Birdie went to the kitchen for the dessert, Daisy said in a rush, "Don't you worry, Mr. Shorty Long. I ain't gonna hit nobody else in the

eye no more. I'm just gonna make people stop botherin' at me
'cause of my skin an' cause of how I look an' all. Mama Birdie
done told me that I gotta stop gettin' so mad. I gotta start
laughin' when people act ignorant." She took her time with the
pronunciation of the word *ignorant*. And for the first time she
saw Mr. Shorty Long smile. He had small, even teeth, and when
he smiled it changed his whole face. The lines fell away from his
eyes and he was younger, more like a boy than an old man. She
picked up her head and smiled, too, forgetting Birdie's edict and
meeting his eyes. He coughed and pulled his napkin from his lap
and dabbed at his forehead. She wanted to make him smile
again. She kept talking.

"Yup, Mr. Shorty Long, it is hot today. Betcha it was in the
nineties, maybe even one hundred degrees. Do you think we
gonna have rain sometime soon?" She barely paused between
questions.

The rattle of the car woke Daisy, and she leaned her cheek
against the cool glass and wondered how soon they would reach
Cold Water Springs and Birdie. She thought of how she would
embrace Olivia Jean right before sliding off the porch into the
car again with Turk. That part nagged at her, leaving Olivia Jean
with a woman the girl had never met, but knowing Birdie, she
and Olivia would be best friends within an hour of the two meeting. And that worried her, too. Birdie was not a woman you
trusted with your heart, and somehow Daisy had to let Olivia
Jean know this before they left her. So how was she to say it?
Honey, I just need you to know some things. I'm leaving you with a
woman that been in jail and that had a few run-ins with the law.

But don't you worry none. She gonna be right with you when you need her. I think she done slowed some since old age come down on her. She ain't gonna do you like she did me. The biggest thing was, even if the words left her mouth, would they be true?

Birdie Abernathy was a thickset black woman who had the strength to beat a man with her fists and a look that could shrivel any part of him worth mentioning. Nobody in town matched her for her tongue or her blackness; her skin was the color of leavings at the bottom of the coal pit, and when Daisy was small she understood power and that power meant big arms and blackness.

Whenever Daisy thought of Birdie, she had flashes—pictures suspended in her mind like those in a big-screen movie, the kind of movie she and Turk went to see in Manhattan every so often at those plush theaters where the colored people could get in but still had to sit in the balcony. But even sitting in the back had not dimmed her pleasure at being in a rich movie house.

She always remained struck by the beauty of such large places and not struck by the fact that they paid the same admission as white folks but could get no closer to the screen than the second floor. There were red velvet seats and a chandelier that hung low enough for her to see the lights and close enough for her to imagine, to dream, to hope that one day she might own something of beauty like the huge bauble that lit up when the show was over. She and Turk always took their time leaving the theater, and other people moved out slowly, too, Daisy thought, because they all needed the magic to linger just a few minutes longer.

She had never been to a movie before Turk took her in New

York. The first time they went, she was in awe about how wonderful things seemed on film, how uncomplicated the problems were, and how everything could be set to rights within the space of an hour or so. She reimagined her life on the big screen—acted out by herself, Daisy, and various other people, bit players, as the movie magazines called them. Of course, there was the mother, Birdie, absent and uncaring; the overseer, Mr. Shorty Long; and the prince, Turk, come to rescue her from Alabama. So even now, having passed her thirtieth birthday, she pictured her life before New York as a series of movie vignettes. She saw a white man on the ground and her mother's fists doubled and then clenched at her sides, her immense bosom pushing up and down from the exertion of hitting a man and knocking him down at the farmers' market.

Mama Birdie and Daisy had stopped to buy melons. The man refused to wait on her until all the other white people were helped, taking people as they walked up rather than the woman who stood with a dancing child at her side. Then, instead of letting Birdie pick what she wanted to buy, he did it for her. He chose the sorriest watermelon Daisy had ever seen, dented on its side, and a cantaloupe whose bottom was turning brown. Daisy had stopped dancing and began to tug on her mama's pink dress. She didn't want to eat that.

With a loud sigh, Mama Birdie asked, "How much?" She was digging into her purse for her money when he told her the price, and she froze. Birdie dropped the money back into her purse. Daisy watched as her mama's hands fell to her sides.

"Beg pardon. How much did you say for those half-rotten melons?"

The man turned red. Daisy held her breath and wondered why some people like herself and the man changed colors when her mama didn't.

"I told you how much already. What, don't you understand plain English?"

"I understand you fine, but I'm reading somethin' else on the sign you got right there," Mama Birdie pointed out. "And I'm thinking that you got things wrong, 'cause that sign say one thing, and something else coming out your mouth."

"Better watch yourself, and don't get uppity with me, gal. Don't think I won't do nothin' 'cause you got that little pickaninny with you."

Daisy remembered that when he said that, Mama Birdie moved closer to the red-faced man rather than farther away. Daisy was trying to make her mother leave; she was pulling the pink dress with all her might, but Birdie didn't budge. The little girl let go of her mother's dress. Daisy twisted her ear and put the first two fingers of her right hand in her mouth and began to suck. She was afraid and always sucked those fingers when she was afraid.

Years later, the Technicolor of her mother's finger pointing stood out as another still movie picture, the sunlight hitting Birdie's hand in a way that highlighted its pitch-blackness against the blueness of that summer morning and then against the dingy white of the man's shirt. There was also the gold kerchief Mama Birdie had tied over her plaited hair that was the same color as the one Daisy wore to cover her hair. That morning, when they were getting ready to leave for the market, Mama Birdie whispered to her as they tied the matching head scarves over their hair, "People gon' stop askin' me who your people is. They gonna know today that you is mine and that I be your mama." Daisy had stood on top of her small trundle bed, and looked Mama Birdie's blackness in the face.

"Yes, you my Mama Birdie. You belongs to me." The girl and the woman chuckled together as Birdie lifted her daughter without groan or effort and set her stick legs on the floor.

"You right about that, Daisy Sweet Mae. I sure is your Mama Birdie. If ain't nobody else in this wide world want me, I know you does." Then they left the house at the bottom of the hill and went walking to the market near town.

What happened next at the produce stand was hard to say. There was the man's version and there was Birdie's version, no one bothered to ask Daisy what she saw. If they had she could tell them that she saw her mama hit the man. She couldn't tell them that Birdie, tired of the nastiness in the white man's nature, had conjured up some of her own nastiness in the form of a fist upside his head. And there he was, felled to the ground, out cold. And there was Daisy, staring at her mother, dropping her wet fingers from her mouth, seeing and feeling raw physical power for the first time yet not understanding it. But she did understand that the bad man who had talked mean to her mother was on the ground, and her mother had put him there.

Birdie shuddered, picked up the bag of fruit the man had laid aside during their argument, and tossed some money next to his unmoving body.

"Next time don't be messin' wid me. I pays what I owes, but I ain't payin' no extra to nobody. Don't you see I got me a little baby to take care of? You must be blind or something." She talked to herself all the way home, and Daisy, for once, did not ask any questions or open her mouth other than to slip in the two fingers of her right hand, sucking on them harder than before.

Daisy's skin reddened to a dusky hue as she and her mother walked back home under a steaming sun, and her feet hurt. Just as they sat down at the kitchen table to have a cool drink of water, there was banging at the door. Daisy stood and followed her mother through the abbreviated hall that led to the front door. It was a sheriff's deputy.

When Birdie opened the door, the man took off his hat. He was pasty white, with a big stomach that spilled over his belt, giving him an untidy look.

"Y'all visit a produce stand today at the farmers' market?"

They let Daisy stay with Birdie at the jailhouse because she had no one else. Birdie told the sheriff's deputy that her daughter had no daddy, no brother, no sister, no relative other than herself. Daisy and Birdie sat in the corner of a big room and watched the movement in and out, watched the handcuffed prisoners marched to their cells or out of the office in shackles to court. Birdie nodded to all of them. The unwritten rule in the South was to speak to another colored person, and the nod was a polite way of speech. Daisy noticed.

"Mama Birdie, how come you know everybody here?"

"I ain't know everybody here."

"But, Mama, they nodding at you; they smiling."

"Colored people do that to each other."

"Why?"

"Humph. Don't know for sure. Maybe 'cause we all been through the same bad times and we telling each other things gonna be okay." Daisy was quiet for a while, and Birdie reached out to stroke her hair, which was long and curled, captured by two pigtails at the side of her head. They had left their matching kerchiefs at home.

"But, Mama Birdie, what bad times you and me been through? We happy."

Birdie smiled. "Yes, we happy. We ain't had no bad times. You and me is great."

Daisy sat on her mother's lap. Birdie reached inside her blouse and produced a peppermint sucking candy that she gave to Daisy, who removed her fingers to make room for the treat. When she finished her candy she laid her head on Birdie's bosom, her fingers roaming across her mother's chest, and finally she rested. They stayed there until Mr. Shorty Long came and picked them up in his truck.

"Your mama lost her temper. I shoulda never bothered with that nasty man," said Birdie.

"You gonna get in trouble?" asked Daisy. From early on Daisy could talk to Birdie like she had good sense, and Birdie answered.

"No. Not this time. But that's jus 'cause he ain't nuthin' but a no-account traveling man. If he hada been somebody else, I would be gone up to the chain gang or worse. Lesson is, I can't let go of my temper like that no more. Ain't got nobody to leave you with, nobody to take care of you. I'm gonna do better. No more trouble."

She was close up in Daisy's face. Daisy took a deep breath and inhaled the body scent that made up her mother. She put her arms around Birdie, burying her nose, taking a chance and licking her mother's neck. She tasted the dark saltiness of heat. When Birdie swept her off the ground Daisy was glad that her mother was strong, and even glad that she had beaten the man down. She knew she'd be safe with Birdie, with her blackness, with the arms that gripped her tighter than tight when they both held on to each other. *No, we ain't had no bad times. My Mama Birdie and me is happy. We doin' great.*

*T*urk's yawn brought Daisy from thoughts of long ago. Now she had a daughter who was going to have a baby without a husband, and she had worries on top of worries. She had never understood why people sang the blues, the deep-down, shaken-spirit kinds of songs that Dirty Red sometimes sang at the corner bar. When he took out his guitar and bowed his head down low so that no one could see the tears as they mingled with the sweat that poured from his conked hair, she had felt his pain, but had not understood it. Now she did. A great sadness had settled on Daisy because of Olivia Jean, and, too, she thought, because of Turk.

The man had never been easy, but he should at least be grateful. She helped provide him with a good, clean home, cooked meals, washed and folded his clothes, and she worked a job that paid her a decent wage so she was able to help pay the bills. Instead of treating her well, he blamed every bad thing on her, going so far as to tell her yesterday that Olivia Jean's getting in the family way was her fault. That if she had paid more attention to the girl and tried to be in his business less, they might not have to rush down to Alabama and leave their daughter with Birdie. Daisy had stared at him for a long time before rolling over in the bed to face the wall.

Rain hit the car, and small rivulets streaked along the window until they thinned and died. Daisy stared, her eyes unfocused, her arms folded across her chest, mouth tight. Thinking of Turk made her angry. Today as he sat behind the wheel of the car, refusing to speak to her, except in clipped monosyllables, or to

Olivia Jean at all, she felt his spirit, malevolent, choking everyone in the car.

She was trapped between an angry husband and a needy child. She knew what she had felt like at Olivia's age with no parents to speak of, except Birdie, who had been in the lockup, and Mr. Shorty Long, the man her mother slaved for. She had been alone and frightened at fifteen. And pregnant, too. Turk should remember, she thought, and then stopped. He hadn't known. No one had.

The storm cleared enough so that the sun started to show, a sickly yellow sun surrounded by gray-black clouds that hung low over the car. She settled into the backseat again, her thoughts drifting in and out of the past.

During most of the summer of 1945, Mama Birdie was in lockup. She was picked up for selling her formula with full knowledge that the town was dry, and Mr. Shorty Long was not going to get anyone out of jail for messing with alcohol even though drinking was his favorite pastime. The problem was that Mama Birdie didn't believe Mr. Long was going to let her sit in jail. She did all his chores, fixed his food, cleaned the house, mended his clothes, and washed and ironed them, too. On Fridays before she left the house on top of the hill, she fixed food for the entire weekend so he didn't have to do anything but warm things up. Daisy often thought that Mr. Shorty Long was one spoiled man.

A sheriff's deputy stopped Mama Birdie while she was making her deliveries. She had to be looking to get picked up, because she did a few things wrong. First off, she drove in the daytime when it should have been at night. Everyone knew that night was the best time for running hooch, especially if it had to be run clear out to the other side of Colbert County. Sheriff's deputies were not going to be on the backcountry roads in the middle of the night waiting for a hooch runner. Things didn't happen like that in Cold Water Springs or in other small towns around the tri-city area, like Leighton, Florence, or Tuscumbia. Birdie was a leading expert on the history of selling formula. She often told Daisy, "Us people got a way of doing things in Alabama, and waiting in the dead of night to catch somebody taking country folk a swig or two, that ain't a fair catch. Shit, tha's almost like puttin' out a net in the lake when fish start jumping. Take all the sport out of catching the fish wid a pole.

"Ain't we got some rights to have a taste?" At least, that was what Mama Birdie used to ask Daisy on the nights when they raced the old truck along the road with the limestone quarries, hugging the curve at the hairpin turn and waiting to pass the grove of old oak trees dripping with Spanish moss that served as a landmark. Once they passed the trees, Daisy knew there were only a few minutes to go before they reached the spot where they had to meet bent old Bugger Pearson on the other side of the road, under cover of night, to trade him out ten quarts of formula for five dollars a quart. Daisy would stand watch while Mama Birdie and Bugger transacted business, Mama Birdie stuffing the dirty bills into her bra as she did with everything she found valuable. Then she and Birdie would run back to the car and take off fast. Because as big as Mama Birdie was, and despite the fact that she had a double-barreled shotgun stowed in the cab, she didn't like to be in the woods when it was so pitch-black she couldn't see her hands before her eyes.

Generally Daisy was with Birdie on a run. She started going

as soon as she turned six. Birdie used her as a lookout and as a decoy. Daisy would be all wrapped up in a blanket with a rag tied over her head. If any deputies stopped them, Daisy acted sick and began moaning. Then Birdie would say something along the lines of, "She got the fever bad, an' I ain't know where it comin' from. Trying to find me some yarrow root so I can make it come down," or she'd tell them they were on their way to the colored hospital in Leighton for help.

Early in that summer of forty-five, Daisy and Mama Birdie had been fussing. Daisy didn't feel like making the runs any longer. She was almost full-grown at fifteen, a teenager who didn't get excited anymore about standing lookout and making a dash to the truck when business was over. And she didn't want to loll her head and pretend to be delirious with fever either. She went with her mother two times in early May. They were stopped both times, and Birdie was hauled off to jail. One deputy had laughed at the yarrow-root story and said that they had used the same lie a few years back. He had let Daisy go because he said she was too young and pretty to be in lockup, and she had been left to drive home alone in the dark. The next time they went out, the same deputy stopped them. Only this time he wasn't laughing. He told Daisy, very sternly, that if he caught her out again, he would take her along with her mother and she would go to jail. Birdie was sentenced to a week in county jail the first time they were stopped, and the second time she couldn't hold her tongue in court and the judge gave her a month. So when Birdie told Daisy she had a new batch to sell in the middle of June, Daisy refused.

"You can buy that new dress you saw in the catalog last week," Birdie said.

"What good is a new dress if I'm in jail? Anyway, Mama Birdie, I don't need a new dress. Other things besides new dresses."

"What's wrong with you?" Birdie asked. She was standing in Daisy's room. Daisy was still in bed, and it was ten in the morning on a Saturday. "You ain't never said no to a new dress."

"Nothing wrong. Just extra tired this morning, that's all. But, Mama Birdie, it ain't a good idea to go back out there with that sheriff deputy on the prowl. He gonna catch us again and—"

"He ain't gonna catch nobody. I'm gonna go in the daytime and do what I gotta do. Next week I'ma get this batch out." Birdie left the room and Daisy sighed. She pulled the covers over her head and turned on her side. Her stomach felt queasy. She closed her eyes, hoping for sleep.

They were at a standstill until Birdie took off in the heat of the day, leaving Daisy chasing after the old truck, yelling for her mother, "Come back, come back, Mama Birdie." All morning long Birdie had been taking a few sips, and telling Daisy that she had to test the merchandise. Daisy told Birdie that she was sipping more than she should and was cutting into the profits. That set Birdie right off. Daisy tried to make her lie down, to rest, but the formula was strong, and Birdie was bound and determined to get in the truck and take her customers the goods. Daisy thought her mother had fallen asleep. Birdie's openmouthed snoring convinced her. But Birdie was only waiting until Daisy left the room. She slipped on a pair of overalls, grabbed her keys from the nail by the kitchen door, and half ran, half fell until she got to the truck. It wasn't until she had backed out of the yard, hitting the fence and scattering the laying hens, that Daisy came screaming out into the yard from the privy house, clothes still half-undone, waving the newspaper over her head. Daisy saw her mother weaving back and forth across the old gravel lane in front of their house and then pull onto the road needed toward Leighton.

Daisy didn't get scared until around midnight, when Birdie didn't make it back home. But there was nothing she could do, no one she could go to regarding her mother. She found a Sears, Roebuck catalog and started flipping through it, looking at the women's clothes and trying to figure out how much material she'd have to buy to get the same look. At three a.m. she put away the book and lay down, cussing Birdie all the while.

"Damn stupid old woman. You better not be somewhere in a ditch. Do, I'ma really hurt you. Why you got to be so goddamn pigheaded all the time?" Daisy fell asleep angry and woke up the next morning looking for her mother, who still had not returned. She dressed to go up the hill to see Mr. Shorty Long.

Daisy sat in front of the man who often made her Sundays miserable. She told him all about Birdie and how she was on the loose somewhere, maybe hurt, in a ditch. She told him about the formula, about learning to make it in the deep country in an old dilapidated house that Birdie said belonged to Queenie Monroe, her own foster mother, and Daisy's foster grandmother.

She told Mr. Shorty Long about the process, making sure the radiator hoses they used were clean so that no one went blind from bad formula, mashing the corn up and mixing it with corn-meal for added flavor. She told everything except the secret ingredient. Mama Birdie had made her promise. After speaking, Daisy couldn't hold her head up. Mr. Shorty Long's steady gaze wore at her; the slight frown on his forehead made her feel guilty.

"Birdie's most likely in jail. If you want to see her, I'll drop you off. If you need a ride back, you can get a lift home."

His voice was cool, very matter-of-fact, as if he didn't care.

"If she in jail, can you help me get my mama out, sir?"

When there was so long a pause that she thought he had either left the room or fallen asleep, she looked up. His face was stretched, and she thought that maybe Mr. Shorty Long was in pain. He looked as if he might pass out.

"I can't help your mother. And neither can you. She's got to want to do better. And she's got to think before she does things. She gets all crazy sometimes and you can't talk any sense into her. No, if she's in jail, she's gonna serve her time. I'll take you to her but I'm not staying."

He got up then and moved close, standing next to her as she sat on the sofa. He picked her hand up and held it briefly. "I'm sorry about the way things are right now. Sorry that I can't help you more with your mother. But people choose a path, and your mama chose hers."

Mr. Shorty Long paused at the door of the parlor, where they had been sitting. "Go on home now and get ready. I'll be down in a little to pick you up." When he left the room, Daisy took a few moments and cried. Then she wiped her face and walked home to get ready.

Sally lurched forward and Daisy fell, sliding to the floor of the car. She heard the hissing sound as a tire began to deflate.

"You all right back there?" And Daisy was angry that it was Olivia Jean and not Turk checking on her.

"I'm fine. Thanks."

Turk pulled over to the side of the road, and the three of them climbed out of the car. He shook his head over the front right tire, circled the car, shook his fist, and finally he kicked the door, leaving a dent. Daisy turned away from him, doing her best not to laugh. The thought of him getting angry over a flat tire when there were so many other things to get upset about amused her. She walked over to the side of the road and watched while Olivia Jean tried to offer her father support, mainly by hovering near him. At first she was going to beckon her daughter. But she thought better of it.

Finally, Turk turned to Olivia Jean, his face contorted, his eyes glittering amber brown, liquid jewels dripping with acid. Daisy heard him clearly.

"Go over there and stand by your mother. Don't bother me anymore. You've caused enough trouble. The best thing for you to do is what you been doing—keeping your mouth shut and staying away from me."

Olivia Jean walked away from him slowly. Daisy did not try to comfort her. She acted as though she had not heard the exchange. She watched as Olivia Jean took her place on the side of the road, behind her mother, with a face just as impassive, emotions erased.

As they watched Turk struggle with the car, Daisy kept thinking that finally Olivia Jean was beginning to learn what life was all about. There was no sense in trying to be good and loving when people only batted you down. Better to be cold than to keep getting hurt. Maybe this rift between Olivia Jean and Turk was not such a bad thing. Olivia Jean had to understand that not even a parent could be relied on when the chips were down. One day, maybe not soon, but one day Daisy knew that Olivia Jean would thank her. Because Daisy was really the one who loved her daughter; look how she had arranged everything. When they started out again, Daisy climbed into the front seat and Olivia Jean returned to the back.

$\mathcal{M}$r. Shorty Long kept his word. He dropped Daisy off at the county jail, nodded to her as if they were strangers, and drove off. Daisy walked up the courthouse steps carefully. She had worn high-heeled shoes and a pink dress. When she finally got in to see Birdie, she was hot, sweaty, and mad all over again about why she was at the jailhouse in the first place.

Daisy and Birdie sat in the jail cell together, swatting at ticks and trying to get the flies from around their faces. It was boiling hot in the room. Daisy thought the place was dirty and smelled as if someone had tried to clean it with Clorox but forgot to get in the corners. She had to force herself to concentrate on Birdie and not to look anyplace else.

"Girl, I done messed up this time. They gonna keep me for a while."

Daisy stared at Birdie and got madder and madder. The burn left her throat and was in the round of her belly. Here Daisy was in the jailhouse seeing about her mama when Birdie was the one who should have been seeing about her.

Birdie put her fingers up to her hair and scratched at a flea that jumped down onto the cot, and rubbed a pea-sized drop of sweat that ran from her forehead past her eye.

"I knows you upset. I knows it gonna be hard for you to get along now, but you gonna hafta be strong."

There was nothing Daisy could say to make her mother

understand—Birdie should have known that there was a problem without her having to tell her. Daisy finally got up from the cot and went to the cell bars, calling the guard.

"Time ain't up yet. You can stay here for a while more, talk to me some. It ain't so bad. Come on, baby, you can stay."

Her voice was soft. So soft that Daisy did feel the pull to stay, to let herself be comforted. The burning came back in her throat, but Daisy stood by the cell bars and didn't look in Mama Birdie's direction.

"Birdie, I'm leaving."

Birdie got up and tried to hug Daisy. But Daisy didn't want her mother to hug her. She stood, cold, while her mother's arms encircled her until they heard the guard coming down the hall with his keys.

"You gonna come back next week, right? You gonna come back and visit your mama, right?"

By then the guard had opened the cell and Daisy walked out, not answering Birdie. "Go see Mr. Shorty Long," Birdie yelled after Daisy. "He got something for you. He owe me two weeks, and he got more of mine that I done saved for you. Go see him right away."

Near dawn they pulled up the gravel road that led to Birdie's house and to the big house that used to belong to Mr. Shorty Long. Daisy could barely make out the outline, but she knew what to look for: one big house up on a hill, and one little house at the foot of the hill, near a small lake that stood as the dividing line between the two properties.

The car shook and rattled as it made its way, and she knew

Turk wasn't happy about the wear this trip had put on Sally, nor about the dent he was going to have to get knocked out. But they had had to do it; Olivia Jean couldn't make it over the next few months with her stomach growing and the whispers that would start and then the downright nastiness. She would have had to leave school. She would have no friends because the other girls' mothers wouldn't let their daughters associate with Olivia Jean. To say nothing of what people would say about Daisy and Turk. Daisy closed her eyes for a moment, willing herself strength. This might not be the best solution, she told herself, but it was the best one for now.

When he finally pulled up to the door of the house at the bottom of the hill, Daisy stretched and reached back to shake Olivia Jean, who curled into a ball in the corner.

"Wake up, girl. We here."

Getting out of the car, Daisy took a deep breath and considered having a cigarette. She had not been to this home since she left with Turk, that last time Birdie had been locked up in June 1945. She remembered the long walk from the jail, the anger in her step, the high heels she shouldn't have worn but she did because someone had told her that if she looked pretty and acted nice at the jail it might help Birdie. But that hadn't worked. Her mother was still there and had to stay for a year. Who was going to take care of her?

"Hey, you," Turk had said, and at first she didn't stop because she hadn't known he was talking to her. She was too busy being upset with Birdie. She had promised no more trouble. Birdie had sat on Daisy's bed, put her hand to her heart, and said that she was going to straighten up, and here Daisy was again at the county jail. And this time Birdie wasn't getting a month. She wasn't even going to get six months. She was going to be there for a year.

The sun was hot, and sweat dripped from her face and mixed with tears. She wiped her eyes with the back of her hand and kept walking, wishing she had at least tried to talk Mr. Shorty Long into letting her drive the truck into town.

"You, there, pretty lady, where you walking to so fast?"

She finally stopped and turned. That was the first time Daisy saw Turk, the first time her eyes widened at the beauty of a man. He smiled at her, gleaming white teeth against skin that had been touched over and over again by the sun and blessed with a tinge of midnight. She could not keep her eyes from meeting his; nothing seemed out of place, the two of them in the middle of the road, dusty, dirty, and hot, both staring without moving.

He took off his hat and swept her a bow. He had a trim mustache in those days, pencil thin, and lips that smiled so hard they nearly cracked. Before she could figure out what he was doing, he sidled in close to her, bent his head, and kissed her mouth, then stepped back and started to sing. She had never heard anyone sing like Turk did then. It seemed as if his whole body were singing to her, his head moving, his hands, legs, and feet swaying. But she couldn't move. Couldn't even say anything. He took her hand afterward and asked her name. She whispered, "Daisy," and he said her name was sweet. When she snatched her hand away, he took it back calmly and pressed it against his heart, and she let him, all the while hearing Birdie, in the very back of her mind, telling her to be careful.

They stood in the road for a while, and she told him almost everything. About Birdie. About Mr. Shorty Long. And about not knowing what she would do in the world without her mama.

He listened. And every time she felt she was getting close to crying again, he'd squeeze her hand and the tears stopped.

Daisy was fifteen the day that she met Turk on the road and opened herself up to a stranger. He was barely twenty.

The next few days were always hard for her to remember, because it was as if the hours became minutes and the minutes seconds. He walked her home and came to see her every day. And on the third day he asked her to marry him and move up to New York City. Daisy told Mr. Shorty Long, who begged her to go see Birdie before she made up her mind. He was changed when she went to see him. The house was a wreck, as though he had pulled every dish out of every cupboard and broke them on purpose. The little man was drunk, too. Although she stepped over the threshold, she didn't go far, even though he urged her in, leaning on the handle to support himself. She told him she was leaving, that she was getting married, that she would be in touch as soon as they were settled. And also that Birdie said he owed her money.

"Wait, Daisy Sweet Mae. You just wait right here for me. Don't go nowhere."

His breath stank. He looked unwashed. But she nodded and agreed to wait. He tottered back. "I have something for you. It's a wedding present. I hope you're very happy. Wait, do I know this man?"

He was so drunk she thought he would fall over soon. "Yes, you know him, remember? And so does Birdie." She was not even ashamed of the lie. When he handed her the ashtray and a packet of bills totaling one hundred and fifty dollars, she smiled, thanked him, and walked out of the house.

"Daisy Sweet Mae, I'm gonna miss you. I'm gonna miss you

something awful. Please take care of yourself. You gonna see your mama before you leave? She gonna want to see you." Mr. Shorty Long fell to his knees at the door. "Girl, did you hear me? I'm gonna miss you."

Daisy nodded. "I heard you, Mr. Shorty Long." But she wouldn't go back. She knew that if she turned to help him from his knees, she'd never leave. So she kept walking, her head held high, her thoughts on New York and her new life with a husband.

They left town five days after Turk proposed.

Daisy finally sent word to Birdie after Olivia Jean reached her first birthday. She was never much of a letter writer, but had tried so that Birdie could know about Olivia Jean and how well Daisy was taking care of her. Once Birdie received the first letter, she answered and enclosed a check, saying that Mr. Shorty Long had put telephones in both the houses; here were the numbers and a check to get Daisy and Turk a phone, too. Daisy did as Birdie asked. Daisy would put Olivia Jean on the line and let her speak, but only for a few minutes. Long-distance calls were expensive. Every once in a while Birdie asked for a visit, if they would come to Cold Water Springs, but Daisy was evasive. She didn't care if she ever saw the small town again.

Mr. Shorty Long died before Olivia Jean turned three.

Daisy braced herself. She had not seen Birdie since that last time in the lockup, and now her stomach heaved and she was unsettled as they made their way toward the little house. She wished there had been some other way for her to help Olivia Jean besides binding her to the crazy woman who had birthed her but never took time to rear her.

The woman who stepped out onto the gravel path was her mother. Daisy knew that in her heart, but her brain had trouble making the adjustment. She was still big but no longer as big; still black, but now her skin was tinged with gray, as if getting older changed the color of her skin, or perhaps it was health that changed it. Regardless, it made Daisy uneasy. And then there was her face. Her mother, the one she remembered, had an easy face, an open laugh. This woman was different. There was a quietness around her eyes, and there were lines around her mouth and forehead that hadn't been there the last time she saw her mother. Daisy wondered that fifteen years should make such a difference.

Daisy held out a limp hand to Birdie, but instead she was embraced and held tightly. "You've grown into a beautiful woman," her mother whispered in her ear, and it took all of Daisy's willpower not to hug her back with as much strength. She pulled away first.

"Birdie, this is Turk, and this is Olivia Jean." Birdie did shake hands with Turk. Then she turned to Olivia Jean and held her arms open. Daisy held her breath. Olivia Jean didn't take to strangers well. She was surprised when the child almost ran to Birdie and stayed in her arms. After a while Birdie pulled back, stroked Olivia Jean's face, and bent to kiss her. Daisy turned away. Turk had gone to the trunk of the car and retrieved his kit and Daisy's overnight bag. He stood waiting, impatient. Daisy went to the back of the car and got Olivia Jean's suitcase. With her arm around Olivia Jean, Birdie led them to the little house.

Birdie showed them into the parlor and they sat, the smells from the kitchen both inviting and familiar to Daisy. But as she sat on the sofa, Turk grabbed her hand, and she turned her head to look at him and he gave her a long wink. And that wink was all it took for the anger she held toward him to burn out. Her heart thudded. She remembered, too.

The room had changed little in the past fifteen years. An overstuffed horsehair sofa dominated the center; a table with a lace doily held a large radio. On the walls were various pictures of people Birdie had once described as her family, even though she had been orphaned at six. The first time Turk had come into the room, he was fascinated by the photographs and asked Daisy about each of them, and was impressed that she knew at least a few words about all of the people who cluttered the space.

She got him a Pepsi-Cola from the icebox, and he put his hat on the back of the sofa and stretched his arms wide. She sat next to him but not too close. He finished his drink in a couple of gulps, put his bottle down on the table near the radio, and, without a word, pulled her to him and started to kiss her.

Daisy knew about kissing. She opened her mouth wide.

"C'mon over here." He made her sit on his lap. She felt him, felt his thing get bigger. He rubbed against her, and then she felt his hands travel under her skirt. She pushed his hands away. That was what you were supposed to do. That was what Birdie had taught her—*No hands under your dress.*

But Turk's fingers were persistent and felt good as they entered that spot between her legs. He pushed her back on the sofa and lifted her dress. But instead of heaving himself on her, something she had expected, he placed his head between her thighs, which she had not expected. She beat at his shoulders, trying to push him off. He laughed, and his breath tickled that place with his warmth. She could not make him stop, and seconds later she didn't want him to. She was breathless, shuddering, rolling her head on the horsehair sofa, and wondering why Mama Birdie had never warned her about this. Birdie had never said anything about tongues.

The next evening when Turk came into the parlor, Daisy had already washed thoroughly and had decided not to wear panties.

They ate together at the kitchen table, helping themselves to the food Birdie had prepared for Daisy's homecoming. There was fried chicken, corn bread, snap beans, and potato salad. Olivia Jean made the lemonade and poured before carefully taking her seat. The four of them ate in silence for the most part. Daisy had a headache. She didn't know if it was because of the trip or because of being back in the house she had grown up in; she thought it was probably both. After eating, Turk stretched his arms and pushed back from the table.

"Well, I know what y'all done asked me to do, and I ain't got no problem with Miss Olivia Jean staying here wid me, but one of y'all got to stay, too." Birdie had collected the dishes and began to wash them in a large steel pot that substituted for a sink.

Daisy was wiping down the table. Olivia Jean was sweeping the kitchen floor, getting ready to grab the dustpan. Turk was sitting with a toothpick, rolling it between his fingers.

Daisy straightened, holding the wet cloth in one hand. "What you mean, Birdie?"

"I say my grandbaby is welcome to stay here for as long as she need to stay, but one of y'all gotta stay wid her. And, as her mama and my flesh-an'-bone kin, I think you the one to stay."

"But I gotta go back to work, I gotta—"

"Humph, the only thing you gotta do is take care of this here

baby and the one she got on the way. That your job." Birdie
stared at Daisy without flinching.

"You trying to tell me how to act? How to be a mama? How
you gonna do that? Huh?"

"Jus' 'cause I might not a been a good mama to you don't mean
I don't know how to be one. Like I said, she can stay here, no
problem, but you gotta stay, too."

Before Daisy could speak, Turk cleared his throat loudly, and
the three women looked in his direction. Olivia Jean stood behind Birdie.

"Daisy, you should stay with Olivia. We can't leave our responsibility with your mama. She gettin' on, and Olivia Jean ain't
always easy." He was very controlled in his speech, and that told
Daisy that he wasn't happy with what Birdie was saying either.
But the fact that he had said she should stay, without talking to
her first, alone, made her weak with anger. She sat down at the
table. She had thought they would work things out together in
New York, without Olivia Jean and without her baby being in
the way. Just a little while ago, while they sat in the parlor, Turk
had winked at her and grabbed at her hand like in the old days,
when they were first together. Now, without even a discussion,
he'd sided with Birdie. She took a deep breath but couldn't look
any of them in the face. Her mouth was dry.

Birdie wiped her wet hands on her apron and moved to the
oven, opening it. She reached in with her apron and removed a
pie, setting it on a shelf below the window. She placed the second
pie next to the first and then turned back to the Stones, Daisy,
Turk, and Olivia Jean, raising her eyebrow because none of them
had said a word for a few minutes.

"Birdie, I don't know what you tryin' to pull here. If I had known you was thinkin' this way, we'd have stayed in New York. You coulda told me so we didn't have to do no twenty-hour ride."

Birdie didn't reply. Instead she gently took the broom from Olivia Jean's hands and started to sweep near Turk. Turk moved his size twelve feet and let the old woman sweep under the table. Daisy noticed that when Olivia Jean had tried to do the same thing, he hadn't moved. Olivia Jean held the dustpan for her grandmother and then went to the back door and threw the contents into the bush, as Birdie instructed her. "Dust to dust," the old woman said.

"Child, could you leave us alone for a minute? We got some things to discuss. Maybe you could walk around in the back, take a turn around the lake. Bet them fish'd love to see your face."

As Olivia Jean passed her, Birdie took the opportunity to brush the girl's bangs from her forehead. And Daisy felt surprised at the way her heart constricted at that gesture. She had to stop herself from saying, *Don't touch my daughter.* She grabbed her purse and pulled out her cigarettes and the lighter, flicking it open.

"You wanna smoke, take it outside. I can't abide the smell in here."

Daisy took the cigarette from her lips and threw the lighter back in her purse.

"Thank you kindly," said Birdie, and sat at the table across from Turk and started to speak to him. Daisy balled her fist and realized too late that she still held the cigarette.

"Shit," Daisy said, and rose to stand by the window.

She stared outside for the most part while Birdie and Turk came to terms about how much money he would send each month for their upkeep. She heard Birdie talk about how much her eggs brought at the farmers' market and how that wasn't enough to keep three people fed, especially with a baby on the way. Turk countered with the sky-high cost of an apartment in New York and losing one full salary. They finally agreed on him sending thirty dollars a month, and they shook hands. Daisy was glad that Turk was doing the business end of this with her mother. She didn't want to deal with Birdie. The adage, "Once bitten, twice shy," ran through her head over and over again, but she cautioned herself that Birdie had done this kind of thing to her more than once or twice. Each lockup, hadn't there been the tearful farewells and the promises from Birdie about straightening up and doing better? And yet she'd gone back to her old ways as soon as she was released. Now here Birdie was again, promising refuge for Olivia Jean with one hand and imprisonment for Daisy with the other.

And then there was Turk. But shouldn't she have known better with Turk, too? He had not proved himself trustworthy either. She knew his ways. And it seemed to her that Turk had jumped at the opportunity to abandon her and Olivia Jean, getting off very easy in paying thirty dollars a month for them to stay buried in Alabama.

Of the three, although Olivia Jean had made the mess in the first place, Daisy felt her the least to blame. After all, Birdie and Turk were grown and had wronged her before. Olivia Jean had not made the right choice, but maybe she deserved more than one chance. Daisy caught sight of her daughter walking in the backyard, headed for the lake. She went to the screen door and walked out to the steps. The air was hot, waves floating around her head, stillness gathered in the yard like before a good, hard rain. It was the time of year in Cold Water Springs when storms cropped up without warning and lightning played across the skies, water drenching the earth, accompanied by the ominous crack of thunder. She remembered nights sneaking to the window and watching the streaks of lightning spread open the night. And how the thunder made her shiver. Someone at church had told her that thunder was God's anger at a sin. Even now, as a grown woman, she still remembered that, and huddled close to Olivia Jean or Turk at the onset of a storm.

The yard was unchanged. There was a large patch of green in the front, and one lone magnolia tree. The gravel road ran through the green up to the porch, which had a large overhang and three steps. The house itself was a dingy white, the same color that it had been fifteen years ago, when Daisy left. She wondered if it had been painted since then. There was some peeling on the steps and near the twin posts that held the roof in place. The thing that struck her most was that there were no flowers. Besides sewing and running moonshine, she and Birdie had kept a flower bed. Now there was only empty space, dry, red dirt packed tightly around the house. Daisy sighed.

Birdie had a few chickens and one rooster. They pecked at the ground but seemed more inclined to congregate in the shade of the chicken coop. Daisy didn't blame them; her choice would have been the shade, too. She decided to follow Olivia Jean to the lake.

The path Daisy took was narrow, bordered on each side by a stand of trees, the only worthwhile natural shade on the land Birdie and she now owned. She could understand why Mr. Shorty Long left the big house to Birdie; Birdie had taken care of him for as long as Daisy could remember. What she didn't understand was why he would have included her in any will.

One night Birdie had called, all choked up.

"Birdie, what's wrong?" It was nine o'clock, and Daisy was waiting for Turk. His shift had ended at five and he should have been home by six.

"Mr. Shorty Long done died. He up and died right after I served him some catfish and watermelon. He put his hand over his heart and fell in his plate. He gone."

Daisy was surprised, but there was a meanness in her the nights that Turk didn't come home when he was supposed to. The type of meanness that kept her from picking up Olivia Jean even if she cried. The type that made Daisy stay up drinking beer after beer until she either passed out on the sofa or he made it home. And speaking with Birdie only made things worse.

"Why you so upset over a cracker? He wasn' nuthin' to you. Wasn' nuthin' to me. You crazy to be carryin' on over some white man."

After a long moment Daisy heard a click. She tried calling back, but something must have been wrong with Birdie's line, because it rang busy. She sat in her seat by the window and kept watch for Turk until she fell asleep sucking on a Pabst Blue Ribbon.

Two nights later Birdie called again, composed. She told Daisy that Mr. Shorty Long had left Birdie the big house on top of the hill and Daisy the little house at the foot of the hill, as well as the land and livestock.

"Birdie, them crackers gonna let us keep all this?"

"They ain't got no choice. He left a will, and the will says all this is ours."

"Well, what we gonna do? Sell it?"

"No, I plan on living in the little house, same as always. Don't know about the big house; we'll see. But I wanted to call and let you know that you own the little house. And I'll move if you want me to."

"Nah. I ain't got no plans now to come back. You stay where you is."

They spoke for a while longer. Birdie asked if Daisy would come home for Mr. Shorty Long's funeral services, something Daisy had already thought of doing. She wanted to. He had been a fixture in her life.

"I done talked to Reverend Walker, an' he gonna preach the eulogy. He somethin' else, that man. Sometimes I think fire comin' out of his mouth when he speakin' the Word."

She changed her mind when she heard who was preaching the eulogy. She told Birdie that she could not get the time off work and hung up the phone a short while later. She considered telling Turk about Mr. Shorty Long leaving her property. But something stopped her. She thought that maybe one day she and Olivia Jean might need a place to stay. Maybe Turk wouldn't come home at all. And then they would be in trouble. When Olivia Jean got older, she'd tell her. But Daisy was glad to have something to hold on to when things got rough with Turk. So the land, like one other secret, was held close to her heart, never spoken of aloud, never dwelled upon for too long, but trotted out when Daisy needed to feel secure of her place in the world. Many times over the years Daisy thought of the house, the flowers in the front yard, and the gravel path that led to it, and smiled. She was a property owner; she owned a house all by herself. With as much frequency, she thanked Mr. Shorty Long, the man who had given her a small measure of independence.

• • •

*D*aisy made her way to Olivia Jean's side and watched as her daughter wiggled a toe in the water.

"Better watch out. Water might have a gator in it." Olivia Jean squealed and jerked her foot away. Daisy laughed.

"Mama, you joking?" Daisy nodded, and Olivia Jean sat down at the edge of the water.

"Ain't never heard of havin' no gator back here, but people do tell of there being lots of 'em in Florida." Daisy sat next to her daughter.

"How come you didn't tell me that you had this in back of your house?" Olivia Jean turned her eyes on her mother, and Daisy was at a loss. She shrugged her shoulders.

"I guess I ain't think nuthin' of it. This was just how things was. Lake always been here, so it ain't no special thing. You know what I mean?"

Olivia Jean shook her head.

"Well, it's like describing New York to people. Somebody might visit there and think it's a big thing to go underground on the subway. But it ain't really nuthin' special to you and me, is it?"

Olivia Jean paused, nodded her head, and then asked, "You real mad with Grandma Birdie, ain't you? You don't wanna have to stay here with me?"

Daisy sighed. "Olivia Jean, this don't have nuthin' to do with me not wantin' to stay with you. It got to do with Birdie bein' full of lies."

Olivia Jean stood up. They locked eyes.

"You full of them, too. You don't want to stay with me. All you ever care about is bein' with Daddy. So you just like she is." Her daughter marched away, and Daisy, angry at first, started to call her back but decided against it. She picked up a rock and threw it in the water, rippling the surface, scaring the fish. She wished she were someplace far, far away.

Mr. Shorty Long was one for throwing pebbles out on the water and watching them skip. He had taught Daisy when she was young, showing her how to aim and throw more like a boy. She wasn't good at it but she enjoyed being outdoors. She remembered him spending the whole day with her, teaching her how to bait a line, how to be still and catch fish. When she was fifteen, and for the first time she was going to be without her mother, Birdie, who was sentenced to one week in the lockup for running hooch, there was only Mr. Shorty Long. But Daisy couldn't count on anyone but Birdie. She needed her mother. She cried like a baby. Her wails were loud, echoing across the surface of the water.

"Ahem."

She saw Mr. Shorty Long through her tears, wiped her eyes, and stood up.

"What's wrong with you, gal? Somebody hurt you?"

"No, Mr. Shorty Long."

"Then why you crying?"

"It's Mama Birdie. She got to go to lockup again, an' she want me to move in with that Lou Willie girl, the one that always be botherin' at me. I don' wanna go there."

"Humph. What your mama done now?"

She lied. Mama Birdie had told her that she was not supposed to talk about formula with Mr. Shorty Long, and she was never to tell him that Daisy went along to the customers, too. "I ain't know, sir; she ain't told me."

"Well, go on home now. I'll see if I can go talk to Birdie tomorrow. Can you stay there by yourself or you need to come up to the big house with me?"

"No, sir, I ain't afraid. And I done already talked to Reverend Walker and he gonna come by."

Mr. Shorty Long stopped and stared at her for a moment.

"Don't let him come to the house at night, gal. Ain't no reason for him to come to you in the nighttime."

Daisy smiled down at him. She was fifteen, but taller than he was by a few inches. She was going to be as tall as Birdie.

"No, sir, he ain't coming in the nighttime. He coming way up in the day, and he gonna bring one of them saint ladies from the church with him."

Mr. Shorty Long nodded and picked up a handful of stones to throw.

"You get on home before it get too dark out here. And don't let him in the house without one of them women. You hear?"

"Yes, sir."

Daisy ran home then, feeling some better to have cried and talked to Mr. Shorty Long. She didn't like that she had lied to him, but she had promised her mother, and Birdie took precedence over Mr. Shorty Long, even if there were times when he acted like family, too. Then she thought about Reverend Percy Walker and the fact that he was to come visit. All the girls in church loved the preacher. When he peeked into choir rehearsal even the grown women giggled. They talked about how words rolled off his tongue like honey. She daydreamed about his visit.

He might even take her to the jail in his fine car, because it was tiresome to have to walk to town every day to see Mama Birdie. Her legs ached from so much walking.

The next day Daisy was up at sunrise, cleaning the house at the bottom of the hill. Company was coming, and she didn't want anyone to say that she and Birdie lived in a dirty house. She shook the rugs, swept the floor, and dusted all through the house. She changed the sheets on Birdie's bed and swept under her own. She went outside to collect the eggs.

When Daisy crossed the yard from the lean-to that served as the chicken coop, the preacher's car was parked up close to the porch. He was sitting on the steps fanning himself with one of the paper fans they gave out in church. In his lap he held his Bible, a great monstrosity of a book, the leather peeled and worn, the gold letters almost smudged off from use. She looked around for the saint lady. There was none.

He got up as she climbed onto the porch.

"How do, Miss Daisy?"

She smiled at him but kept her eyes down, the way Birdie told her to do with adults. *Be polite, but don't look your elders in the eyes. It's a sign of disrespect.*

"Miss Daisy, I do declare, you looking older and older each day. You sixteen now?"

"No, Reverend. I'm fifteen."

Daisy sat on the porch in the glider while he leaned back on the steps and talked about her soul. He kept visiting all through-out the week Birdie was locked up. And he came the next time Birdie went in, too. Daisy couldn't deny that she liked the attention. He started to bring her things, pretty trinkets, a flower, books. She let him into the house, out of the heat of the day and into the cool of the parlor. She pretended that he was courting her and that she was Lovey, his wife.

He kissed her hand each time he left. As they sat on the sofa he whispered thickly in her ear and complimented her on her figure, how she kept everything so clean, said he was sorry that her mother wasn't taking better care of her. Daisy nodded; this was the second time Birdie had been put away in the county jail within the last month. She wouldn't be out for another three weeks. His arm snaked around her waist and he kissed her full on the mouth, his breath smelling of formula, of the white lightning that her mother distilled and drove to the outer parts of Colbert County to distribute.

And finally it happened. One dark night he showed up crying, telling her how he had tried and tried to resist temptation but she had him by the heart, that he just needed a little of her kindness, just enough to keep him going. There wasn't a lady prettier or sweeter in all of Alabama. She beat out Lovey, who didn't love him anymore. Could she spare a little of her beauty for an old fool?

Daisy spread her legs then, trembling. She watched herself as he heaved on top of her, huffing and puffing and spending himself in less than a minute, and wondered why everyone made such a fuss over something so fleeting. Love? A moment, a groan, and then over? He cried again as he zipped his pants. He begged her not to tell anyone, most especially not his wife, Lovey. Daisy sat on the edge of her bed and nodded. He kissed her hand again, and as he left he promised to come back, but he never did. By the time Birdie was locked up for the third time, in the middle of June, Daisy was expecting Olivia Jean and didn't know what to do.

.   .   .

*D*aisy stood by the water. She bent to pick up more stones and began by launching a big one across the surface of the lake. She still couldn't throw. The stone only skimmed the surface twice before sinking. Things were not close to turning out as she had planned. She felt out of control, off balance, and very, very angry. Birdie again, messing with her life. She had to stay with Olivia Jean when all the while she had meant for her and Turk to have some time alone so she could talk to him, get him to accept the new baby. Go to the movies. Walk Manhattan together like they used to when they were first married and she was pregnant.

*T*he people walking the city scared Daisy. She had to keep her eyes down, because when she didn't the men approached, and she wanted nothing to do with them. But she found that if she kept her face lowered she got lost. Manhattan was for her only when she had Turk by her side. No one risked speaking to her when she was with him. Her husband was a tall, wide-shouldered man who had a knack for either charming people or scaring them to death. Daisy liked this in him and felt safe as he navigated her through the crowds, one large hand at her waist, the other holding on to his hat.

She didn't question the late nights at first. She knew he loved her. He just had a streak in him; maybe like Mr. Shorty Long, who was a gentleman until the nights he hit the bottle hard and thundered through his house on top of the hill until no one could talk to him, not even Birdie. Her mother was forced to sneak in once the commotion had died down and pick up the shattered lamps and bric-a-brac and eventually Mr. Shorty Long, too. He always keeled over right next to the bed, as if he aimed for it but could not quite make it.

It was a payday Friday in October when Daisy decided to follow Turk from his job in a factory that made books. She waited by the side of the building as he walked out with a group. When the metal door opened, the heavy smell of printing presses and ink flooded the area. She held her nose and waited for the men to pass a distance before she followed. They were quiet, weary, and they stood together waiting for traffic to thin before they crossed the street to the subway. They shuffled across two lanes of traffic, and Daisy was struck by the fact that they were all old men and Turk was not. He looked like one of them when he came out, but crossing the street changed him; he stood taller suddenly; he smiled and raised his hand to say good-bye. He didn't go downstairs to the subway as the rest did; he kept walking and she followed behind.

Daisy was four and a half months pregnant in late October. She carried the baby high on her stomach, and no one noticed unless she said something about being in the family way. She looked like the teenager she was, not yet sixteen, a few pimples still on her face, awkwardly tall and perhaps on the heavy side. She was wearing a disguise of sorts, an outfit from the throwaway bin at the Salvation Army: a bulky white shirt, a midcalf herringbone skirt, with ballerina flats. She knew she looked a fright, but she told herself that this adventure was in service to her marriage, and she stopped the internal dialogue she had about not matching and how the skirt rode up in back because of the girth of her stomach. Daisy had never felt so unattractive. She threw a jacket over her arm before leaving their apartment.

A girl can be invisible in the city, she thought. She was one of many colored girls with hair caught up in white barrettes on either side of her head and who roamed the streets in New York with freedom. But even if there was a look or a short pause as eyes shifted over her stomach, she was still invisible, and that was what she wanted. Invisibility. Obscurity.

Daisy stayed less than half a block behind him. When he went up Liberty Avenue and sauntered inside an old Italian bar, she sat waiting at the curb, her feet crossed like a swami's and her head slightly bowed, facing away from the door. Only the thought of so many men inside kept her from going in. At fifteen Daisy did not like men, only Turk. Each time the door opened, she hid her face between her hands. One man tripped over her and told her to "get the fuck out the way"; another accused her of smoking too much dope and told her that she had better "get home to those kids or else." She told him she would, and her solemn nod encouraged him to walk away.

A couple of hours later Turk passed close enough to her so that she smelled the beer on his breath as he belched, punching his fist into his upper chest. She waited until he crossed the street and rose to follow him.

He seemed not to know where he was going. She followed him anyway. Three times he went up and down one block, neither turning to the left nor the right but slowing in front of one gray, soulless building. It was the kind of three-story home that told no story. There was no garden, only concrete and a black door.

The fourth time Turk made as if he were going to pass the house altogether, but he stopped and stood in front of the gate, then grabbed it open. Daisy felt her heart leaving her chest, but if asked she could not have said why.

A girl could be invisible in the city except to other girls. Someone saw Daisy.

"Whatcha doin'?" a small voice called to her after Turk had made his way up the stairs and into the building. "You done passed by here three times like that man. Whatcha doin'?"

She couldn't have been much older than Daisy, but she had a stroller in front of her, pushing it gently back and forth. Daisy could not think straight. "That my man. I gotta follow him 'cause sometimes he gets lost. Like sometimes he sleepwalks."

"Umph. Then he be sleepwalkin' a lot to that house over there. In fact, he done sleepwalked here every Friday night that I knowed of and went right on out, too, when he woke up on Saturday." The girl laughed and woke up the baby. Daisy stood frozen, her hand on the gate, her mouth dry.

She didn't want to think about it. About how she stole into the house because the door was open and crept up the stairs, pausing at each landing, wondering where Turk might have gone, until she heard his voice, singing. She stopped at the apartment. Again, it was open. An invitation.

They were sprawled on the entryway floor, his pants at his knees, and she was taking him from the back. There was no room for Daisy to step over them. No place that she turned where she did not smell sex, did not see their bodies. She choked, bent double, and then started to vomit. She heard the woman screaming and Turk's shouts, but all she could think about was purging the sight of them from her belly. Getting rid of everything in her body. Giving it to Turk and the no-name, big black-assed woman who serviced him. She wanted them both to have all of it.

Afterward, there were days at a time when she did not leave the apartment. She kept the doors locked and bolted, the windows shut, the lights out. She drank coffee and beer whenever she got a chance. The coffee woke her and kept her from sleeping all day, and the beer helped put her to sleep at night.

Turk moved like a shadow around the apartment, but she would not allow him to come near her. She wanted to see the big house on the hill, to sit at the table with Mr. Shorty Long again and answer his questions. She wanted her room and the Sears catalog, her sewing machine, the lake between the houses. She wanted, more than anything else, to hear Birdie humming her tuneless songs, dressed in purple, brown, and gray, with a pair of size-ten red shoes jammed on her size-eleven-and-a-half feet. But there was no Birdie to run to. Her mother was still in jail. She had to deal with Turk, who tried singing to her and coming in from work on time and sitting with her in the airless apartment. He bought her vegetables to eat and milk to drink, soup for her stomach, and begged her forgiveness. But she couldn't look at him. All she saw was his behind stuck in the air and the woman trapped under him. Only it wasn't his behind. It was Reverend Walker's. And she was the one trapped. Wherever she looked, there was a wall.

Daisy couldn't help it. She didn't want to but there was no one else. She went back to loving Turk. She waited for the time when he came home from the book factory, smelling of burned metal and ink, only to turn her head away from him, not wanting to seem too hungry for his presence when she was; she would have eaten him whole if it meant that he would not be with anyone else. So she watched and waited and grew bigger with another man's child. And sometimes she cried because there was no home and no other love to go back to, no other love but Turk in her life.

*T*hen came the Friday night when her pains started. She knew the tightening in her back was a labor pain. She got up from the chair and got her purse and walked down the stairs slowly. Mr. Willie Boyd and Mr. Jerry Boyd sat on the stoop, and both hurried to rise and nod at her as she passed.

"Is everything all right, Mrs. Stone?" She could not tell which one asked the question.

"I think the baby is on the way."

Then things became a blur. One took her hand. The other said he would stay to tell Turk, and somehow she was whisked to the hospital. She sat in a wheelchair, and a cheerful nurse took her to a room. The woman smiled and asked her what she was going to name the baby. Daisy shrugged. She had a stabbing pain, worse than the ones before. The doctor came and examined her. She didn't know what to say to anyone. All she kept thinking was that she was only fifteen and where was Turk?

She took a deep breath. The pain came in waves but it was bearable. For the first time in months she began to think with some clarity, the way Birdie had taught her to think. And she found the secret to Turk and love as she lay panting in the bed, sweaty and alone. Sometimes it didn't matter if a person loved another with all their being, like she loved Turk. Love wasn't enough. She had another contraction. It might be that nothing would ever be enough for Turk. But she vowed that she would keep on trying, keep loving him the best way she knew how, and maybe one day she would be able to forgive him and herself for all the history and bad things that had happened.

Someone wiped her brow. They raised her from the bed and opened her legs. The smiling nurse, Olivia, was holding her hand, encouraging her to breathe harder, to push. Daisy felt strong now, now that she knew what she had to do with Turk. She pushed.

Then there was the awful tearing, and her own self making pitiful noises, grunting. They laid the baby in her arms and she looked and could have screamed. Such a shriveled little package. Such a raisin thing. She held the fingers, touched the little toes, kissed her. Something twisted inside her breast. The nurse was smiling at her. That was when she decided.

Turk came much later. He paced around the bed, a big man holding himself in. When they brought the baby to her again and she held her out to him, he shook his head.

"I already done seen her." He paused as if searching for something else to say.

"She don't look like you. The doctor say she healthy, was screaming up a storm when he hit her bottom." He came to stand by the foot of the bed. "Next time we gonna have us a boy, okay?"

Daisy stared at Turk for half a second and hugged her baby closer. She had already decided that there would be no next time. She was going to speak with Nurse Olivia before she was discharged.

PART THREE

Birdie

*B*irdie's father died first and then her mother, coughing deep in the night. No one knew what to do with her, so they took Birdie into the deep woods to the local healer woman, Queenie Monroe. Queenie took one look at the child and started laughing, loud and deep. She told them that she would be glad to keep Birdie.

Birdie remembered the day by squinting in her brain. She was almost six. Queenie took hold of her tiny stick arm and held it against her own big oak tree arm and laughed even harder.

"You couldn't be more mines if I hadda birthed you my own self," the healer woman had said.

Looking at a picture of Olivia Jean, Birdie knew the feeling. Like maybe she spit Olivia Jean out and not Daisy. Like maybe things would have been better all the way around if that were the case. *Boy, God sure was a joker,* Birdie thought.

She stood on her front porch, a woman close to sixty, big, robust, and as inky dark as a velvet night in the country. She held herself erect, nose turned westward, sniffing the air, sensing the rain to come through the aching joints in her body. Though no clouds appeared and the sun shone harshly through the foliage of the magnolia tree planted for shade years back, she trusted her aged bones more than her eyes. Rain was on the way. She spit over the edge of the porch, a mixture of saliva and snuff, hacking a wad of mucus afterward. "Hope they get here soon and don't get caught in this rain." She spoke aloud to herself, a habit she'd developed over the last few years. She went back inside to boil water for tea.

The problem with living, Birdie thought, *is that you can't see the future. Everything is all tied up in a knot in your stomach—the pain, the truth, the knowledge of death waiting just past the next step, maybe even the next word.* When Birdie thought of the future beyond a week she began to make up what would happen. Made it as good as she could and then as bad as she could, knowing that the real happening would most likely fall between the two.

Daisy had called in the middle of the night. It was late enough that Birdie's heart jumped and she had to take a few deep breaths before answering the telephone. She reminded herself that she was the only colored woman in Cold Water Springs to have a telephone, courtesy of the late Mr. Shorty Long. She closed her eyes and puckered her lips in the general vicinity of heaven, where she assumed Shorty now resided.

"Birdie, I got some news for you." Daisy was not one for wasting time on long-distance calls.

There were shadows on the ceiling of Birdie's bedroom, made from the swaying magnolia tree. Although it was summer, a fine breeze bent the branches and fluttered the bushes that sat around the edge of the house. She was tired because arthritis, a constant nagging companion, would not let her sleep the way she wanted to, even after hours spent sweeping, cleaning, cooking, and, in the midnight hour, prayer.

"Spit it out." She hadn't meant to be so harsh, so impatient. But sometimes Daisy made her that way. And, too, there was the pain.

"Olivia Jean is gonna have a baby."

Birdie couldn't answer right away. She choked and managed to spit some phlegm in the handkerchief she kept by the bed. Then she tried to remember when she had last dreamed of fish, the harbinger of birth, but could not think clearly enough before Daisy's voice shot at her again through a crackling phone line.

"Did you hear me?"

"Yeah, I heard you, Daisy. The baby gonna have a baby. What y'all gonna do?"

"I was hoping you could help us out. I was hoping Olivia Jean could come down with you for a little while."

Daisy's call was more than a week ago. Now she sat and waited and thought and decided against praying. Seemed like whenever she did pray, the opposite of what she prayed for happened. So nowadays she moved her thoughts around in her head, back and forth like a saw on green wood. She knew that the devil was just waiting for her to show some kind of partiality so he could turn things around. But she felt that now that she had a notion of where he went on these kinds of things, it was best to keep her feelings under wraps.

She did wish she were still a hard-drinking woman. A shot of something strong might bring relief—to her aches and pains, to her fears. But too much drink, like too much rich food, was now forbidden. Her routine was set. She could down a shot of whiskey every now and then, eat a piece of red velvet cake on occasion, and bed Lupe Rawlins once a month, but that was about all her body could stand by way of enjoyment. The drink was surefire, the cake, if it was baked by Amelia Lee, was delicious, whereas Lupe's night maneuvers might not always be counted on to ease the hunger that gnawed between her legs. But she suspected that had more to do with her never being satisfied rather than a lack of talent on his part.

"Woman, you is greedy is all. Stone-cold greedy. Naw, naw, don't touch it. Can't you see the little fella is tired?"

"Good God, Lupe, I ain't been your way for over a month. You tellin' me once is all you got? You ain't saved up no more than that for me?"

"Birdie, we both is near dying. Almost dead for sure. You lucky I ain't already done gone, with you strangling my neck with them legs of yours. Now, move on off me. I gotta catch my breath."

Lupe's hand rested on his heaving chest. "Don'tcha ever think about anything but lovin', don'tcha ever?"

Birdie thought she heard a quaver in Lupe's voice and that he might start crying. "Yup. I think on a heap of things, but since I can't change 'em, I mostly keep my thinking to myself."

They were dressing, moving slowly. Lupe stooped to pick his shirt up from the floor and cussed when he saw a button missing. In Birdie's frenzy to undress him it must have popped off.

"Dammit, Birdie. You gonna hafta take it easy from now on. I ain't got but three shirts. Gonna take me at least an hour to thread the damn needle to sew the button back on. Where's the dang-blasted button, anyway?"

"Button right here, old man. Stop your fussing." What she didn't tell him was that she had found it between her butt cheeks. Some things Lupe was better off not knowing. She put the button on his nightstand, the only piece of furniture in the room besides the bed.

"Don'tcha ever think about dying, Birdie? Where we gonna go next? Who we gonna see when we get there?" Lupe sat on the edge of the bed, shirt buttoned crooked, with a sigh that came all the way through his skinny chest.

Birdie paused. She was in the middle of pulling up her girdle, and that always took a lot of effort, what between easing it up over her rolling thighs and holding in her stomach. But it was worth it, taking her watermelon-sized belly and squeezing it down to a svelte honeydew.

"Don't know those answers, old man, and I ain't really looking for 'em." The shoulder straps to her bra fell in place with a loud snap. A moment staring at Lupe's bowed head softened her. She walked over and helped him off the bed, pulling his zipper up and giving his private parts a tender smack.

"But I tell you what, if I get there afore you, I'll wait on you— but you better hurry up. Bet they got lots of studs up there could use a hand with they pants, just like you."

"You ain't nuthing but a crazy old woman, you know that? You 'bout plumb crazy." But he was smiling and so was Birdie. She kissed him on the cheek, and they held hands as they walked out of the little bedroom at the back of his house.

At the door he put his arms around her and was ready to give her a good-bye kiss. His tongue was poised, his hand gripping her butt firmly, when she stopped him with her hands on his chest, covering three-quarters of it without opening her fingers wide.

"Honey, I can't kiss you now," said Birdie.

He opened one eye and then the other. "Why not, woman?"

Birdie put her head down. "I done took a little dip o' snuff."

Lupe sighed and let her go.

"I wanna come by next week," Birdie said. Her hand was on the doorknob.

"Woman, if you see me next week, it gonna be to hold my hand. Don't be comin' over here thinkin' you gonna get you some. That ain't gonna happen."

She slipped away with Lupe still fussing, nodding his head for all he was worth and shaking a fist in her direction. She smiled to herself, thinking how she might come back again next week with a lemon pound cake and a carton of milk. Then maybe Lupe could be persuaded to show her more of the affection she craved. Birdie had to laugh outright. Here she was, walking with a swing to her step, feeling like she was thirty instead of past sixty. No aches or pains today, just the joy that came from good loving.

Sometimes the breeze in the morning carried the smell of dew-kissed grass and muddy earth. And Birdie would stop to fill her lungs because Shorty was still a part of the land, loamy and rich. Her head would tilt in the direction of the wind as she drank in the scent of her first and only husband, Shorty Long. A dead man tied to the land, whose smell lingered long past the time when it should have receded like an old lavender sachet pushed to the back of a drawer. Birdie found herself haunted by his smell.

He never showed up when she willed him to; as in life, Shorty had his own way of handling things. More often than not it was just after she caught catfish from the lake, scraping the scales and finally chopping its head off, that the briny smell brought a memory to her. And she would look down just as her knife made to slice through the bone and flesh, and catch a glimpse of Shorty—some forgotten look, some mischievous glance that raised the hair on the back of her neck and made her long for the days when they walked the land together or fished in the lake. It was unsettling to have a dead fish remind her of Shorty, but at least it was only fish and the occasional morning breeze. And land. And, of course, snow.

Snow fell the year they married and covered the ground, an early frost that surprised everyone. Birdie went out in it barefoot and full of laughter. Shorty followed her.

"Birdie, dammit, where your shoes? Hold on, woman. I'm coming after you. I'ma catch up."

But he was no match for her, and she slid from his reach, running through the woods in between the two houses they owned— one big house, built for the master, the place where Shorty Long resided, and one much smaller, built for the servants, where Birdie lived, officially. He finally stopped, breath curling in front of his red face, bent double, gasping for air.

"You gives up, Shorty Long, you gives up?"

"Naw, ain't never gonna give up to ya, woman. Never."

That was when she stopped moving and slipped closer to him and allowed him to draw her into his arms. She sighed as his fingers ran through the hair she considered coarse. All she could think of was her lack of beauty. Only Queenie and Shorty Long had ever said she had any looks. The children at school ran her home more often than not with cruel words. One nicknamed her Onion. Said she was so ugly she made him cry. The teacher had laughed. That day Birdie left school and never went back. All the learning she needed she had already. Years later she took the job Shorty Long advertised in the newspaper: "Domestic needed to clean house, cook, and wash clothes." She had been twenty. Now she was thirty.

She began to feel cold. He noticed her trembling and took off his coat and wrapped it around her.

"Woman, I would pick you up and take you home, but I can't say for true that we'd make it back up that hill. Next time you get a dang fool idea like running in the snow, just run around the house once, okay?" His color deepened, becoming a rich wine as they walked toward shelter.

They stopped on her doorstep. "You comin'?" he asked her while averting his eyes. She knew he wanted her with him all of the time. But things were too dangerous in the South. They could not live openly as man and wife, so they lived as employer and domestic, not even sharing the same roof for fear of retribution. The thought of night riders made Birdie shudder. Shorty Long moved closer and hugged her tightly. "You better get on inside before you take a chill."

"Gonna make some stew and bring it. Be over later."

His smile was quick, and he reached to kiss her lips before she could turn away. He touched her stomach.

"I'll see y'all in a while."

The eggs were boiled and pickles chopped finely for the potato salad. She stared her one unnamed hen down, caught her, and wrung her neck with an easy twist of the wrist, and then a swift chop on the tree stump outside left the broken-necked hen headless as well as nameless. She plucked the feathers outside, too, quickly, moving from one part of the body to the next, happy that the hen was plump and not scrawny, thinking about whether to serve collard greens or snap beans. Snap beans won out, and she went around to the smokehouse to get a big piece of fatback to season the pot, while the blood drained from the upside-down hen, settling in a pail. Back inside the kitchen she immersed the plucked chicken in water and let it sit while she prepared the butcher block for cutting and eviscerating it. She lifted the heavy skillet from its place under the sink, seasoned the bottom with lard, and placed it on the unlit eye, looking around for anything else that had to be done before she started with the knife. She never liked to be interrupted when she had the knife. She snapped her fingers and twirled around. She had forgotten the corn bread. She mixed the eggs, cornmeal, baking powder, and flour, greased the pan, and poured. Then she started chopping up the hen, concentrating on the plucked body, moving it this way and that on the butcher block, splitting the breast, hacking the legs cleanly from the torso.

"I'm glad I didn't name you nuthin'. I woulda been sad about tearin' you up like this." Birdie talked aloud to no one in particular. Her habit was to talk all day long on some days and be entirely silent on others, depending on what direction the spirit moved her. She started to sing one of the old songs:

Devil ain't showed,
Devil ain't showed,
His ol' face 'round here.
He know he can't come after me,
He know he can't come after me,
'Cause I'm a-Jesus bound, you see,
Devil ain't showed his ol' face 'round here.

But the last line spoke to her and she stopped, her fingers bloody, one hand raised with the knife, the other clamped around a wing. She shouted out so that the sound reverberated through the house. Birdie had to laugh, because even to her ears she sounded like a frog on its last hop.

"Lord, you done give me a lot of blessings, so I guess I can't complain that you ain't gave me no singing voice. But it shore woulda been nice to be able to hit me some notes every once in a while."

The old woman finished cutting up the chicken, prepared the batter, and started to hum. She smiled, thinking about the sweet butter she had in the icebox and the buttermilk she would sample as soon as the first pieces of chicken cooked through and through. The thought of a big piece of corn bread sitting in a glass of buttermilk made her mouth water. She was preparing a feast for Daisy, the daughter she had not seen in years. The daughter bringing home a daughter whom she had never met. She paused, wiped at a tear, and went on cooking. She was happy that she was going to see her baby again—Daisy Sweet Mae, and Olivia Jean, her grandbaby. Birdie was happier than she had been in a very long time. She thought that any cook worth her salt knew that food tasted better with a few tears mixed in, so she cried a little more and waited for her family.

Warm weather came early to Cold Water Springs that year, and Birdie took every opportunity to be out-of-doors. She had walked two miles into town believing that it would be good exercise for the baby she was carrying, but what she got was worn out before she made it to the dry goods store. She used a white lace handkerchief to mop her brow and neck. The few lessons she learned about being a lady from her surrogate mother, Queenie Monroe, emphasized the fact that a true lady always wiped the perspiration off before anyone could see. While Birdie didn't mind Shorty Long seeing her sweat, she didn't want Amelia Lee Harper, the owner of the store, to see her skin pop with wetness or her hair sticking straight out like she had never run the straightening comb through it earlier in the day.

Birdie squared her shoulders before opening the door, smoothing down her dress and licking her lips. The little bell jingled as she walked in, and she smiled in anticipation when she crossed the threshold.

Right away she noticed that Mrs. Harper was busy, flitting around the store like a woman on fire, and it wasn't even eleven yet. Birdie nodded to her and began her rounds. Although Amelia Lee didn't nod in return, Birdie took no offense. The woman was helping other customers. And if she had nodded back to Birdie, a colored woman, some one of her customers might have taken their business elsewhere. While Birdie didn't like being treated second-class, thought her money was as good as anyone else's, she understood the situation for what it was and knew it wasn't going to change anytime soon. She had a list and a basket. She started to shop.

After a few moments Birdie was lost. She weighed heavy brocades and stiff velvets in her hands, trying to get a sense of the fabric, how it would feel against her skin. She thought of colder weather next year. Perhaps Shorty Long would like a robe for Christmas, cherry red with green piping? Her fingers lingered over a purple taffeta, but even she knew better than to request a yard of taffeta. Where would she wear it? Her inner eyes saw Shorty Long dressed in black tie and tails with her on his arm, resplendent in purple taffeta, fingers encased in long purple gloves. Her hair was topped with bold purple feathers, and from her pierced ears dangled gold earrings. In her mind's eye he led her onto the dance floor, and not a single person moved before they began to dance. But it was not the staid waltz. The music was rhythmic, throbbing. They did the hucklebuck first, and from there—

"Hey, you, you Onion, what you doin' with that taffeta? You're not buying it, are you? I don't think it goes with your black skin."

Only when the laughter started did Birdie come to her senses and notice the group of white women scattered about in the store. It was the notorious Ladies of Colbert County. They got together once a month to shop in town and eat lunch at a club member's house. She cursed herself for not looking around before coming in out of the heat. She wanted no trouble today. She turned, trying to ignore her attacker, but the woman wanted to be heard.

"I'm just trying to help. Maybe once you drop that pickaninny of yourn you'll lighten up some. Oh, on second thought, maybe I should call it a half-breed pickaninny." There was muffled laughter in the room. Birdie allowed herself to take one long look at Mrs. Jennifer Montgomery, a pale-faced, bucktoothed matron who was rumored to sleep during the Episcopalian service on Sunday. Sleeping during a service was unfortunate but generally forgettable. Except Mrs. Montgomery had the audacity to snore. Sounds suspiciously like snorts came from her very unfortunate mouth. Behind her back, her fellow parishioners had started to refer to her as Mrs. Mount-gomery. Not everyone knew the joke, but some colored servants, the invisible but not hard-of-hearing servants, took it back to their homes and talked of it over back fences. Mrs. Montgomery was notorious for her mean ways and bad temper.

Birdie drew herself up and stood tall. "Missus Harper, I be back later when things ease up in here. But I want you to cut off some of that there calico. 'Bout half a yard. Give it to Mrs. Mount-gomery. Put it on my bill. I do believe she needs a new muzzle." With that, Birdie turned her big body out of the shop amidst the "humphs" and the "oh, dears" and the "uppity nigger" comments. She was so angry that she walked the two miles back in half the time it took her to get to town, the heat working on her hair so hard that by the time she reached home it was standing wildly on end. She caught a look at herself in the mirror and moaned. The baby moved, and for a moment she forgot her anger.

"Ain't nuthin' wrong wid your old ma bein' any color but what she is. An' me an' your daddy gonna loves you even if you is as black as a tar baby. Ain't make no difference to us. Not one lick."

She smoothed her hair and started to get dinner ready, her mind already finished with Jennifer Montgomery.

One Saturday before sundown, Birdie and Shorty Long had fishing poles, bait, and sandwiches ready by the edge of the lake. He had pulled a chair from the big house outside, because she would not be able to rise with ease from the ground. Her stomach, round and hanging low, made them both laugh. She lumbered now instead of walked, and he smiled deeply whenever his eyes met hers.

Her line skipped over the surface of the water. Shorty Long lay in the grass next to her feet, kneading them with his hands. Every so often he asked her how she felt and if she had everything she needed.

They didn't hear the men approaching, because Shorty was humming loudly and out of tune.

"You be quiet, Shorty Long. You scarin' the fish away."

"That how you let a nigger woman speak to you? You got any sense, boy? You can't let no nigger talk to you like that."

Birdie's pole slipped from her fingers and she rose.

"Seem to me she ain't just no plain nigger woman, not with that belly of hers. This here your black bitch?"

There were four men in all. Birdie was puzzled over their sudden appearance. She had heard no car from the road, no footsteps. But there was a truck parked near the dirt road that led down the path to the water. Birdie glanced at Shorty Long and she could read his mind; after all, she had worked for him ten years before they married. He had not been paying attention either. From the set of his jaw and the way his eyes were narrowed she knew he was afraid—not for himself, but for her and the baby. Without thinking, her hand rested on her belly.

Shorty Long nodded in Birdie's direction, and for the first time in all their life together she obeyed him and moved away, toward her little house, eyes to the ground. The baby kicked, the skin across her abdomen tautened, and she tasted bitterness on the side of her tongue like in the first days of her pregnancy.

Just before she reached the house she turned into a stand of peach trees, sidling close to the bark of one, her eyes and ears directed to the men. She stood very still, fruit on the branches keeping her hidden. She was glad they hadn't started to harvest the trees, although they had talked about doing it for days.

"We ain't care that you got some of tha' there dark meat, but you disrespectin' our wives. You can't have no nigger maid actin' like she better'n our white women. Boy, you should know that."

One of the men had swept off his hat and wiped his brow with a yellow handkerchief. Another took out a cigar and struck the match on the side of his arm while he made himself at home in the seat that Birdie had left.

"Be one thang, too, if she was even pretty, high yella or something like that, but you went out of your way to get you some extry-dark pussy." He was not a big man, and he might have been lost in Birdie's seat except that he was at home being small. He leaned forward once he had the cigar lit and peered up at Shorty Long. Birdie saw her husband's clenched hands, how his legs were planted firmly on the ground as though he were braced to strike.

"Ain't no need to talk foul." It was the preacher, dressed in a stained tan suit. His hair curled around his ears, thin and stringy, falling forward so that ever so often he had to tuck it back and away from his face, which was pitted with old acne scars and livid, new red ones. He didn't take his eyes from the ground, staring in the vicinity of Shorty's bare feet.

"Shorty Long, we come to tell you that you can't go carrying on like you been doing. This here is a sin. Ain't no white man and colored woman supposed to be together like y'all is, and in public, too. Our women is up in arms. It's a scandal. And it's gotta stop."

The man glanced up and saw that Shorty Long had his attention on the water and had picked up a stone from the ground and skipped it across the surface of the lake.

"Boy, you hearing what we got to say? You listening? There gonna be trouble if you don't cut out your doings with that woman."

No one spoke. Shorty bent and picked up another stone. He lifted his arm but before he could throw, the first man, the farmer with a nasty handkerchief and the ugly mouth, caught his wrist and held it as he moved in so close to Shorty that Birdie wondered if the men kissed.

"I heard what y'all got to say; now get your hands off me and get off my property." Birdie heard controlled rage in his voice. Shorty Long had only ever been angry with her once like that— the first time he proposed and she refused to marry him. By the second time, a year later, she had agreed.

"Long, your property ain't gonna help you and ain't gonna help that nigger woman you knocked up neither. Nuthin' ain't gonna help you."

"Well, what you gonna do, boys?" And it was not so much what Shorty said as how he said it. He used a whisper voice that hissed at the end. A tremor ran up Birdie's spine.

"Don'tcha worry none. We find something to keep us busy, what with all them titties your nigger bitch got."

Birdie heard a muffled roar as Shorty put his head down and dove into the man's stomach. She backed away from the trees, and as she did she felt a thin stream of water trickle down her leg, and clutched her stomach. She did not want to turn from where the men wrestled Shorty to the ground, pummeling him, fists sinking into flesh, his body thrust against the ground. But she had to turn, had to get to her house. She panted with the effort and wondered at her body, so fast and fleet before the baby, now so hobbled and slow with it pressing to the center of her being. She was bent over with one hand on her belly as she opened the door of her home and reached inside.

Minutes later Birdie made her way back to the clearing. She aimed for where the men fought. A jackrabbit skittered across her path. She brought the rifle sights up to her eye and aimed at a tree near the men, who wriggled and fought together as though they were one body with many arms and legs twisting in the earth.

The shot was close enough to frighten them all and make them roll off Shorty, who had been using his torso and legs to twist and kick and bedevil the hands that pinned his shoulders. The farmer moaned, clutching a bloody ear. The cigar-smoking man clutched at his chest, heaving big gulps of air through his mouth. The preacher remained most untouched, aiming and giving Shorty one last kick of dirt in the face, and then turning to challenge Birdie, who cocked the trigger as if to shoot again. This time she deliberately aimed at his heart. She kept the gun steady even though a contraction rippled across the small of her back.

Finally Shorty stood. Birdie could see the blood and dirt on his face, the way one eye closed and the other moved wildly from man to man.

He went to stand next to Birdie, daring to put his arm around her shoulder. She shook him off and stood straighter. The men filed past as Birdie kept the rifle honed on them. As the truck pulled off, Birdie sagged, handing the rifle to Shorty, almost falling on him.

"Baby coming. I got to get inside."

Throughout the night rain fell in torrents against the house; the thunder boomed, shaking the floors, walls, and rafters; while darkness fled for seconds at a time when lightning struck. Amidst the chaos of the storm, Shorty Long sat with Birdie, holding her hand sometimes, wiping her brow at others, and wishing that he knew what he could do to make the birthing go easier for her. When thunder clapped and a fleeting streak of lightning crossed the sky, he could do no more than press his lips against her forehead and make promises to a God he'd long ago sworn not to believe in.

"We can still get to the hospital. Let me just go and crank up the car. You need a doctor, Birdie."

There was candlelight in the room, a dozen or so white tallow candles placed near the headboard, on the dresser, and wherever he could find room. Earlier, during her contractions, Birdie made him go collect them from all over her house and light them and put them where she directed. He'd been crazy with fear even then, his hands trembling so much that he could barely strike the matches. When she laughed at him, called him a baby for being so nervous, his fingers obeyed and his heart slowed so that he could hear again and concentrate on what he was doing. He was always grateful for her laughter, to hear the fine, throaty volume that rose swiftly from inside her and flowed aloud at the smallest things, like tasting honey from the comb or plucking a flower from a bush. To Shorty Long, Birdie's laughter was her beauty, more deeply felt than the earth underneath his feet. He leaned his head so that it was on her arm, and she stroked him as if he were her child.

"Ain't going."

"Birdie?"

Shorty raised his head, and if Birdie had opened her eyes she would have seen his tears.

Without warning she grabbed his head down again and mashed it to her bosom, a guttural howling coming from between her clenched teeth. He thought he would pass out if she didn't let him go. He opened his mouth to take in air.

"Aargh. Aargh. Haaaaa. Get down there, Shorty. Get down there and catch that baby."

He stumbled to the foot of the bed, where her legs were splayed open, and closed his eyes until she shouted, "How the hell you gonna catch wid your eyes closed? Open your god-damned eyes."

With a great grunt and heave Birdie pushed and Shorty Long caught, arms receiving the small mass of flesh and blood that was his own. Had anyone ever told him that he would be able to look at the sight of Birdie split asunder and still love her, even he would have been surprised, knowing his natural disinclination for blood and unpleasantness. But he was a man of heart and love encased in a small body. Holding the baby, umbilical cord attached, seeing Birdie, spent from her labor, was enough to link him to her forever.

Shorty Long did as he was told, clearing the lungs, cutting the cord, bathing the child as it trembled and squawked, a little bird. He did everything, finally wrapping her in the blanket that Birdie had prepared and taking the baby girl to lie in her mother's arms.

In the time that it took for him to do these tasks, Birdie had fallen asleep, hair wild and covering her pillow. He shook her shoulder gently and laid the baby down. His hands went to her sweat-drenched hair, and he smoothed the tight curls from her forehead. He kissed her brow and then kissed his daughter, who was trembling, quiet and yawning. He wondered if she needed to nurse. Birdie opened her eyes and stared.

"It's a girl, ain't it?"

"Yes. It be a girl."

"Humph. Then her name gonna be Daisy, on account of her being so bright and yella. You all right with that?"

Shorty Long hesitated, glancing around the room, watching the flickering candles. There were other names he might have preferred. But he remembered his promise to the God he didn't believe in and nodded, because no matter what, he believed in keeping promises. When she was struggling on the bed and the pains were racking her body, he'd prayed for her well-being, for the health of the baby. In return he'd promised God that he would not argue with Birdie anymore. The least he could do was let her have her way, too. Maybe they might even add "Cordelia" some other time.

"I'm all right with that. It's a good name."

• • •

While it didn't take Birdie long to heal, other things changed between Shorty Long and her. Shorty helped her around the house, cooked the meals, and rocked the baby for hours at a time. Birdie would wake from a nap and there he was. She never had to rise in the middle of the night. As soon as Daisy cried, Shorty would appear at the doorway, patiently waiting for Birdie to wake before he placed the baby to nurse.

In the old days he might have teased and asked to watch. But now he slipped away, leaving only the flickering light of a candle to keep his wife and baby company. He seemed to know the moment Daisy was finished, the moment when Birdie's head lolled forward, and despite her best efforts, her eyes closed. He held a well-fed baby and stroked Birdie's hair, pressing her head down into a pillow, finally laying the baby in the cradle by the bed and stealing away into a darkened house. He would find his seat by the fire and sit for hours, staring at the licking flames, quiet until Birdie slipped from the bedroom before sunup to cook breakfast at the wood stove.

On the first night that Daisy slept through without waking, Shorty Long gathered his things and moved back to the big house. Birdie stood at the doorway and watched him. She went to the cradle and fingered the blanket and bent to sniff the child. She smiled a sad smile as she lifted Daisy from her bed.

"Poor baby. You ain't got nobody but me now. Poor little yella thing."

• • •

*M*an, is you crazy? Put that dang-blasted gun down." Birdie heard her foster mother, Queenie, next to her window, speaking to Shorty Long.

"Miz Queenie, ma'am. I ain't know it was you. I thought—"

"I knowed what you thought. But I ain't them. They up at my place, drunk. Had too much formula, the extry-special kind I makes up just for friends like 'em."

"What we gonna do?" Birdie imagined that Shorty Long had lowered his gun in the dark night, with the wind blowing across his face and the sound of a lone hooting owl. Birdie thought she heard fear in his voice. But she could not blame him if it was there. He was a man who no longer slept, who prowled night and day, waiting for the night crawlers to attack.

"I been studyin' on that. Thinkin' how to make them leave you and mines alone. I done got me an idea. Let's go inside so I can see that pretty baby y'all done made and tell you how we gonna deal wid these here skunks wid white sheets."

*T*he next afternoon, as Shorty Long slept well into the day, Queenie sat at the kitchen table in the house at the bottom of the hill and sipped a cup of coffee laced with her own formula and told Birdie all about the happenings of the night before, when she and Shorty Long spent time together taking care of a few worrisome problems.

" 'Here, take 'em by they legs an' drag 'em like this.' Tha's what I said. We was workin' as quiet as we could, an' we ain't neither one of us gentle when we draggin' these here white boys to the truck we had waitin' in the back bushes. They was not gonna be

gentle with my people, so I ain't figure I gotta be no ways gentle
with them. When we got 'em loaded up, we took 'em deep in the
woods, deep an' far. And, when we got to the big tree, the one
wid the legs in the earth dug in, I told that Shorty Long boy of
yours to stop so we could unload these here piss-assed white
mens. The night ain't had no moon, so we had to make do wid
that one kerosene light we had. Them mens still passed out
when we got there, an' it were easy to roll 'em out the truck. Like
I said, I ain't care 'bout no gentle. Then me an' that boy start
pullin' the clothes off 'em, threw 'em around like they might been
doin' if they was havin' a party. Then we spread 'em out naked an'
put them together. And I was laffin' to myself all over, cacklin' so
bad I had to stop an' hold myself up to breathe. Them white men
ain't gonna know what happen, but they gonna be naked an' on
each other. Ain't gonna be no more trouble from them again,
'cause they gonna be too busy tryin to 'member what happened,
first thing, an' then when they can't, they gonna be too busy tryin'
to prove they men, for the second thing. I done thought of puttin'
honey on they privates so somethin' might come along and get
'em goin', but I ain't want they dicks to get chewed off. One of 'em
had a mighty oak, an' that sure would have been a shame. But I
fixed 'em, all right. Put some heads where they ain't supposed to
go, an' some hands too. They ain't gonna have no thought of
botherin' nobodys else. Not for the rest of they natural-born days
they ain't. My girl gonna be left alone.

"An' I looked at that Shorty Long of yours hard before we split
up. I wanna understand what you see to make you cross that line
that ain't supposed to be crossed. But ain't nothin' there but a
mannerable white boy, an' I still don't understand. I figure I don't

have to know. Maybe he got a mighty oak tuck in his pants, too. But whether he do got a mighty oak or a mighty acorn, I guess I ain't never gonna know. An' if you happy, I'm gonna be happy. Now give me my granbaby. She a fine one."

Queenie sat with Birdie for the better part of two days, holding and rocking Daisy, singing the old spirituals, filling the little house with her strong alto voice. Then the conjure woman got up the evening of the second day, kissed her daughter, and walked out. Birdie never saw her again.

*B*irdie heard the car pull up and had to steady herself. She stood in front of the mirror in her bedroom and talked to herself before going out to greet her family. "Ain't no use looking too excited, 'cause I know Daisy ain't gonna act like she want to even hug me. I gotta act friendly but I ain't pushing nuthin'." She fixed a welcoming smile on her face and went to the door.

Daisy was not the fifteen-year-old girl who left her. She stood nearly as tall as her mother. Olivia Jean was short and petite, and Birdie wondered if they fed her at all. And then there was Turk, a big, solid man. Birdie took a dislike to him right away. She didn't know what it was, but she kept thinking that he had a shifty-eyed look and that she wouldn't trust him near her chicken coop.

After she fed them and they settled down, she took the broom from Olivia Jean and shooed her out of the kitchen. Birdie closed her eyes for a second. She didn't want to hurt Daisy, but it seemed as if hurting was the only thing they were doing anyway. Even with all the good food she'd cooked staring them in the face, no one said more than a word or two between bites. And the way that man ignored his own flesh, not moving his feet out of the way when Olivia Jean was trying to help sweep the floor, made Birdie's blood start to heat up with a slow fire. But she knew what she had to do.

Her voice was steady when she announced the plan, ending with, "One of y'all got to stay, too."

She didn't dare look at Daisy. If she had, she knew she wouldn't have stuck to her decision. She would have given in to the daughter she had failed before. But Birdie knew that now, to demand any less than that Daisy stay with her own child would be another, even worse failure. She felt it in her bones just as sure as she knew when rain was in the air and when the frost was liable to linger for more than a night. Inside she cringed when Daisy turned from her and she had to talk money with Turk. But she willed herself to do it. This was the cost of not being brave so many years ago and going away when she should have tried harder to stay. The love she had inside for Daisy was not going anywhere. It was going to lie like a shovel on top of her heart.

Later that night, when everything was still inside the house, she rose and went to the chair she kept by the side of the window and sat, pressing her forehead against the coolness of the pane. She sat there until first light, moving in and out of prayer, in and out of dreams. She shivered as the sun rose to warm the day, and stood.

She thought about going to see Lupe and taking a pound cake and Olivia Jean with her.

PART FOUR

Of One Accord

$\mathcal{D}$aisy couldn't say she was surprised when Turk stopped calling after a few weeks. She kept telling herself that things would get better once she got home to New York and he saw her. He'd come back down south in Sally to pick her up, and she would shake her hair out for him to see, like she used to do when they were first married. They would open all the windows as the car ate the miles between Alabama and New York. And he would sing to her, like he used to in the old days. His voice would soothe her nerves.

Perhaps she'd write to him about how her mother thought he had deserted them. It wasn't anything Birdie said, but the fact that she didn't say anything at all that set Daisy's nerves on edge. Maybe his knowing that he wasn't well thought of would get him to acting more like a husband and a father. And then, too, it was the way Birdie walked around with her old man Lupe, the two of them laughing and giggling like newlyweds, even holding hands. They were sickening. A couple of times she caught them kissing, and she and Olivia Jean had felt very uncomfortable. They weren't used to that type of goings-on.

She was lying in her bed with the window wide-open, moving restlessly under the heat. Indian summer, people called it, when the oppressiveness didn't lift and a faint breeze brought even smaller relief. But staying in her room was better compared to having to be around Birdie and pretending to be polite; or acting as if Olivia Jean's swelling belly didn't bother her. *She done cost me so much.* She knew that children were supposed to cost; that was the way of the world. But with Olivia Jean, she felt as though her payments were beyond what should have been required. After all, hadn't she left her family and friends, agreed to marry the first man that came along, and been mostly miserable ever since? Except in bed. That thought sent a flood of red-hot feelings through her body. She flipped on her side again, her face to the window. There was a knock on the door. At first she didn't answer; then there was a louder knock.

"Come in, Birdie." She didn't bother to hide her exasperated tone. Neither did she turn over.

Birdie didn't waste time. "Turk ain't sent no check. Dat mean we short of money an' you gotta go to work. I done already talked to Missus Amelia Lee Harper at the dry goods store in town. Told her how you was a good seamstress and all. 'Bout how you make them clothes up north for white women. She want you to come by tomorrow. Lupe say he can give you a lift if you wants."

By the time Daisy flipped over, Birdie had already left the room, closing the door with a loud click. Daisy sighed and thought about all the places she would rather be than Cold Water Springs, Alabama.

*T*he next morning Daisy was up early, waiting for Lupe on the front porch when he came by in his beat-up truck. He jumped out, opened the door for her, and held it until she was seated. Daisy felt her color rise to the roots of her hair. Only Turk had ever done that for her.

"Thank you kindly, Mr. Lupe. . . ." She stumbled, because for the life of her she didn't know his last name and wasn't sure what to call him.

"Miss Daisy, please calls me Lupe. It's all right wid me. Everybody calls me Lupe. Real name is Lonnie. But my mama always did call me Lupe."

"All right, Lupe. An' please call me Daisy."

"Why, that be my pleasure, Daisy. You know, that sure is a pretty name."

Daisy's heart did a quick *thump, thump*. She was sure he was going to make a pass at her and she was going to have to slap him. She held her purse tightly in her hands, ready for the feel of his gnarled fingers on her knees.

"Yup," he said, "Birdie tole me how she named ya. Said you came right out an' looked like sunshine. That woman is somethin' else, ain't she? Can talk up a blue streak an' dress like a queen. Wear all them colors like nobody else."

Daisy felt relieved and ashamed at the same time. She was used to men making advances, saying things they shouldn't just because she might laugh or smile at them. It didn't matter if they were young or old. But the older ones were the worst. Every old man reminded her of Percy Walker.

"You know, your baby girl look like her, too. Next time you get them up close, look 'round them eyes. And they mouth. Didn't know better, I'da thought Birdie spit her right out."

Lupe talked all the way into town and didn't leave from the front of the dry goods store until she came back to tell him that she wouldn't be getting off work until four.

"I'll be back then. Don'tcha go tryin' to walk home. I'll see you at four, Daisy."

And the way he added that "Daisy" at the end made her smile. She turned and went back inside the Harper Dry Goods Emporium of Cold Water Springs to Mrs. Amelia Lee Harper, her new boss.

Amelia Lee Harper knew a good thing when she saw one, especially when it came to business. She took Daisy's measure from the first, and before the small cuckoo clock that she kept on the front counter signaled twelve, she called every client she had ever had in three counties to tell them about the new colored girl all the way from New York City. Daisy was booked for a solid month after only a few hours. And Amelia Lee, being a woman of good sense and intelligence, decided to pay her a reasonable salary and a small commission on each dress that she made for a customer. While it wasn't half what Daisy made in New York, it would do what Turk failed to do, and that made Daisy, if not happy, at least happier than when she had been given the news of her husband's latest failure.

·   ·   ·

Olivia Jean, Birdie, and Daisy sat down to supper of pinto beans with fatback and rolls steaming hot with butter. "I hope these beans taste good. I ain't cook like this in a month of Sundays. Not since Dr. Hicks say I gotta lay off the fatback. I chopped up a big onion and put it in the pot with the fatback with some salt and pepper first. That let the onion flavor the food," said Birdie. The dinner was supposed to be to celebrate Daisy's new job. Birdie had asked her what she wanted to eat and had gone to town especially to pick up the pinto beans.

Olivia Jean noticed that Daisy picked at her food, moving the beans around in her bowl and letting her rolls get cold before she took a bite. But Olivia Jean was hungry. The baby kicked with every mouthful.

"Grandma Birdie, this is some good food," she commented as she watched Birdie pull out her teeth and set them on a napkin beside her plate. Daisy pushed back from the table then and stared at the teeth, wrinkling her nose like something stank.

"Birdie, do you think you could put your teeth back in or maybe take them off the table?"

Birdie was just getting ready to put a big spoonful of beans in her mouth. She was bent forward over her plate. Her mouth was wide-open, but when Daisy spoke it seemed all the enjoyment went right out of Grandma Birdie, and her spoon dipped back into the bowl without getting any more. Olivia Jean put her spoon down, too. As hungry as she was, she was upset at Daisy for fussing. She thought about how her mother had torn into a piece of barbecue chicken and licked her fingers afterward, or how she would taste a batch of stew and use the spoon again to stir. One time she even caught Daisy running her tongue over a bowl after her ice-cream dessert.

"Mama, Grandma Birdie gotta eat with her teeth out. She can't chew as well with them things in. It doesn't taste right."

First Daisy pretended that she didn't hear Olivia Jean and that she wasn't going to pay her any mind. But Birdie and Olivia Jean joined forces. They had already stopped eating. The spoons remained in their bowls. Then they folded their arms across their chests and both turned their eyes on Daisy, who glared right back at them.

"Eat how you want. I'm finished." Daisy rose from the table and pushed her chair away, scraping it against the floor. Then she picked up her dishes, grabbing them from the table and trying her best to make more noise. At home Daisy would have been all over Olivia Jean for doing the same thing. When Daisy left the room, Olivia Jean and Grandma Birdie went back to eating. Olivia Jean felt better without Daisy's long face at the table. Sometimes it was a chore to be around her mother, especially now that there was Grandma Birdie, who was almost always happy. At least she could enjoy her food. She was grateful for the pinto beans, onions, and fatback. They'd never eaten like this at home. She reached for another roll and covered her face when she got a little bit of gas at the table. Grandma Birdie threw her head back and laughed at her for being embarrassed.

"Girl, gas is a natural thing. You supposed to let it go. Get sick if you try to keep it in. You don't need to be sick. Let it out."

Olivia Jean didn't know what got into her. She felt so good sitting with Grandma Birdie that she did let it out. And then Grandma Birdie let it out. The table sang with their farts.

Birdie's farts were long and deep, like a foghorn, and Olivia Jean's little toots came out like a trail of pebbles. Birdie laughed and laughed, and so did Olivia Jean after a while. Together they finished the whole pot of beans and fatback and almost the whole pan of bread. Olivia Jean felt sorry for Daisy, sitting wherever she was sitting, alone. But it was her mother's own fault. She could be with them laughing and having fun and not worrying about what was so proper and right all the time. Sometimes all a person needed was to be with somebody who made them laugh. But to Olivia Jean's knowledge, her mother had never been the laughing type. She used to smile a bit, especially at Turk, but nowadays Daisy walked around unfriendly and not smiling at all.

Olivia Jean had asked Grandma Birdie about Daisy after they had been in Cold Water Springs for a few weeks. By then Olivia Jean felt comfortable with Birdie, who kissed her every morning and called her "Sunshine" and acted as though she was glad that Olivia Jean had come to stay. Birdie said that Daisy was missing Turk. Then Olivia Jean almost understood, but it was hard to imagine how missing Turk had Daisy acting the same way as when she was angry with Turk when he didn't come home in New York. But Olivia Jean was not slow; she left Daisy alone. She didn't ask her mother to feel her stomach, even when the baby started to move and poke hands and feet in all different directions. Instead she told her Grandma Birdie about it. And Olivia Jean didn't say anything about not being able to fit into her clothes anymore. She began to wear the two big dresses they had bought right before their drive down south. She'd wear one for two days, wash it in the tub, and then wear the other for two days. She wasn't going to ask her mother for anything that reminded her that she was away from Turk because of her daughter's big belly. Olivia Jean would have to make do with the clothes she had.

I don't know if you've noticed it, girl, but they's two types of people in this world." Birdie was talking after dinner as they sat on the porch. There was no cool air, but sitting outside was better than sitting inside, where it was stifling hot. Olivia Jean heard crickets in the distance, singing with their legs. She batted away the moths that danced around the screen door, attracted to the kerosene lantern. Her grandmother kept talking. "They's fat people and skinny people. Now, take me, for example. I'm a big woman. Some people might go so far as to say I'm fat, but never to my face. But I ain't fat because of my butt or my big legs." Birdie pulled up her dress and shifted on the porch to better show legs, brown and dimpled, seemingly unending in length and width. "Not even because of my belly." She let her dress go and placed her hands on the sides of her stomach and squeezed the flesh between her fingers.

"Naw, I'm a fat person because I always want more. I want to eat more, to love more, and laugh harder than anybody else. I believe God put me here on this earth to live fat. And I ain't a bit ashamed." Birdie sat back and belched before she took her tin cup again for a long sip. She used the back of her hand to wipe at her mouth. Olivia Jean giggled, but Daisy, looking out over the yard, was silent, her body almost rigid.

"Now, you, Daisy. You my only born, and I do hate to get after you, but you gotta understand. You was born skinny. I pushed you out and near about jumped outta my skin when I saw how little you was. Shoot, you didn't even want no milk. When I put you on my titty you was plain disinterested. I knew you was gonna be a skinny person then. Knew it right off the bat.

"Now, really, ain't too much wrong with being skinny except y'all don't know what you want. Can't make up your mind what you want to eat, so y'all ain't never eatin'. Always sayin' such and such look good. That peach cobbler smell sweet, that carmel cake just look like it would melt in your mouth. Well, Daisy, why don't y'all go on ahead and have you a little nibble? Stop worrying what people gonna say and how they gonna act once you set your teeth into something. Go ahead on. Get fat."

Daisy had been sitting quiet, holding her tin cup by the handle. Not once had she put her head up to glance at Birdie. When she slammed her cup on the top porch step, Olivia Jean was startled.

"Why I got to be the one that's skinny?" Daisy yelled, and Olivia Jean trembled. As she sat with her mother and grandmother, she smelled the anger and sweat, like rancid fruit, drifting in the air between them. The bitterness rose like yeast kept overnight.

"But that's all right. You go on," said Daisy. "You be fat. Let me tell you about your fat self. You fat people want too much. Y'all take and take and take and don't let nobody else get a chance to get they goddamned hands on the food to eat. I can't get to no peach cobbler. Soon's I get my spoon ready and I reach for the Pyrex dish—the shit is gone. You sit up there and talk about me not tryin' nuthing out—ain't nuthing left to try once y'all get to it." Daisy had stood; her fists were clenched and she was almost crying. But her voice was strong, carrying its frustration into the deep night.

Olivia Jean was trying to stand, her hand on her belly because the baby was moving. In the few minutes they'd been on the steps she'd stopped enjoying the summer air that kissed her face. Now she was feeling hot and uncomfortable. She felt a strange witness to this fight: Daisy and Birdie going at each other; the preliminary rounds over, the kid gloves trampled the very first day they arrived in Cold Water Springs. Tonight, two months after their arrival the punching had begun, and Olivia Jean felt a huge need to duck.

"All I done heard from you and from Turk is, 'Relax, Daisy; enjoy life, Daisy; don't worry about anything, Daisy.' Well, who the hell is supposed to do the worrying? Who, Birdie, who? You tell me. You fat people get on my fucking nerves."

"Now, you don't mean that, baby," Birdie said.

"But I do mean it, Mama. I do."

There was a quiet patch, and Olivia waited before trying to get up again. She knew they were upset, but now she was starting to be upset, too. Why did she always feel as though she was caught up in the middle of their problems, even when her name had not been mentioned? She sighed. All the peace she had felt in the evening air was gone. All she wanted was her bed.

"I ain't never heard you call me nuthin' but Birdie all your grown life. It's a pure-dee joy to hear you call me Mama." The way Birdie said it, the way there was a hopeful note lingering in her voice, calmed things down some.

Grandma Birdie got up from the porch and offered her hand to Olivia Jean, pulling her up easily and smiling down, first at Olivia Jean and then at Daisy. She offered her hand out to Daisy, too, who refused it and stood on her own.

"Daughter, I didn't mean to upset you with this here talk. You can be fat, too." She put her hand on Daisy's face, her finger stroking her cheek. "I'll help you learn."

Daisy shook her head so that Birdie's fingers fell away from her face.

"I'm happy with what I am, Birdie. Just leave me alone." Daisy picked up her cup and went inside, letting the screen door slam. Birdie and Olivia Jean were standing together on the porch. Birdie glanced down at Olivia Jean.

"She do wanna be fat. She just ain't know it yet."

"Grandma Birdie, which one am I? Am I fat or skinny?"

"Olivia Jean, I do declare that you are the fattest granddaughter in the world. And I am proud to have such a big one livin' in my house."

When she smiled, even in the dark, her teeth lit her face and it was like sunshine in the midnight sky. They went inside.

The next morning Birdie and Olivia Jean were standing together in the kitchen washing dishes. Daisy had not joined them for breakfast. As soon as Lupe had poked his head through the door she had ducked out, not bothering to even say good morning.

"Grandma Birdie, let Mama go home. She don't wanna be here with us, with me, and I don't want her to stay. I feel fine being with you now," said Olivia Jean.

Birdie concentrated on her big pot, the one she had cooked pinto beans in the night before. There was a scorched part that she had to scrape with a knife and then use a scouring pad and elbow grease to help loosen.

"What make you think she ain't wanna be with you?"

Olivia Jean swallowed hard before answering. While she knew the truth, it was a hard thing to say aloud, especially to someone she had only started loving. "She ain't never much cared for me. She loves Daddy, beer, sewing, and butter pecan ice cream; that's about all."

Birdie took one last hard swipe at the pan, and water flew from the basin soaking Olivia Jean's top. She shivered. The water was cold.

"Humph. We'll see. But all I want you to worry 'bout is takin' good care of yourself an' that baby you got on the way. That your job for now. All right?" Birdie dried her hands on her apron, while Olivia Jean waited by her side. "Dry your hands and take you a walk up the hill. Get some air. Be good for you."

Olivia Jean turned to go. Her fingers were on the doorknob. She was trying her best not to let Birdie see her crying. Olivia Jean knew Birdie would never cry.

"Child, I need you to think 'bout somethin' when you out. Everybody made different. Sometimes what you see ain't all there is to know. Especially with your mama. She done had it hard. She was just a bit older than what you is now when I had to go away. To jail." Olivia Jean's eyes widened. Birdie nodded. "Yes, I said I went off to jail. Doing things that I hadn't oughta done. So I went away, an' before I could get back, your mama ran off with your daddy. She had you an' I wasn't nowhere to be found. She had to do it all by herself. She ain't forgive me yet. I don't think she mad at you so much as she can't let go of bein' mad at me." Birdie sighed, and Olivia Jean reached out and took the old woman's hand. Birdie smiled. "I'm sure glad she brought you to me, though, Olivia Jean. I'm glad that I'm gettin' to know you. We just hafta be more patient wid your mama. She gonna come 'round soon."

Grandma Birdie took her apron off and shooed Olivia Jean from the kitchen because she meant to sweep and straighten up. As she grabbed the broom she said, "I can't get to nuthin' standin' and talkin' to you all day," but the woman smiled as Olivia Jean left the room.

That same night, after they finished their dinner in silence, Birdie stopped at the screen door and glanced outside at the velveteen sky, sprinkled with sequins. The evening was calm; the leaves on the magnolia tree turned in the wind, and the scent of the white flowers flooded the night. She was not a poet, but she felt the words well in her heart wanting to burst. She thought of an old spiritual, one the choir used to march into the church with, "Going to See the King," and began to hum it down low, in the middle of her belly. The words were in her mind: "Mother don't go; Father don't go; Sister don't go," when she saw the curl of smoke on the porch and stopped.

"Daisy."

There was no answer. Birdie opened the door and walked out. She still had a dish towel in her hands.

"You know, I'm tryin' to give you a present and you steady droppin' turds on me and Olivia Jean, an' I ain't 'preciatin' it." Birdie's voice was strong, forceful.

"What you talkin' 'bout now, old woman?"

Birdie reached down and caught Daisy's arm so that the cigarette went flying, and Daisy cried out, twisting away.

"Uh-uh. You gonna listen to me. I'm tryin' to do for you what nobody ain't done for me. Tryin' to make sure you don't lose your girl like I done lost you." Daisy stopped moving and looked up at her mother, who dropped her arm.

"I made a promise to you an' I broke it. Went on to the big house an' left you out in the world. I shoulda knowed better, but I paid for it. Ain't had no good idea where you were or how you was doin' till after Olivia Jean got here. Then you writes an' tells me that I got a grandbaby by the name of Olivia Jean." Daisy stood and walked to the cigarette that had rolled to the grass, pressing it firmly into the ground to make sure it was out.

"Now, I done give you the chance to take care of your own daughter, an' you too busy bein' mad at me to do things right by her. She need you now, an' all you doin' is goin' on 'round here wid a long face, makin' everybody miserable."

"You ain't right, Birdie. I am too takin' care of Olivia Jean." The women were now face-to-face.

"You ain't doin' nuthin' but draggin' that fat lip of yours to the ground an' actin' like bein' wid your husband more important than bein' wid Olivia Jean. If you don' learn nuthin' else while you here, you need to learn ain't no man more important than your flesh an' blood, the baby you done squeezed out from between them legs. An' if you ain't get it, you gonna wind up jus' like me. Gonna have yourself a daughter that can't even stand to be 'round you, won't even call you 'Mama' unless she forget how much she hate you for a minute and slip up on the name."

Daisy leaned in close, so that the two women were almost touching. "You right about that, old woman. You got a daughter that can't stand the sight of you."

Birdie nodded. She looked out over the sky again before leav-

ing the porch and Daisy, who had been able to find another cigarette, sat alone, in the dark beauty of the night, and thought
ugly thoughts of her mother.

*D*aisy dragged out of bed the next morning. Nightmares had
troubled her sleep. She dreamed of Birdie, Turk, and Percy
Walker. In each she had the notion that should one of them
touch her, she would shrivel and die, like the Wicked Witch in
The Wizard of Oz did when water singed her skin. Of the three,
Birdie got close enough and killed her. Daisy saw the old
woman's gnarled hands reach inside her chest, ripping the core
out, taking the heart still pulsing and dripping blood. As Daisy
slid to the ground, she wondered, *How could my own mother kill
me? Doesn't she know the rules? Mothers are not supposed to kill their
daughters.*

On waking, her tongue was dry and the back of her throat
hoarse, as if she had called out during the night. Birdie and
Olivia Jean were at the breakfast table when she left. She nodded
vaguely in their direction, but they were talking and did not notice as she slipped out the door and into Lupe's car. That was fine
as far as Daisy was concerned. She still carried ill feelings toward
Birdie from the confrontation last night, and now the dreaming
only made her feel worse. She wanted to go home to New York,
but since Birdie had made that impossible, Daisy decided it would
be best to stay out of her mother's way. There were too many old
wounds set to ooze open and a good likelihood of new ones de-
veloping soon. Olivia Jean and Birdie were close already, and the
time they spent together increased their bond and left Daisy out.

Riding with Lupe did not restore her balance. She was used to having time alone to think. In New York, even with the noise of the subway, her mornings on the way to work were quiet, no conversation required, none anticipated. But Lupe was a magpie, and she felt compelled to at least pretend to listen, which took effort. She had to nod, and even smiled once or twice. She was exhausted by the time she reached Amelia Lee's. Lupe ran to her side of the car door and offered his hand and helped her down from the cab gently.

"Daisy, if you not feeling well later on in the day, you got my number. You call me and I'll come get you and take you home to Birdie. She'll fix you up just right." He didn't wait for her to answer. He got back in the truck, waved to her, and took off. She walked into the store.

Daisy and Amelia Lee had settled into a routine. Each morning when she arrived Daisy stopped at the front desk, where there was a schedule of appointments in a small, leather-bound book. Next to the client's name was a general description of what Daisy had to finish or begin on a project; she might have a hem to be basted or a waistline to let out or cuffs on a sleeve to shorten. Once she had an idea of what the day looked like, she began to set out the materials she would need, including her sewing kit, shears, colored threads, chalk, etc. When she checked the book today, Daisy sighed. A wedding party was due in at eleven. She went to the back room and pulled a few bolts of Spanish lace that had only just arrived, and an ivory-colored satin in case the bride-to-be might be interested in seeing that combination. The dress pattern had already been chosen and ordered.

Amelia Lee was waiting when she made her way up front again. "I put on a kettle of water. I thought you might like some peppermint tea." Daisy was surprised. She had never been offered anything in Brooklyn at the department store where she worked. The older lady smiled. "Relax, Daisy. Our clients won't be here for a while. You're caught up on everything. Have a seat for a few minutes. Your tea will be ready soon."

Daisy sat and drank her tea. When the wedding party came in at eleven she felt better physically, but she was still in disarray emotionally. In New York she knew where she stood. She was Turk's wife, Olivia Jean's mother, a colored employee of a large business that paid her well but that had never treated her as more than a worker. If she had to guess, they probably hadn't even missed her leaving. Other colored women were waiting in line to get her job. That was how things were in the big city. One person left; that person was replaced. Quick as snapping fingers to a jive beat.

But here in Cold Water Springs, her place was changing from what she was used to it being. Instead of her knowing exactly where she fit, things were scrambled, and she felt challenged every day, by Birdie, by Olivia Jean, by Lupe, to become someone she didn't think she knew how to be, and perhaps didn't want to become.

Before she came down south, everything had been clear. Get Olivia Jean to the country and bury her where no prying eyes could see the baby growing in her stomach. She and Turk would decide the rest after Olivia Jean gave birth. They, husband and wife, had been united in their thinking. At least Daisy had thought they were together on this issue. But apparently they weren't. Turk deserted them, no money, no calls, no nothing. And it was Birdie, a woman whom she had long ago written off as a betrayer, who had stepped in to do the things that her husband should have. Her mother had provided a roof over their heads and had helped Daisy find employment and made sure, with Lupe's help, that she was able to get to work every day and back home. And since she had started working and bringing in a paycheck, Birdie asked only that she do the smallest of chores around the house, and made sure that Daisy and Olivia Jean were well fed and that the clothes they wore were washed clean, pressed, and ready in the mornings. Birdie was taking better care of them than Turk ever had. And that was very sad.

After the bridal party left, Daisy asked to be excused for the rest of the day and called Lupe for a ride home. All she wanted was her bed. She was tired of thinking, tired of feeling, and, truthfully, tired of all the problems life was handing her. But more than that, she was building a fierce anger against Birdie, whom she believed to be the architect of all of her current woes. Yes, she was a savior; she had done good things to get Daisy and Olivia Jean on their feet; but hadn't she been the cause of the fall in the first place?

When Lupe picked her up, she was quieter than usual. She slipped in the house and into her bedroom without making a sound except a sharp click when she shut her bedroom door. When she fell asleep this time she was confronted with two Turks, two Birdies, one tall Olivia Jean, and one baby Olivia Jean. The next morning she went searching for a bowl, filled it with water, and slid it under her bed. She was determined that the witches riding her back would fall off and drown.

Olivia Jean was sitting on the porch with her mother and grandmother, hoping for stray air to touch her face, but the flies kept lighting on her skin, so she didn't have any peace. Daisy and Grandma Birdie were on the steps. They had gone into town and bought Olivia Jean an old rocking chair. They put a pink ribbon on it. When Olivia Jean went to touch it, to run her fingers over the smoothness, she couldn't help it. She started to cry.

"Now what you all cryin' 'bout? Ain't no need to cry." Grandma Birdie took her hand.

"Go on, now," Daisy said. "Sit yourself down. This chair is for rocking." Daisy had started to say that the chair was for rocking her grandbaby, but she couldn't get that part out yet. She was having trouble thinking about being a grandmother.

The baby startled Olivia Jean by turning and stretching. She put her hand over the little foot and pushed it back in before she sat down in her new rocking chair. The cushion felt good on her bottom. She stretched out her legs and leaned back with her eyes closed. She had trouble thinking that Daisy and Birdie had done something together, like going into town and picking out something for her, but she was glad. Maybe this was a first step.

So, there they all were, Olivia Jean rocking, Daisy and Birdie using paper to flap away the flies. If they had been in New York, Daisy and Olivia would have been sitting on the stairs in front of their building, waiting for Turk to come home. And when it got to be way past time for him to show up, Daisy would have been fidgeting and getting mad. Now she was almost calm, wiping her forehead every once in a while and grumbling about the heat.

The sun went down and the wind picked up some and the night creatures started singing and talking to one another. Olivia Jean kept rocking with her eyes closed. When they first arrived in Cold Water Springs and they had sat on the porch at night, she thought she would go crazy with the quiet. But now she knew better. The country was as noisy as the city in its own way. "A body has to listen differently, that's all," said Birdie. "Use different ears than them city ears, gal, an' you'll hear we got some loud stuff goin' on down here, too."

Grandma Birdie had proved right. Now Olivia Jean listened to the sounds every night as they rocked on the porch. She knew the easy ones right off the bat: the screeching of a hoot owl, the sound of crickets trying to attract mates. The harder ones, like rabbits rustling through the bushes or the occasional fox crossing the gravel-lined yard trying to get in the henhouse, she had yet to hear. Birdie said they'd come with time. She'd develop a sense of country that would tell her all about what was going on in the dark as well as what was happening in the day. When she asked Birdie where Birdie had picked it up from, the old woman smiled. "Oh, I had me a mother that loved the outside so much, that's 'bout all we done when I was little. We was in the moonlight all the time learnin' 'bout the undercover goings on."

Now, as Olivia Jean inclined her head toward the woodpile because she thought she heard a skittering sound in the short stacks of lumber piled on the side of the house, Daisy's voice sliced through the night.

"Birdie, who my daddy?"

"Why you asking? You ain't never asked me that before." Birdie had taken a full minute to reply, and even in the darkness Olivia Jean knew she was surprised.

"Don't know why I'm asking. Just wanna know." There was a challenge in Daisy's voice.

"What if I tells you that I don' wanna tell you? That it ain't gonna make you no kinda difference to know."

"But you don't know that, Birdie. You don' know how I feel not having no daddy and not even havin' no name to call or say to myself. I wanna know his name."

Olivia Jean stopped rocking and held her breath. On the one hand she was tired of Daisy always having an issue with something. They were having a good time on the porch. Then Daisy had to bring up things that made them all uncomfortable. But, on the other hand, she was torn up with curiosity. She had never thought of having a grandfather. What if he was still alive?

"Daisy, it ain't gonna be a good thing if I tells you. You ain't gonna like it, not one little bit. Why can't you be glad that you got me? I ain't the best mama, but I been the best you got. Ain't a mama enough?"

That was when Olivia Jean started to side with Daisy. *A mama ain't enough,* she wanted to tell Birdie. It was her daddy, Turk, who had loved her no matter what, until she got in the family way. It was her daddy who smiled at her when Daisy was angry and who slipped her candy when her mother made her cry. Olivia Jean thought Daisy had a right to know the name of her daddy. Maybe knowing might lift some burden in her heart.

"Grandma Birdie?"

"Yes, child?"

"I think you should tell my mama about her daddy. Everybody needs to know about their daddy." Daisy lifted her head in disbelief. Olivia Jean knew what she was thinking before she could open her mouth.

"I'm gonna tell my baby when the time come. I'm gonna tell

her all about her daddy." Olivia Jean rose and excused herself. Birdie would tell her later about her mama's daddy. But she figured they needed to talk alone.

"Good night, y'all."

"Good night, baby," said Grandma Birdie.

"Good night, Olivia Jean," said Daisy.

Olivia Jean paused at the screen door. Birdie was looking off into the night as if remembering a long time ago, and Daisy's eyes were glued to the ground at the bottom of the porch.

*B*irdie took a deep breath while she waited for the screen door to close behind Olivia Jean. After the quick whistle of air and the soft bang of the aluminum hitting the door frame, the two women sat without speaking. Daisy began to squirm, twisting to glance up at Birdie, clearing her throat, dusting a twig from the bottom step. Finally she said, "You gonna tell me? You gonna let me know my daddy's name?"

"Ain't all that simple."

"How it not simple? Just say it."

When Birdie stood, the porch step she had been sitting on rose up, too, relieved from her weight. She looked out on her yard, turned to catch an evening breeze, and suddenly felt chilled to the bone when one caught her the wrong way. A woman of signs and indications, she rubbed her thick arms back and forth.

"I know you wanna know about your daddy, but first you gotta know about me. You ain't never asked me no questions 'bout where I come from or where I been. You ain't never showed no interest in me. Them pictures in the parlor, they ain't really my family. Just told you that so you'd have someplace to come from.

Maybe tha's why you ain't never asked nuthin'. Thought you had all the answers, right?" While she was talking, Birdie thought, *This here is because of that baby coming, all because of Olivia Jean. A new baby stirs up dust that's been settled, dust that don't need to move 'cause can't nobody see it under the chair or behind the sofa.*

"Birdie ain't my full name, you know. It's Birdie Air. Before she died, my mama told me that I looked like a little baby bird when I was born, hair standing up and all, mouth open, eyes closed, ready for a titty. So she named me Birdie 'cause that's what I looked like, and then she named me Air 'cause she wanted all the good things in life for me. She tole me she wanted me to fly, to get up and away from Alabama, where she been a slave an' was still livin' her life like she was one. Colored people back then was hopeful. They knew someplace better was out there for they children, someplace where they didn't need to be 'fraid of them night riders an' could make a good livin' from the land an' not be no sharecroppers, always in debt an' robbin' Peter to pay Paul. I know y'all got hope, too, had hope for Olivia Jean. That she gonna have a better life than you done had, than her daddy. Tha's what hurt really, don't it? Now you think she not gonna be able to make it wid a baby?"

Daisy nodded. But it was more than that. Olivia Jean was smart; she had the book-learning sense to take her anywhere she wanted to go and she had wasted it all on a boy who either wouldn't claim her or she was ashamed to claim. And then, God help her, Daisy blamed Olivia Jean for driving Turk away. She blamed Birdie also, but Birdie wasn't her daughter. Birdie was a grown woman who could handle the weight of Daisy's dislike and mistrust. Hadn't they been at a distance for fifteen years because of the same issues? Those years hadn't broken Birdie.

What she felt was not fair to Olivia Jean, or even logical. Turk had driven Turk away. She said that to herself at least a dozen times a day. Now it was a matter of believing it.

Birdie continued. "I grew up in these parts. You know my mama died when I was 'bout six, an' the local peoples didn't know what to do wid me. No other colored family would take me up, ain't no one had extry to feed 'nother mouth. So they took me out to the woods by Queenie Monroe, an' she took me as her own girl 'cause she ain't had none. Went to school up till the chil'rens run me off. Had to learn me a trade. I learned to clean, keep house, an' cook. Tha's what a colored girl learn in the South if she ain't got no school sense. Tha' an' keep babies.

"I was goin' from place to place to keep house, cook, an' clean for peoples. But no matter how good I was, people was 'fraid of the fact that I had been wid Queenie, that I was big and wouldn't hold my mouth shut like other gals they could get. I was havin' a hard time makin' any kinda livin', an' ain't nobody wanna marry me. Too big for most mens, too ugly for the others.

"Tha's when I heard 'bout Shorty Long. People say a single man looking for somebody strong to help on a little farm. Say need to be able to cook an' clean some an' not be 'fraid of no hard work. I shows up at the front door. Place was raggedy. So, I start cleanin' it up. Man look me up an' down an' he grin. Say, 'You a big gal, ain't you?' I can't help my mouth. I say, 'An' you a little man, ain't you?' He say, 'It depend on where you looking.' We both laugh, and he say that I got the job.

"That was Mr. Shorty Long. He your daddy."

Daisy stood up. Her eyes were blazing; her fists were clenched. "All this time you coulda told me that that little cracker was my daddy an' you didn't? He was right here with me, an' the both of you lied—didn't let me know? I hate you, Birdie. You ain't done right by me, never. Don't expect me to love you an' don't expect me to sit up here with you an' cry over no damn Shorty Long." She went into the house and slammed the door.

The breeze in the air had picked up, whistling through the magnolia tree that gripped the earth in the front yard. Birdie remembered the summer morning she had planted the tree, more than thirty years ago, just after Daisy was born. She remembered the way the earth felt, its moistness between her fingers, the dark richness that tempted her first to lick and then to open wide and swallow a handful. She had rolled it in her mouth, then held it in her bottom lip, the gritty, sweet soil, and felt satisfied with the one taste of earth she'd ever had. She and Shorty Long had stood in front of the fledgling tree, and Birdie had bowed her head and prayed that the Alabama soil might nurture the magnolia just as her milk and love might nurture and provide guidance to Daisy. Tonight she wondered why the sweetness of that moment in time lingered even in the face of all that had changed over the years. She doused the lamp and went inside.

*B*irdie waited a week, until the rawness in the pit of her stomach had started to work itself closed. Daisy was in the front yard throwing feed at the chickens that Birdie kept. Amelia Lee Harper had decided to give Daisy two Saturdays a month off. She couldn't afford to have Daisy so tired that no sewing got done at all.

The sun was starting to slide down in the sky, and Olivia Jean was following her mother as if she were a baby chick herself. Birdie strode out of the house and planted herself in front of

Daisy, arms folded, face scowling. When Daisy stopped, feed still in her hands, Olivia Jean bumped into her mother and the bucket went flying. Birdie didn't move an inch.

"You mad at me an' I'm mad at you. I done told you I was wrong for leavin' you the way I did, an' I'm even tellin' you now that maybe Shorty Long an' me shoulda told you that you was ours. Maybe. But you was wrong for up an' leavin' an' not tellin' me like you did, an' for sayin' them disrespectful things 'bout your daddy the other day. I can't abide nobody talkin' no stuff 'garding Mr. Shorty Long. That man took care of you an' me, an I ain't havin' it. Plus, you walkin' 'round makin' us miserable. We can't eat the way we want, can't laugh, can't joke, nuthin'. Daisy Sweet Mae Stone, I challenges you to a wrestling match. We gonna settle this once an' for all. If I beat your ass, you gonna get in line an' start treatin' me an' Olivia Jean better. See, I know what you thinking."

"Dammit, what is you talkin' 'bout? You as crazy as a bedbug. Ain't nobody gonna fight your old gray ass."

The slap rang out; the red mark across Daisy's skin from Birdie's palm was so vivid that Birdie swallowed hard. Olivia Jean put her hands to her mouth and stared at her grandmother.

"You gonna fight me or you gonna stand up here and let me kick your ass? 'Cause I sure feel like knockin' the shit outta you today."

Daisy lifted her face, put her hands to her jaw, and worked it to make sure it wasn't broken. She felt heat in her stomach. She thought about Birdie's leaving all those years ago, about Turk's deceptions, then and now, about Olivia Jean's baby, and finally about Shorty Long. She burned to hit somebody, too. "Let's go then."

Olivia Jean stood, confused, head moving back and forth, trying to see if the two women were serious. Her hand was on her stomach.

Birdie marched across the front yard and to the side of the house by the woodpile. She stopped in front of a small depression in the ground where the rain had left a circle of mud a couple of inches deep. She took off her long red skirt and orange top, flinging them on the ground, and stood in her bra and panties. "Come on wid it," she yelled to Daisy. "Come on." Olivia Jean's feet were rooted to the front yard, until she figured out that she could see better from the porch. She kept rubbing her eyes. She could not believe her grandmother was standing there, practically naked, ready to fight her mother. She sat down on the lip of the side porch, shaking her head and waiting. She wondered if craziness was something that she could inherit. The baby kicked sharply.

Daisy saw a big, powerful black woman, with a large curved belly and arms the size of a man's, step into the mud and set her legs apart, bracing for a fight. "I ain't gonna hurt you too bad. You my daughter an' all, but you gotta be taught a lesson. I'm tired of the way you actin' 'round here. Tired. When I was in the lockup, we used to eat women like you for breakfast. Women who think they too good to learn an' know everythin' 'thout listening. You sittin' up here in my house, disrespectin' me an' the mem'ry of your daddy. The one that gave you this place to run to in the first place. You ain't too old to learn some respect. Shoulda beat your ass a long time ago. Knocked that damn chip off."

"Is that so? You gonna teach somebody somethin', huh? You ain't got nuthin' to teach me, old woman, nuthin'. 'Cause you ain't know shit. You jus' a stupid old lyin' colored woman; that's what you are."

Daisy transformed right in front of Olivia Jean's eyes. She became bigger, and she stepped into the mud in seconds, ripping her clothes off, throwing them in the dirt, too, reveling in the freedom of not caring.

"Olivia Jean the referee. The first one get pinned is the loser. Ain't gonna be no hard feelin's. Nuthin' like that." Birdie was moving around in the mud, trying to get a feel and a toehold.

Daisy, rid of clothes, strode over to Birdie and, without a word, jumped on the older woman and at once they were writhing in the mud, struggling with body on top of body, grunts coming from both of them. Olivia Jean slipped off the porch, trying to see who was on top, but as soon as one almost touched the ground the other got a second wind and turned things over again.

Mother and daughter found themselves locked thigh against thigh, breast against breast.

They were wrestling so long the mud dried, caked, and became green. Although Birdie had strength, Daisy had agility and was able to twist from Birdie's grasp. Birdie's arthritic hip began to pain her, and her butt hurt. But still she felt good. Rolling in the mud, the sun shining, her daughter and her, wrestling it out. She had thought for a long time about how best to give Daisy the release she needed from the anger that was tearing her insides up. Then one night she remembered the jailhouse, and the fights. She had gone crazy for a time after Shorty Long told her that Daisy had left and he didn't know where or how to find her. Every day Birdie fought, climbed into the ring and fought until she dropped from exhaustion. Daisy needed the same. She had to have a target, someone who made her angrier than anyone else. Birdie was glad to be that target if it meant that the demons that drove her daughter to meanness might be eased. If this fighting might lead to some measure of peace in their home, she was all for trying it.

They had been wrestling for about half an hour when they heard, "Y'all, I gotta pee an' I'm hungry. I'm goin' inside," Olivia Jean yelled, and the two women looked in her direction in between grunts. Birdie had been in the process of trying to grab hold of Daisy's leg that was right out of her arm's reach. Daisy had Birdie in a headlock and was trying to lower her to the ground. Birdie yanked Daisy's hair and they both fell to the ground with a huge thump. Daisy squealed.

"Why ain't y'all take a break an' come back to this some other time? I'll make us all some grilled-cheese-and-baloney sandwiches. And some lemonade, too."

Birdie had managed to stand, and Daisy pulled herself up by digging her hands into the bottom of the mud pit and pushing up. She had a fistful of mud, ready to fling it in Birdie's face. They were circling each other, feet buried in the mud. Birdie stopped and held up a hand.

"Daisy, this here a tie until later?"

"Guess so. If Olivia Jean hungry, we gotta stop. She won't be here to see me pin your ass." Daisy stopped moving, too.

"Watch your mouth, girl." Birdie was breathing hard, her hands on her hips. They both took a moment.

"I got something here for ya. I been done had it, but you won it fair an' square from me. I ain't sayin' you beat my ass or nuthin', mayhap you came close, but you ain't done it." Birdie left the mud pit and went to her clothes, which she had flung in a pile on the ground.

Olivia Jean knew it cost Birdie; anyone could see that plain on her face as she reached inside her blouse pocket and pulled out the little envelope, the kind she sent her bills in every month. She looked tired. Her hands shook. Olivia Jean moved closer.

Birdie took her time and opened the envelope, letting it flutter to the ground when she got what she needed from it. It was a sheet of folded paper, and when she opened that she took out another piece of paper. It was a photograph.

"Take this. This the only picture I got of us. I don't need it. Got his face in my mind. You need it so you can remember." Birdie and Daisy stood close. Daisy nodded and held out her hand, and Birdie laid the picture in her palm. There was enough light by the side of the house with the kerosene lamp hanging from the hook for the picture to be illuminated.

Olivia Jean couldn't wait to see it. A picture of her grandfather, Shorty Long. Without thinking Olivia Jean walked into the mud, feet sinking and toes wriggling in the mess. She was at Daisy's side as they both stared at Mr. Shorty Long and Grandma Birdie, his wife.

The photographer had Birdie sitting. He'd had to, because she was so much bigger and taller than Shorty Long. The picture itself was perfect, not frayed at the edges, not worn from handling. Almost as if it had never been touched. But Olivia Jean knew her grandmother better than that already. She knew that Grandma Birdie had pulled that picture out in the dead of night and held it reverently in the palm of her hand, memorizing Shorty Long's face, tracing the lines over and over again with her eyes.

"We was in New Orleans," Birdie told them. "They allowed such things as colored women and white men to take pictures together there, to do all kinds of things together in that city. Now, generally it was white men with part-white women, quadroons or octoroons, they called them. This man let us go on ahead and take a picture, even though I was dark to the bone and not skinny like them other ladies in the city. Shorty Long paid him some extra. That's why the photographer ain't make no fuss. Ain't opened his mouth except to tell me to sit straighter. 'Sit like you a elegant lady,' he said to me, and I did my best.

"We had already been in front of a minister that morning and told him and God that we was gonna stay married. I know what y'all thinking. How we get married, 'cause they ain't allow no white man to marry no colored woman in them days, right? Well, money said a lot, and your daddy"—here Birdie paused and nodded at Daisy—"had some money and was ready to pay for what he wanted. The minister just listed me as white on the paper and made us promise to hurry up and get outta town.

"Shorty said that we had to get our picture taken. That every bride and groom should at least have that. It was September twenty-fifth, 1929. That was a yellow dress, and see that feather there?" Her fingers traced the feather that curled around the pillbox hat she wore tilted to the side. "That was an orange feather. I liked them colors together a lot. Orange and yellow, with just a touch of peacock blue on my neck with that scarf. Shorty Long laughed at me that morning when he saw me all dressed up. He said that ain't no man ever had such a beautiful, colorful, colored wife. And he kissed my hand, acted like I was a queen." Her voice broke then, and Olivia Jean thought it strange that Birdie should still grieve over this little bit of a man who barely topped her while she was seated, after all these years.

Olivia Jean saw that her grandfather had been a good-looking man. The sepia background highlighted the contrast between him and Birdie. Her skin became black-brown instead of her ordinary blue-black tone, and the mass of her hair was gathered up under the hat. Shorty Long stood military straight at her side.

He had a mustache, a pointed chin, and big eyes with thick brows. Olivia Jean ran her fingers over her own eyebrows. Grandma Birdie smiled.

"Yeah, baby. You do look like Shorty Long. You favor him greatly. He was small and you got his chin. I see it whenever you get mad."

The three of them had been standing in the mud for a while. Flies buzzed around, and they knocked mosquitoes off every few seconds. Birdie had been waiting for Daisy to say something, anything.

Olivia Jean walked to the front of the porch, headed for the doormat, mud oozing between her toes. Stepping in the mud had been a secret enjoyment to her, never having walked barefoot in mud before. She began to wipe her feet as she listened to her mother and Birdie.

Daisy cleared her throat. "Thank you, Birdie. I appreciate you giving me this picture of my daddy and you." The "and you" part was an add-on and came a half a beat after "daddy."

Birdie paused. "You're welcome, Daisy."

"Why don't y'all go on down by the lake an' wash off? I'll get the food ready," said Olivia Jean.

As Birdie stepped from the mud, Daisy grabbed at her arm.

"You one lucky old woman. I was about to nail you. Olivia Jean just ain't wanna see you pinned."

"You wasn't about to do nuthin'. Please. You got my teeth?" Birdie headed for the lake. Daisy stopped first. "Take this and put it away for me, Olivia Jean." She gave her daughter the picture.

Olivia Jean grinned as she opened the screen door. She started humming, a habit she picked up from Birdie, under her breath, and wondered, fleetingly, what in the world her daddy was up to in New York. Here she was with Daisy and Grandma Birdie, and they were acting better to each other than they had been acting, and that was a relief. And they were all going to sit at the table and have a meal together. Things were feeling different than they had been in New York. It seemed to Olivia Jean that in Cold Water Springs, Alabama, people couldn't run and secrets couldn't hide. Birdie forced them out in the open. She wrestled them out no matter how difficult. While it might not be the best way all the time, Olivia Jean thought, it seemed to have been the best way this time, because it had helped Daisy.

She paused before closing the screen door behind her. She could hear Daisy and Birdie from the lake out back. They were singing a good old spiritual, "The Battle Hymn of the Republic," with Grandma Birdie singing the bass part. By the time she reached her lowest note, Olivia Jean had already seasoned the pan and was ready to fry the bread.

Olivia Jean didn't find the church impressive. She'd seen much bigger ones in New York. Or at least passed by bigger ones, because they weren't a churchgoing family.

Grandma Birdie's church wasn't grand on the outside. Brick steps led up to a whitewashed plank building. The floors inside were wood and polished to a high gloss. There were some stained-glass windows, but when you got up close you saw that some were only drawings of stained glass taped on top of windows held open by iron bars.

The Sunday Grandma Birdie got up and said that they were all going to go to church with her, Olivia Jean found herself turning her head toward her mother. She didn't know what she was going to wear. Her two dresses barely fit any longer.

"Grandma Birdie, do I have to go with you?" Olivia Jean asked.

"Yes, ma'am. You gotta go to church. We go to church to thank God for all He has given us and to pray with other Christians." She moved closer to Olivia Jean and dropped her voice to a low whisper. "I know that you ain't gone to church much. I don't necessarily care for going neither sometimes, but you gotta learn about Jesus, God, and the Holy Ghost. And you got to get out and meet the people. Best place for that be church. Go on now...." Grandma Birdie flapped her long arms, shooing Olivia Jean back into the bedroom. Olivia Jean paused with her fingers on the doorknob, thinking that Birdie really looked like a bird, tall and storklike, black and graceful the way she was standing by the stove with the sunlight streaming all around her.

There was water in her washbasin and she started to bathe. She was thinking about Turk and Preston and how they would fall in love with the baby once she had it, and how things would change. *Daddy will have to do more than say he is sorry when he finally gets back down here. He will have to get on his knees in front of me and apologize. Preston will have to act right, too. He can't be going into a closet with a girl and getting her in the family way and then telling her that he is not going to be a good father. He's got to be good.*

She stood with a washcloth on her belly with what she knew to be a stupid smile on her face when she heard the door open, and there was Daisy standing in the room with her.

"Look, I been working on this here outfit for you. You wanna wear it to church today?"

At first Olivia Jean tried to cover her body, one arm thrown over her breasts, the other across her stomach. Then she shrugged. She did not have enough arms to cover anything. Besides which, Daisy was not looking at her but at the dress that she was holding out to Olivia Jean like a peace offering.

The color drew Olivia Jean to the dress. It was yellow, a bright-sun-in-the-morning color that pulled her to touch and stroke the fabric, forgetting that she was naked, with pendulous breasts hanging and various other body parts open to Daisy for the seeing. Her thumb and forefinger pressed the fabric, the weave soft and buttery.

"Mama, this for me?" There was wonder in her voice.

"Who else it gonna be for? See, I did you a special pattern and let the front out some, you know, down there so it'll fall just right. Hurry up and try it on, 'cause we only got a little while before we gotta leave. Might need to put a couple of stitches here and there, but we got time if you hurry." Daisy laid the dress on her bed, and before Olivia Jean thought too hard or could make up a reason not to, she grabbed her mother and hugged her.

"Olivia Jean, get some clothes on before you catch your death." Grandma Birdie was at the door, grinning and toothless.

"That's right, girl, c'mon, now. Get going." But the words Daisy said didn't have their usual edge, the hardness that Olivia Jean had come to expect when her mother gave her directions. After Daisy and Birdie left, Olivia Jean stood by the bed, her fingers caressing her new dress, imagining the envious looks of the other girls at church. She was suddenly excited about going.

•   •   •

Olivia Jean wasn't paying attention to the preacher speaking in front of the church, because it was too hot. She reached around her Grandma Birdie to get one of those funeral parlor fans stuffed in the back of the pew that Birdie and Daisy were using to stir the breeze some. Other women were doing the same thing and Olivia Jean wondered why they had the heat on so high when it wasn't cold for November. Olivia Jean felt one trickle of perspiration that paused at her jaw and then went under her chin. She was getting ready to lean over and ask Birdie if they had to stay for the entire service when she felt her grandmother's body stiffen. That was when she began to pay attention to the man in the pulpit.

"Ah, we, uh, got some people in this here congregation that think they above everybodys else. That they can come in the Lord's house and not repent of they sinning ways."

Daisy took a deep breath like a hiss, and on the other side Birdie picked up her hand, pressing it hard. Olivia Jean still didn't understand. Birdie looked down at the girl, and Olivia Jean covered her grandmother's big knuckles with her hand and smiled up at her. More sweat had started at the top of her head, under her bangs, and she was trying to fan it before it slid down the whole of her face.

Then the preacher said, "And they coming from the city with they loose ways, trying to act like it's all right to sit up in His house without begging pardon, without asking for forgiveness. We can't let this kind of behavior pollute our church. They can't come in here and make having a baby out of wedlock all right with our children here. They just can't."

Olivia Jean gasped. The man in the pulpit was talking about her. Her eyes flew to Birdie and then to Daisy. Birdie gave her a look that said to calm down, and squeezed her hand. Daisy's mouth was set in a straight line, and she did not look in Olivia Jean's direction. Her attention was on the preacher, the Reverend Percy Walker.

He wasn't much taller than Olivia Jean. While he talked he pulled a handkerchief from his breast pocket and held it to his brow. He didn't use a paper funeral-home fan with a wide Popsicle stick in the middle. They were close enough up front to see how it was still folded and square as he mopped the front of his face, his brow, and then the back of his neck.

He took his time. Perhaps he was waiting for Olivia Jean to rise, for some response from Birdie. Olivia wondered if maybe she should stand. She didn't know these people, the old weathered faces in the pews, fanning themselves and looking in her direction. She felt her stomach clench. She felt like throwing up.

For the first time since she got in the family way she felt dirty. She shouldn't have gone in the closet. She had made a mistake. She was a loose woman. The short, dark preacher with the handkerchief was telling everyone, looking at each of his congregation in turn but pointing a finger at Olivia Jean.

The fan dropped from her fingers and slid to the floor. Olivia Jean tried to stand, but Birdie held her as if she weighed nothing, her arm a steel bar keeping her from rising. Olivia Jean glanced up, confused. Why would Birdie want her to stay and hear talk that made her feel she wasn't any good? Hadn't the man just said something about how she didn't belong in God's house? But Birdie smiled, a grim smile, and nodded her broad white hat in Daisy's direction. Olivia Jean hadn't noticed that Daisy had stood up, and remained standing as the preacher continued to speak about loose women and the part they played in the Bible. He said something about a whore, and Olivia Jean's face turned hot. She could no longer hold her head up. Her chin settled into her chest.

"Excuse me." Daisy's voice was no louder than the fans that moved about them, and Olivia Jean knew that the preacher didn't hear her, although he couldn't have helped but notice that she was standing in front of him.

"Excuse me?" This time her voice was louder, and it caused him to stop midsentence and trail off about the wages of sin.

"I said excuse me, Reverend Walker."

"Yes, Sister Abernathy?"

"No, my name is Stone. I am married and my name is Stone. Mrs. Daisy Stone. Reverend Walker, is you talking about my child, Olivia Jean? About her being in the family way? You saying she loose?"

Olivia Jean heard the whispers rising against her, rising against the swish of fans in the room. She looked up.

He took a deep breath and swallowed. Olivia Jean thought he looked scared.

"Well, is you gonna answer me? You talking about my daughter?"

"Well, now that you ask, I most certainly am talking 'bout your daughter. You got some nerve."

He didn't get any further, because Birdie stood then and pulled on Olivia Jean's arm gently to get her to stand, too. Olivia Jean felt on display. She started saying her multiplication facts inside her head, because she couldn't think of anything else, and she didn't want to give this man the satisfaction of seeing her tears.

"Let me tell you this, you little stunted piece of shit," said Daisy, and there was a shocked silence and then furious intakes of breath, so that the church was hotter than before.

"My child is a good child and she doing wonderful in school. She a straight-A student." People were talking now, leaning back and forward, using the fans to cover their mouths, not even bothering to whisper.

"School ain't the only thing she studying up there in New York City," he said, and someone in the congregation laughed. "She need to beg the church's forgiveness and ask the Lord to forgive her, too, before she come back up in this church."

Daisy snatched Olivia Jean's hand, and they were out of the pew in seconds. Her mother stopped and faced the pulpit, making Olivia Jean look, too.

"My baby ain't got nothing to be ashamed of, not like some other folk up in this place. I love her, and God surely loves her and she don't need to say she sorry to nobody up in this piss-ass church." Daisy turned, and walked toward the back of the church. Olivia Jean followed.

"Well, don't you bring her back here until she ready to say she sorry for being loose. She's not welcome in this church, in this church where we worship Jesus Christ in Spirit and in Truth, until she can come up here and say she sorry for being a whore."

His words felt like a sting on the back of Olivia Jean's head, and she turned to take a look at this man who was speaking about her as if going into the closet with Preston made her the worst person in the whole world. She did the only thing she could think to do, the only thing that made sense to her, because she'd never had a fight with a grown-up. She licked out her tongue. He dropped his white handkerchief and some of the church members shook their heads in her direction. "Incorrigible," she heard someone mutter as Daisy led the way out of the church.

Daisy slowed down and took Olivia Jean's arm. "Put your head up," she hissed. "Start loving that baby in your belly the way you supposed to." Daisy was so close, she smelled of soap and sweat and the talcum powder she used under her arms. Olivia Jean caught her eye, and for a moment no one else mattered.

Daisy and Olivia Jean had reached the back of the church, but Birdie was still rooted to the floor next to the end of the row where they'd been sitting. She faced the pulpit. No one moved.

Reverend Walker had managed to bend over the large hill of his stomach to retrieve his handkerchief. For a fleeting moment Olivia Jean felt sorry for him. His oldness and meanness had not prepared him for Daisy or for Birdie.

He was trying to ignore Birdie. He looked around, and his gaze settled on the deacons of the church, the men in the first row. He nodded at them. Some nodded back, as if to say that he was right in how he had dealt with Daisy and in what he had said about Olivia Jean. But he shrank before Olivia Jean's eyes, his shoulders hunched, and she could see he was preparing for Birdie. Olivia Jean said, "Lord help him," under her breath, before she remembered that he had called her a whore.

"Miz Birdie, you got something to say, like your daughter?" He tried to sound bold, as though he were not afraid, but he was, and anyone looking at him knew it. He gripped the podium and leaned forward.

"Nah, Reverend Walker, I ain't got nuthin' to say to you. But I'm gonna be talking to somebody tonight. Fact is, I'm already a-talking to Him. Asking Him 'bout his virgin mama, you know, Mary? The one that got in the family way and didn't have no husband but God? And then I'ma ask him 'bout that part in the Bible 'bout casting stones and such-like. You ain't preached that part in a long time. Reckon you done forgot 'bout that story, huh?"

Birdie pulled herself up even taller. She turned toward Olivia Jean and Daisy, smiled a big smile, and then they saw her hands. For a moment Olivia Jean couldn't figure out what Birdie was getting ready to do. She bent at the waist and flipped her dress up, right at the pulpit.

"Reverend, you can kiss my a-s-s." She said this in a loud voice as she wriggled her hind parts at him. Then she stood, smoothed her dress down, and smiled again at Olivia Jean. There were hisses and murmurs traveling across the church. One lady jumped up at the front of the church and started screeching about how she couldn't believe the goings-on. Another sagged in her seat right as Birdie was shaking her butt at the preacher.

The last Olivia Jean saw of Reverend Walker, he had stepped down from the pulpit and was helping the ushers with the woman who had fallen out on account of Birdie flipping her dress up.

But they had forgotten the fourth member of their church-going group, Mr. Lupe Ray Rawlins. He awoke to the commotion, looking around as if he had lost something. As Reverend

Walker helped fan the unconscious woman and barked directions at the ushers, Mr. Lupe slipped out of the pew, caught the Reverend's eye, and held up his index finger to excuse himself as he rushed to catch up with his ladies.

Daisy heard Birdie and Olivia Jean settle in for the night and waited for the sounds of the evening to seep through her door before she got up and sneaked outside. She had a jacket with her and a pack of Pall Malls. She agreed with Birdie one hundred percent—Olivia Jean shouldn't have any smoke around her—but tonight Daisy needed a couple of puffs.

On the porch she slipped onto the glider and took a deep breath. It had been an impossible day. Reverend Walker had the gall to stand in front of the congregation and tear Olivia Jean down as though he didn't have any sins, as if he had been squeaky-clean all of his life. He must have forgotten that Daisy was someone who could set the record straight. She lit a cigarette and sucked on it, trying to get the initial high she always felt when she'd been away from them for a time. The top of her head floated for a minute. But she was still alert enough to hear the car engine.

The lights were turned off as the car traveled over the gravel- and rock-strewn path to the house. She bent down to grind the cigarette out and paused to take one last deep draw. Her heart was pounding. She hoped it was Turk. She could picture his bald head, his sweet mouth. She rose and moved to the front of the porch and waited as she heard the car door close a short distance away. She wondered if she should run to him or wait until he got to the foot of the stairs and throw herself in his arms. She was nearly singing: *My Turk come to get me. My Turk.* Then she saw him clearly as he moved into the light and her heart fell. Percy Walker had come calling.

She didn't wait for him to climb the steps. She stood with her hands on her hips, blocking his way. "What you doin' here?"

"I came to try to make amends. I know I ain't been right by you, and I came to say I'm sorry."

"You truly is a sorry son of a bitch." Daisy felt good saying those words. "And stupid, too." Percy sat on the top step without being invited. Daisy's foot was near his behind, and she felt tempted to begin kicking him off the porch. "Reverend Walker, you done said you sorry. Now you can leave."

His voice was barely a whisper now, ragged, rasping, begging. "But can you forgive me?"

She leaned forward, and even though she knew he couldn't see her in the darkness, she smiled.

"Forgive you for what? For what you said about Olivia Jean, or what you did to me, or both?"

He dropped his head. She saw how his shoulders slumped and how his white shirt stood out sharp and clear, almost iridescent now, as midnight approached.

"See, I forgave you a long time ago for what happened. After all, I got me a beautiful baby girl out of it. I forgave you enough to come back to this here town, to come back to the church where they got you up in the pulpit. I told myself that you deserved to be forgiven. After all, I was to blame, too. I ain't had no sense. No sense at all. Thinking I done fell in love with no preacher. Just 'cause you talk so smooth and wear some good clothes and had a car to take me to my mama." His head fell lower and lower on his chest as the words tumbled from her lips.

Her voice never rose above a whisper, but the anger pulsing through her body was a live thing that jumped and danced between the two of them on the porch.

"But today? Is you crazy? You got up in front of all those people and you talked about your own daughter like she was a tramp. You pointed your finger at her, and ain't nobody ever pointed nuthin' at you. You ain't nuthin' but an old disgrace. Ain't fit to be called nobody's pastor."

Sixteen years of keeping the secret welled up in her throat. She bent down next to him on the porch and grabbed the lapel on his coat and drew his face close to hers.

"Did you hear what I said? Olivia Jean is your daughter. I was pregnant before I left here. I had to go. Had to marry Turk, but I couldn't tell him. I ain't been able to tell him all these years. It would break his heart. And hers, too. Now, if she was ever to find out that you with your sorry preachin' self was her daddy, she sure as hell would be messed-up. Don'tcha think?"

The screen door opened behind them and Daisy jumped. Her hands dropped from his lapels and she heard him sigh. She had felt him tremble before, when her face was in his and she had ahold of him, making him listen. Now Daisy's heart stopped. She hadn't wanted anyone to find out. Ever.

*B*irdie put the kerosene lamp by the door and stepped through the frame. She was dressed in a blue woolen nightgown with a scarlet velvet robe tied around her waist and a scarlet silk scarf around her hair. She was holding a black stick that she used for chasing stray dogs off her property. She marched down the steps of the porch and stood in the yard.

She paced ten steps to the middle of the yard, all the time counting aloud, and started dragging the stick around in a circle. She hadn't said a word to either Daisy or Percy.

"Mama, what you doing?"

"I'm drawing me a circle."

"For what, Mama?"

"It's what they calls a fightin' ring. I'ma kick this mutha-fucker's ass." She whirled around and marched back to the step where Percy was sitting and caught him by the collar. She pulled him off the step into the yard.

"Now, Birdie, we can handle this some other—" began Percy.

"Naw, we can't. We can't handle this no other way than for me to beat the shit out of you. Right here. Right now."

She half dragged him into the circle, where he stood, glancing at Birdie and then at Daisy, not knowing where to turn or which one to talk to.

"Birdie, this here is crazy. I know I done wronged Olivia Jean, and I come to apologize."

Birdie stopped. She balled her fist and brought it back near her side, then with lightning swiftness landed an uppercut to his chin. The good reverend stumbled. He fell to one knee.

"It ain't only Olivia Jean you done did wrong. I hear tell you took advantage of my baby girl. I hear tell you Olivia's daddy. You did all us wrong. You ain't nuthin' but a fat, evil man, an' I be sorry for Lovey. She ain't deserve some old lecherous man like you."

With her right hand this time she landed a punch to his stomach and watched him double up and land fully on the ground, retching. "Get up. I ain't finished with you," Birdie said.

Percy was slow moving, hardly able to pull his body from the dirt.

"Mama Birdie, please. You don't have to do this. Mama, stop."
Daisy's voice was frantic, cutting through the darkness. She didn't
want Olivia Jean to wake up.

Birdie planted her feet, and as soon as Percy made it off the
ground she swung and connected with his eye. He groaned and
tumbled over again. She began to move in the circle, fist weaving, chanting, "Get up, get up now. 'Cause I'ma give you some
more."

Daisy came down from the porch step and caught Birdie's
arm.

"Mama, you gonna wake up Olivia Jean. Please stop. He ain't
worth it. I don't want her to know."

"You hear that, Preacher?" Birdie spat. "My daughter say you
ain't worth me finishing you off. Maybe she right about that. I
don't know. But I'ma leave you alone right now. If you ever come
on my property again, if you ever speak to my grandbaby or ever
try to speak to her or my Daisy again—" She stopped and moved
closer to the man. "I promise you, I'll cut your head off. Do you
hear me?"

Percy rose from the ground. He walked to the car, his gait that
of a defeated man. He moaned with each step. A few seconds
after he closed the car door behind him, the ignition roared, and
both women turned to the screen door, hoping that Olivia Jean
had not heard.

They watched until Percy Walker disappeared into the night.
When the silence was restored, Birdie turned to Daisy, opening
her arms. Daisy hesitated for only a second. But as she laid her
head against her mother's heart, there were no tears, not from
either of them.

"I ain't fit to be your mama. I shoulda knowed why you left. Dammit."

Daisy pulled away from the embrace first but held out her hand, and Birdie took it. They walked back to the house.

"Mama, I don't want Olivia Jean to know. She don't need to know."

"I ain't gonna tell her. And I ain't gonna tell Turk neither. But that preacher might. What we gonna do to stop him?" asked Birdie.

"I don't know what we gonna do. I don't know." Daisy shrugged her shoulders.

They came to the screen door.

"Mama, where you learn to fight like that? I ain't never seen no woman throw punches like you did. And when you had me in the mud the other day, I thought you was gonna break my back."

"Learned that in the jailhouse. I'll tell you the story one day. I gotta teach you and Olivia Jean how to box. Might come in handy."

"Sure might, Mama. We have to wait on Olivia Jean, though. Can't teach her fightin' until she have that baby."

Olivia Jean was asleep when she first heard the noise in the front yard. She went to the window to peek around the new curtains Daisy had made. Her room now had pink lace curtains threaded with ribbons. Daisy had sewing fever and was making Olivia Jean dresses and helping decorate a room that looked like the kind of room that Olivia Jean had always wanted. Daisy had changed since they left New York. Olivia Jean wondered if Turk had changed, too. She guessed she wouldn't have the answer to that anytime soon, since they hadn't heard a word from him in months. Daisy put on a good act, but her eyes turned red and stayed red once she'd been crying. Besides, Olivia Jean had been through this before with her. Turk was an expert at leaving and coming back again when he got ready or didn't have enough money to play another hand of cards or buy one last drink.

As Olivia Jean stumbled to the window that night, she thought that it might be Turk coming back to Cold Water Springs. Then she saw Daisy nose-to-nose with the man and knew it couldn't be her father unless he'd shrunk. She finally recognized Reverend Walker and was puzzled as to why he would be coming to their place so late at night. She didn't have to wait long for an answer. Birdie shot out of the house, her voice angry and carrying through the closed window.

At first the shock had Olivia Jean wringing her hands and sobbing. She moved from the window and sat on the edge of her bed, wondering what she should do, what she could do about the situation. When nothing came to mind she climbed back into bed and turned to the wall. She didn't know what to think except that the world no longer made sense to her. How was it that the only father she'd known was not hers any longer and that a person who had called her a whore was?

One morning, as Birdie went out to hang the wash, five crows sat on the clothesline. According to *The Farmer's Almanac*, it was the first day of winter. She noted the trees and their seasonal desolation and marked some for the woodpile. This was the time for wood to be chopped. After the wash she would tackle that chore.

She loved the heft of the ax in her hands, how her muscles strained as she cut through the wood. She squinted at the sun, again eyeing the birds. They hadn't moved.

She put the laundry down and stood on the back porch, studying each of the crows in turn. One shifted on a leg; another turned sideways, his black agate eyes firmly on Birdie, as if daring her to enter the backyard. Finally she said, "Humph. Not today." And hearing her voice, the crows took flight. Birdie stared as their black bodies soared across the sky, and then she picked up the wash again.

Olivia Jean appeared at the door as Birdie stepped into the yard.

"Grandma, did you call for me?" she asked.

"No, baby. Just talking to some old crows." Birdie flung a white sheet across the line, pulling a clothespin from her apron. Olivia Jean came by her side and reached down into the laundry basket, but Birdie stopped her by lightly slapping her hands away.

"Girl, I done told you that there ain't nuthin' for you to do but sit down and relax. That baby gonna be here any second now, and then you gonna have your work cut out for you. Go on and sit down up there. I can handle this here wash."

Olivia Jean climbed the three steps again and sat in the straight-backed chair that Birdie kept on the back porch. The wind blew her hair gently around her face, and when Birdie turned to make sure that Olivia was sitting, the older woman marveled at the beautiful picture that Olivia Jean presented: her big belly, the smooth skin, and the soft, dark hair that moved with the wind. For a moment she paused, and then she turned again to her work, picking up a brassiere to hang on the line.

"Grandma Birdie, I been meaning to ask you a question."

"Well, spit it out, girl, ask away." Birdie smiled at Olivia Jean and began to clamp the wooden clothespins on her blouse, in the gaps between the buttons.

"Why you wear so many colors, so many different colors all the time?" Olivia Jean inclined her head and Birdie looked down. She was wearing blue, pink, and purple and a pair of soft brown moccasins that did not hurt the corn on the side of her big toe.

Birdie shrugged and hung another sheet, pinning it to the line. She raised her voice to carry over the wind and the clothes that flapped on the line.

"What you really mean is, why I wear these here loud colors and I be so black? Right?" Olivia Jean didn't reply, but when Birdie turned in her direction she nodded, suddenly ashamed.

"I guess a black-as-night person just supposed to keep with wearing some old blue or brown. Ain't supposed to wear nuthin' that make me seem blacker, right? Well, let me tell you something." Birdie picked up the empty laundry basket and headed for the steps, where she paused, looking up at Olivia Jean. "Colors ain't only for white folks and high yellas. All us got a right to colors. That be one of the first things Queenie Monroe taught me when I went to live with her. She said, 'Big, black women got a right to feel good, too.' And colors make you feel real good. Leastways, they make me feel good."

There was no anger in Birdie's voice, no hidden jealousy for not being lighter. Olivia Jean thought of Preston and shivered. His skin was like the midnight sky, and she had thought he was beautiful. But other friends of hers talked about dark-skinned colored people. As a child she had looked in mirrors and thought that she would be prettier if her skin were lighter. There was even one time when she thought that it was a shame that Mama had married Daddy. Why couldn't she have found a lighter man?

"And another secret Queenie done told me." Olivia Jean leaned in close so that she and Birdie were almost touching. "She say that no matter how black or ugly you think you is, there gonna be somebody that loves your black, ugly self. And that somebody ain't gonna think you ugly. They gonna think you is beautiful. And that's the honest-to-goodness truth."

After a moment Olivia Jean said, "Grandma Birdie, how 'bout if you ain't exactly ugly but you got a baby? People don't forgive women that have babies without a husband, do they? Ain't no boy gonna wanna be with me after I have this here baby, is he? My own daddy ain't even wanna be near me." There was a hysterical edge building in Olivia Jean's voice. Birdie reached her hand out and grabbed Olivia Jean's, which had been flying about in her lap. She squeezed and held it tight. Olivia took a deep breath and looked into Birdie's set eyes and calmed.

"I can't promise you that you ain't never gonna have no problem about this baby coming. Some days jus' livin' is a problem. But I can say that one day the right man gonna come by and you'll feel it in your bones. He'll look at that baby you have and say that it don't make one bit of difference. An' he gonna make room for you and this child that God puttin' in your life. Wait and see."

Birdie offered Olivia Jean a hand in getting out of her seat. Once Olivia Jean had shuffled her feet inside, Birdie stood looking at the sky. Gray clouds drifted low, and she thought that rain might hit before nightfall. But the wash would be dry and ready to come down way before then. And she could get the firewood in, too. She searched for the crows but they were gone. "Good," she said. "Don't need any more of them bad-luck birds around." She let the door slip from her fingers and went into the house to find heavy boots and gloves to wear out to the woodpile.

Mama, I heard you outside with Olivia Jean this mornin', and you sure 'nuff a liar." Daisy was baking a cake, standing in the middle of the kitchen with a large mixing bowl and a spoon, stirring in the flour, crushing the small lumps that it made in the batter. Birdie didn't have a sifter.

"How you figures that?" Birdie had finished chopping the wood and was sitting near the kitchen stove, half-asleep.

"Tellin' her that it don't matter none 'bout the baby. You know it do too matter. People ain't as bad as back in your day, but they bad enough. She gonna have plenty of rough days 'cause of the baby. You seen how them church people acted." Daisy was stirring faster now, some of the batter spilling out of the bowl until she took a deep breath and slowed.

"You think it gonna do her any good to know that right now?" asked Birdie. She was alert, her eyes focused on Daisy.

"Olivia Jean ain't gonna thank you none for tellin' her no lie. She ain't that type of child." Daisy sat at the table with Birdie. She put the bowl down and slumped forward.

"Well, I ain't done lied to her neither. Jus' told her the truth as I sees it. Somebody might jus' come along that ain't care none where that baby come from. All she gotta do is sit tight." Birdie was firm.

"Humph. Well, I'm glad to know you still believe in fairy tales." Daisy shook her head.

"What done got you up on a high horse today?"

"Mama, you fillin' her with stuff you ain't even believe. You talkin' to her 'bout color, too. Like you really believes what you say."

Birdie raised her head up and met her Daisy's eyes. "I do believes what I say 'bout the color of a man's skin."

"Mama, all you used to do when I was runnin' 'round here barefoot was grab me and tell me how pretty my yellow behind was. All you could talk 'bout was how I was like the sunshine, or how my name was Daisy 'cause of my color. Shit, I went to school one time and said what you said an' had to fight 'most every damn body in there. They said I was uppity an' colorstruck. You was proud of me bein' high yella. I ain't never heard you say you was proud for bein' black. I ain't never heard you say no such a thing."

Birdie sighed deep down and nodded.

"Daisy, you is right. I can't lie. I done tried to be proud of being as black as I am. I can even hear Queenie talking to me sometimes, the way she use ta when them old colored chil'rens ran me home from school callin' me names 'cause I was blacker and ashier than all them. Your daddy was a comfort, too. That why I know there is somebody for everybody, 'cause he use to be callin' me his black pearl. But you is right. I was sure 'nuff proud of you 'cause you was light, an' wadn't nobody gonna be callin' you ugly or chasin' you up and down the street or asking you to roll your eyes at night so they could pick you out by the white parts. I was sure glad you was never gonna have to go through none a that." Birdie had to look away. Her voice was choked with emotion.

"Birdie, I ain't never knew it was so hard for you." Daisy's eyes were gentle as she stared across the table at her mother. She had not known that someone so strong might still hurt at the thought of childhood taunts.

"An' you ain't never gonna really know, and you ain't got to. An' I'm happy you ain't got to. Bein' a blacker-than-coal woman is a mess, somethin' I ain't gonna wish on nobody. But you think on this: If Olivia Jean have herself a blackberry baby we gotta be ready. Gotta be ready to train that baby an' Olivia Jean to be proud. Not to hang no head about they color. Not to let nobody chase 'em. You an' me gotta make sure they know to be proud."

Daisy nodded. "Okay, you right, Mama. We gotta make sure they all right with they color. I'll work with you on that."

"Look up under that sink there Daisy an' pull out that jug. We gonna have us a little taste on this here agreement," Birdie said with a big smile.

Daisy found the jug, uncorked it, and started looking for a couple of clean glasses.

"Don't need no glasses." Birdie tipped the jug and took a long swallow, and then handed it over to Daisy. Daisy tilted the jug up to her lips, taking as long a swallow as Birdie. She wiped her mouth with the back of her hand, and both women hooted.

Olivia Jean appeared at the kitchen door. "What y'all gettin' into in here?" she asked.

Birdie winked at Daisy. "Not for you to know this year, little woman. You still got some other things you gotta learn before you can be wid us."

Later that night Birdie swayed in front of the mirror, touching her face, her skin. There was a difference now from when she first came knocking at Shorty Long's door almost forty years ago. Lines around her mouth, puffed half-moons under her eyes. Gray threads ran through her hair, the widow's peak entirely white. Somewhere there was the girl who Shorty Long kissed and who kissed him back. There was a black pearl buried within, somewhere. One tear slipped down her cheek and she wiped it away quickly. One thing she knew for sure: Black-as-midnight women didn't do no crying.

Olivia Jean could tell that Mr. Lupe was surprised, but he kept on talking when he was supposed to talk and he was quiet otherwise, even though his leg must have hurt. She had kicked him hard under the table to get his attention. She needed to speak with him in private to ask a favor. She was impressed by the fact that he didn't let out a sound and only tilted his head a little in her direction. Olivia Jean could tell that Mr. Lupe Rawlins was a man who could keep a secret.

They were seated around the table at the big house on Sunday having dinner. It was the middle of December. Birdie had said that the little house was too small to have a real dinner and that they should use Mr. Shorty Long's table at the big house. She meant that everyone had to put on shoes and comb their hair and that she had to keep her teeth in even though the meat didn't taste as good when she chewed it. But things were different in the big house. First off, it was big; not by a little but by a lot. There was the formal dining room and the formal sitting room and the guest bedroom, and there was indoor plumbing; Mr. Shorty Long had put in two bathrooms before he passed. Daisy had taken Olivia Jean by the hand and showed her every room as soon as she found out that Mr. Shorty Long was her daddy. When they came to the dining room she was crying a little, telling Olivia Jean all about the Sunday dinners and how she had to sit and answer all of her daddy's questions about her week. She broke down then and had to go off by herself to walk outside and get some fresh air. Olivia Jean let her be and waited by the breakfront, running her hands over the wood. She wondered why it was that Daisy was having such a hard time with the fact that Mr. Shorty Long was her father. As far as Olivia Jean was concerned, Daisy should have known her daddy was a white man because of the color of her skin and the way her hair waved and didn't kink up at the first touch of water.

She started to ask Daisy why she was so surprised about Shorty Long, when Daisy came back inside smelling of cigarettes. But she didn't on account of how red Daisy's eyes were and how her mouth trembled, as though she were just holding on by a thread. That was when Olivia Jean cussed Turk Stone a blue streak in her head. He'd let them both down, and she did not know whether she could ever forgive him.

But she thought, Did it really matter if she forgave Turk Stone or if he broke down and forgave her? After all, she was not his real daughter. If he heard the news, would he be relieved? Was she relieved? That was an easy one to answer. No, she was not relieved to find that Turk Stone was not her father. She was surprised, maybe as surprised as Daisy had been to discover Shorty Long was her father. It was like being turned upside down. Everything you thought was the truth was a lie, and the lie was the truth. Poor Daisy, Olivia Jean thought. At least Olivia Jean had had a flesh-and-blood person to hold for a while, even if he was fickle and her love didn't mean anything to him. Daisy had a photograph, some memories of Sunday dinners, and a house. Between the two, Olivia Jean counted herself as the winner.

After Daisy finished giving her a tour of the house, Olivia Jean grabbed her hand and squeezed it hard. Daisy was surprised but squeezed back, and they walked down to the little house hand in hand until they reached the door. That had been one of her favorite Sundays.

Now every Sunday they were supposed to eat in the big house. Mr. Lupe was their invited guest, although he might as well be family, as much time as he spent around them all. Olivia Jean smiled at him, and Mr. Lupe kicked her under the table, too, just as hard as she had kicked him. She almost made a noise but remembered how he didn't, and she kept on grinning. When it came time to serve up the food, Olivia Jean told Grandma Birdie that she wanted to fix Mr. Lupe a plate herself. Birdie stopped and half smiled at her, but she said, "All right."

Birdie had often told Olivia Jean that the best way to a man's heart was through his food. She was determined to get on Mr. Lupe's good side by serving him a substantial portion of food. She went to the pot Birdie had simmering low on the stove and fished out the biggest pork chop she saw. Then she put some white rice on the plate and went back to the pot with the chops. White rice was best with gravy when the gravy was thick and heaped on top and mixed in with a little spoon. The collard greens were ready, and she made sure he had a generous portion.

"Next week we not gonna serve you from the pots like that," Daisy said. "We got plenty of gravy boats an' bowls we can put the food in." She frowned at Olivia Jean as if to ask her why she hadn't used the right things for the table. When Mr. Lupe took a bite out of his pork chop and declared it the best pork chop he had ever eaten, and then wondered out loud about the possibility of seeing the governor and proclaiming it "Daisy Pork Chop Day in honor of the mighty fine meat Daisy done prepared," her mother smiled and the frown lines relaxed around her brow.

Olivia Jean sat in her seat next to Mr. Lupe and bided her time. Just in case the kick earlier hadn't been enough, she winked at him whenever he turned her way, and spilled her cup of water over his pants. Daisy fussed, but Mr. Lupe looked as if he were going to fall out laughing. He finally excused himself from the table and went out front. Olivia Jean counted thirty seconds and limped out, too. He was waiting for her, leaning against one of the wood pillars on the wraparound porch.

"This sure is a mighty fine house Mr. Shorty Long built. The kinda house that gonna last and last."

He was talking to Olivia Jean, but she wasn't in the listening type of mind. She wanted to ask for what she needed in a hurry. Daisy and Birdie would be out soon.

He reached inside his pants pocket and pulled out a pipe. He had it in his mouth and was drawing on the light when she asked him.

"Mr. Lupe, I want you to take me to see my father."

He started to cough. She rapped on his back. When he got clear he said, "Olivia Jean, your daddy clear up in New York. I can't—"

"I didn't say I wanted to see my daddy. I want to see my father."

Mr. Lupe was tall and thin, his face full of lines. His lips barely opened when he spoke. His teeth were stained from years of coffee and tobacco.

"Must be something I'm misunderstanding. You gotta explain

this to me." They were standing on the front porch of the big house that faced the lake. The surface was calm and blue, the water lapping gently at the shore.

Mr. Lupe and Olivia Jean stared ahead while she told him about the night Birdie beat the preacher, her father, until he could barely walk to his car. Mr. Lupe was quiet for a spell, and she held her breath thinking that Birdie was going to fly out of the house any minute and her plans would be ruined. She'd never get to speak a word to her father.

"Humph, you sure you wanna go talk to Percy Walker?"

That was when she turned to look up to Mr. Lupe. Olivia Jean had the feeling that as bad as Birdie beat the old preacher up, Mr. Lupe could and would do worse if she wanted him to. His eyes were deep and warm, and they told her that she had his protection. She looked down.

"I've got to see him, Mr. Lupe. Mama ain't gonna take me, and neither is Grandma Birdie. And I don't know where he lives, except for it's someplace in town, maybe near the church. You the only person I know that can do it."

"What you gonna tell your mama and grandma about going wid me somewhere? You gonna lie to them?" Mr. Lupe was staring out at the water. He could have sworn that a catfish jumped on the surface and flopped back down with a big splash. He thought about bringing his fishing pole by next Sunday.

"Well, I ain't exactly gonna lie. I thought I'd ride into town with you tomorrow when you take Mama into work, an' then maybe we could stop an' see him then."

Mr. Lupe took a long puff from his pipe and then sat on the edge of the porch.

"If you plannin' on goin' to town tomorrow, best you get to bed early. I'm leavin' at nine sharp. Your mama have to be to work on time."

"Thank you, Mr. Lupe. Thank you." She almost jumped, but she remembered the baby just in time. Instead Olivia Jean put her hand on Mr. Lupe's shoulder. He reached across and put his bony fingers on top of hers.

"If you changes your mind, I ain't gonna be upset. You can always change your mind," said Lupe Rawlins.

But he should have known better than to think she'd let this go. She was Birdie's granddaughter, after all. Olivia Jean went inside to do the dishes and the sweeping before heading to bed. She listened to the soft murmur of the trees in the wind and the voices of the adults as they wafted under her window, sitting and talking their dinner off. She dreamed of her father, the real one, the one who might speak to her and forgive her for what she had done wrong. The one she might have a chance to turn around.

At breakfast Daisy stared at Olivia Jean, and Birdie lifted her eyebrows. Olivia Jean didn't usually get up before nine, but here she was, dressed and ready to go to town with Mr. Lupe and Daisy.

"You all right?" Daisy was concerned, and she laid a hand on Olivia Jean's cheek.

"I'm fine. I just want to go into town an' see things a little. I asked Mr. Lupe. He said it was fine with him."

"That's what all that talkin' was 'bout last night on the front porch, you wantin' to go into town?" Birdie asked. She was wip-

ing the table down with a washcloth after their breakfast of oatmeal and bacon.

"Yes, ma'am. I wanted to ask Mr. Lupe if it would be all right
to ride with him and Mama."

Daisy and Birdie exchanged suspicious glances. Olivia Jean
would have laughed if she hadn't been so nervous.

Olivia Jean climbed into the cab with Mr. Lupe, and Daisy sat
in a chair in the back of the truck and held on to the sides. Mr.
Lupe drove very slowly, only twenty miles an hour, into town.
When he stopped, he rushed to the back and held out his hand
for Daisy to step down. Olivia Jean opened the door of the cab
and half slid down by herself. She was curious about the dry
goods store where Daisy worked; the place that swallowed her
mother every day from nine thirty until four thirty. It had to be
different from New York. Daisy never complained now—not
about her fingers hurting, not about people treating her badly
and not about money.

Daisy went in first, and Mr. Lupe held the door for Olivia
Jean. Olivia Jean paused for a moment, expecting someplace
spectacular to appear as soon as she entered her eyes. She was
disappointed. It was an old country shop with bolts of material
stuck this way and that: colorful, patterned material, ridged and
velvety, but fabric just the same. There were two jars sitting on
the counter, filled with buttons. One held only white buttons, a
sea of shimmering seashell whites, and the other held buttons of
every color, reds, blues, greens, and even purples. She walked to
the jar with the colored buttons and stared at it.

"You must be Birdie's grandbaby," said a stooped old woman. She was so bent that she was barely taller than Olivia Jean. "Y'all favor, an' then you went right to the button jar with the colored buttons. Birdie love herself some color, don't she?"

The woman had gray, flyaway hair and crooked teeth that seemed to be pushing at one another to get space in her mouth, but she smiled at Olivia Jean anyway and held out a hand.

Olivia Jean stayed almost an hour. She saw Daisy seated at a sewing machine that was near the back of the store, close to a window that was propped open with a stick. The sun was pouring in and the tree was rustling because of the wind. Daisy was talking to herself as she moved the cloth around the sewing machine with her feet gently tapping the pedals underneath.

*W*hen they climbed into the truck to leave, Mr. Lupe was quiet until the engine started and he began to drive.

"Ain't no shame in changing your mind," he said. "From what you done told me, nobody knows you know about him anyways."

"No, Mr. Lupe. I gotta go meet him." What she didn't say was that she didn't want to lose another father. Maybe she could talk to Percy Walker, convince him that she wasn't the worst sinner he had ever met. Maybe he would forgive her. Olivia Jean wanted a father again. And it seemed to her that Reverend Walker was the only chance she had. Turk was already gone.

They stopped in front of a small house and she thought it was beautiful: flowers all over, lining the walkway leading up to the house, spread in all types of patterns in the yard. Mr. Lupe was with her the whole way. She wanted to tell him that he could stay in the truck, but there was something in the set of his jaw that stopped her.

Olivia Jean rang the doorbell, and Lovey Walker answered. When she saw Olivia Jean she blushed and tried to say that the preacher wasn't home. Mr. Lupe came in handy then. "Miss Lovey, his car is in the carport. We know Percy ain't a walking man. And it ain't right for you to be lying for him. We not here to cause no trouble. This here young lady jus' wanna have a few words with him. Ain't gonna take much of his time."

There was a moment when both Lovey and Olivia Jean stared at Lupe Rawlins. It was the most Olivia Jean had ever heard him say at one time when he wasn't joking or fooling around. Her heart skipped when Miss Lovey invited them across the threshold and told them to have a seat in Reverend Walker's study.

The room was bare except for one picture of Jesus, his head crowned with thorns, his blue eyes fixed heavenward, and three rivulets of blood running down his forehead. There were three folding chairs facing the desk. Books and papers were scattered in piles on the desk, in the corners of the room, and on one of the folding chairs. Mr. Lupe pulled one chair forward for Olivia Jean first, sat in the other, and pulled off his hat. He had not allowed Miss Lovey to take it, maybe because it was so sweat-stained and old. Now he passed time twirling it in his bony hands, stopping every so often to pluck at the red feather at the side. Olivia Jean cleared her throat.

"You ain't let Miss Lovey take your hat."

"This be a hat your grandma made for me. I don't let nobody touch it."

The preacher came in then, and that shut them both up.

There was no warmth in the man. He stared straight at Olivia

Jean, but she would have bet money that he didn't know who she was. She touched her belly. His eyes darted there, too. He knew her. Then she searched his face. They shared the same wide jaw, the same smooth forehead. But his eyes were old, shrunken into his brow.

He nodded at Mr. Lupe. "What can I do for you, Mr. Rawlins?"

"I ain't come here for me. This little lady here want to talk wid ya." Mr. Lupe stood up. "I'm gonna go right over there by the door, Olivia Jean. So, if you needs me, all you gotta do is call my name. I ain't goin' far." He moved over to the door then and leaned against it, his back turned away from the preacher and Olivia Jean. There was a moment when she thought she saw something slide across the old reverend's face, like maybe his heart was yammering inside his chest as loudly as hers was, but she changed her mind when she saw how cold and closed his face was toward her. He sat down at his desk, riffled through some papers, and then turned his chair halfway facing her, as though he couldn't stand the thought of Olivia Jean.

"What can I do for you, Miss Stone?"

"I ain't told my mama or Grandma Birdie that I was coming here today. They woulda been mad. But I had to say something to you." The preacher was silent. Olivia Jean was getting more nervous by the minute and more afraid that perhaps she had made a mistake. The man didn't like her. She could tell by the way he wouldn't meet her eyes.

"I know 'bout you being my father. I heard that night you came over to the house. Kinda hard not to hear all that commotion." She paused, giving him a chance to respond, but when he didn't she continued.

"You said in the church that day that I should come beg your pardon for what I did to get in the family way. I came to beg your pardon. I didn't mean to sin or to be loose. I did something I shouldn't have done, and I was wrong. Will you forgive me, and . . . and maybe we could start over again? I promise I ain't bringing no bad city ways—"

He cut her off. "Young lady, I don't know what you're talking about regarding me being your father." She lifted her eyes to see that he had turned and was again searching through the papers on his desk. His voice was terse, distant. And proper. "But I do know that the only one that can forgive you for your sins is Jesus. You'll have to get on your knees and ask Him. If you'd like for me to pray for you, I certainly will. I think you should probably be getting back home now. I don't think your mother and your grandmother would approve of your being here. Mr. Rawlins?" She was surprised at being dismissed so quickly, as though she didn't matter at all. Olivia Jean stood. But he did not stand to walk with her to the door; he did not look up from his papers.

Her neck was hot, and she felt the saliva gathered on the sides of her mouth. She didn't remember walking out, but she did, Mr. Lupe's arms supporting her. At the bottom of the stairs leading from the house, she paused and was sick in the flower bed. Mr. Lupe had to pull over by the side of the road once. He yelled for Birdie as soon as he parked the car. She came flying from the house, trying to get to Olivia Jean, who pushed her away and was sick again in the graveled driveway, on her knees. She kept saying, "Dear God, forgive me. Dear God, forgive me." But it made no difference, because she knew He hadn't heard. If her two earthly fathers refused to hear, why would God be any different?

•   •   •

Olivia Jean sensed the raised voices before she could figure out what was wrong. There was a wet cloth pressed to her eyes, but even though she could not see, she could hear.

"How you gonna take her to that man? Are you crazy?" It was Birdie. Mr. Lupe answered, but it was in a much lower voice.

"You need to leave this house, Lupe Rawlins; you leave this house now."

Olivia Jean swung her feet over the edge of the bed. When she tried to stand, the room swam.

"Grandma Birdie, Grandma Birdie," she yelled. Something fell over.

"Baby, you got to get back in bed. Dr. Hicks done been here already. You got an ear infection, a little fever. Your mama rode in town to get you a few things to make you comfortable."

"Grandma Birdie," said Olivia Jean, "it wasn't Mr. Lupe's fault. I made him take me. I didn't want you or Mama to know."

"Child, don't you worry about—"

"Grandma Birdie, if you make him go away, I'm going away, too. I'll get up out of this bed an' I'll leave you like Mama left you, an' I won't come back."

"Baby, don't say that." Birdie's face and voice were anguished. She held on to Olivia Jean's hand.

"Grandma Birdie, I love Mr. Lupe. He can't be leaving. He our family. Promise me that he not going nowhere. Promise?"

"Promise."

"And, Grandma Birdie?"

"Yes?"

"Please don't tell Mama I know. She'll tell me soon. I just got to give her some time. It's a big secret."

"Young lady, you get yourself back in that bed right now. How you gonna be talkin' to your elders like you can tell somebody what to do?" It was Mr. Lupe. Olivia Jean smiled up at him, and he smiled back. Birdie made her put her feet under the covers and tucked her into the bed again. Olivia Jean asked if he would stay with her for a while. He pulled the rocking chair from the corner and folded himself in it and sat, not saying a word, and that was fine with her.

$\mathcal{R}$ight before the New Year's celebration, one of the congregation ladies called the house. It was two thirty in the afternoon. The woman was breathing hard over the phone. She said it was an emergency. Reverend Walker was dying, on his deathbed, and could be drawing his last right now. But he wanted to see Daisy and Olivia Jean. He wanted them to come quick to the house. Would they please make it over to the house as soon as possible? Miss Lovey had asked her to call because she didn't want to leave his side. Olivia Jean and Mr. Lupe had been at the Reverend's house only two weeks ago.

Daisy put the phone in its cradle and went in the backyard to find Birdie, who had the big house rug slung over the empty laundry line and she was beating it with long, practiced hits, almost as if the rug were human and she was enjoying some type of game. Olivia Jean was nearby, sitting with a book on the inside of the doorway, tucked in a blanket, sipping hot chocolate.

"Mama Birdie, Miss Lovey had one of the saints from the

church call to say that Percy Walker gettin' ready to kick the bucket. They say he could go any minute."

Birdie did not pause in her beating of the rug. Nor did she sound breathless when she responded. "Did they now?"

"Yes, Mama. He wanna see me and Olivia Jean before he pass on."

Birdie gave another solid *thwak* and rested the broom on the ground.

"Really?"

"Yeah. That's what they said. I was wondering if you could take us? We gotta get there soon."

"Why you wanna go there? What he got to say now that's so important?"

By this time Olivia Jean had abandoned her book and had come outside with a shawl wrapped around her shoulders.

"Mama, who was that on the telephone?" Olivia Jean asked.

"One of the ladies from the church. Percy Walker seem like he dying, an' he wanna talk to you an' your mama. You ain't owe him nuthin', an' I was jus' tryin' to figure out whether we should even tell you 'bout the jackass," replied Birdie.

Olivia Jean stood for a moment. At first she looked at the ground. "I already know he my father. I heard you all that night." She was trying her best not to cry.

Daisy trembled. She took a deep breath. "Olivia Jean, I am sorry I didn't tell you sooner 'bout Reverend Walker bein' your father and Turk not. But whoever your daddy is, you got to know that I love you. What happened sixteen years ago over an' done. I got me a beautiful daughter out of it, an' I know I'ma blessed woman. So I know you disappointed that your daddy ain't your daddy, but I hope you forgive me. I ain't mean to cause no harm all them years ago. I was jus' young. I ain't know no better."

"Okay, y'all go ahead and hold each other for a while," said Birdie. "Then we gonna go see this man before he pass. Let's hurry up an' get over there an' back. We all got a lot of things to speak on later. But I jus' wanna tell y'all that I'm happy y'all here. I know it ain't been easy, not for any of us, but things workin' better'n I thought they would."

The old woman grinned as Daisy took her daughter in her arms and squeezed and kissed her on the forehead.

"Oh, an' by the way, we movin' up to the big house this week. I done decided that we need us some more room."

"Mama Birdie, we moving to the big house?" Daisy was almost laughing. "We not gonna hafta sneak up to the bathrooms no more?"

Birdie shook her head. "No more sneaking. The house ours. Shorty Long left it for us all to use, an' we gonna use it. Best damn house in Colbert County sittin' up there an' ain't nobody in it. Sin an' a shame."

Only Olivia Jean was quiet.

"What's the matter, gal, you ain't happy we movin' up in the world?" asked Daisy.

"I'm happy. Really I am." She smiled at her mother and grandmother. "I'm just sorry that Mr. Percy Walker dyin' and that Daddy's not here." She couldn't put in words what she felt. But there was a coating of happiness that fit snugly around her heart from being with Birdie and Daisy, but when she thought about the men who had been important in her life, there was emptiness.

"Well, we can't worry 'bout them now. We got to hurry up and get to town," said Daisy. Birdie nodded in agreement, and the three women went inside to get ready.

*L*ovey Walker was sitting in the parlor when they arrived, her face pinched and ashen. "Y'all just missed him. He went on home not ten minutes ago." Her voice was composed, her face full of emotion.

Birdie started at the news. She had not believed the telephone call. Percy had been dying for years from all types of complaints.

"The doctor say his poor heart give out, what with the weight and all the ministering he been doing lately. Things was too much for him." Lovey shook her head. Her fingers had been busy with her needlepoint. She rested it on her lap and motioned to Olivia Jean.

"Child, could you come here for a moment?" Lovey patted a seat next to her on the sofa, sliding over to the right so that Olivia Jean could comfortably sit. Then she reached out a hand to Daisy and held it firmly while she looked from Daisy to Birdie.

"Percy asked me to beg your forgiveness. That's why he was wantin' y'all to come. He wanted to tell y'all that he was sorry for speaking like he did to you in front of the congregation. He said that everyone got their crosses to bear, and that he ain't had no right to make Olivia Jean's harder. He say the same thing 'bout you, Daisy. He was real sorry."

Olivia Jean, who had started to cry at everything lately, let out a loud "Ohh," and tears began to flow from her face. Lovey gen-

tly told her to go on in the kitchen and find a napkin to wipe her
face.

Birdie waited for Olivia Jean to get out of earshot. "You lying.
Percy ain't left no such message."

Lovey picked up her sewing again, finishing off a stitch before
she replied, "You right. He ain't apologized. Just told me the
truth before he went on." She paused again. "You'd think he'd
know better than to tell the truth before he died. Not like he ain't
seen a thousand people die before and heard the truth from 'em.
And then seen how the truth mess up everything. I'm telling y'all
now," Lovey said, "don't wait until you ain't got but a breath left
to tell the truth. That ain't right for nobody."

Olivia Jean came through the door then, bringing a glass of
lemonade that was precarious, given her new propensity to drop
things and spill. She offered the glass to Lovey, who smiled at
her and again made the young girl sit next to her.

"Y'all don't mind if Olivia Jean visit a spell with me do you?
I'm waiting for all the menfolk to get finished here. There's the
doctor, the undertaker, and they say they gotta find at least six
strong men to move him. I told Percy he oughta ease up off all
those biscuits and molasses. That man ain't never listened to nobody."

Daisy and Birdie left then with a picture of Olivia Jean sitting
next to Miss Lovey while the older woman hesitantly brushed
her fingers over the girl's protruding belly.

Birdie reached into her bodice front and withdrew a small
snuff tin, took a big pinch, and nestled it between her bottom
teeth and her lip, breathing a sigh of satisfaction. Daisy stopped
in the middle of the road to light up a long-needed cigarette.

"Mama, I never did tell you about Reverend Walker and what happened." Daisy took a long toke on her cigarette.

"Ain't no need to tell me nuthin'. I already done heard the story. Church folks always talkin' 'bout Eve an' how she made Adam fall. I say that Eve was a lone woman up against her husband an' Satan, an' she did the best she could. You did the best you could. Ain't nobody can blame you for nuthin'."

When Olivia Jean got so big that she couldn't move around much, Daisy and Birdie made her sit in whatever room they were in and she had to do her chores from a chair. They had her shelling peas or snapping green beans at the kitchen table. Although she couldn't do the fancy stitches that Daisy could, Olivia Jean could baste a passable hemline. Daisy put her to work to keep from seeing her constantly stroke her stomach. But every so often Daisy would get up and stretch from beside the window, where better light streamed, and walk over to where Olivia Jean was sitting. Sometimes she'd smile and tell Olivia Jean that she was doing a fine job. Other times she'd wrinkle her nose and go back to her seat and get a small pair of sewing shears and cut the thread out of the hem, explaining to Olivia Jean that she was working too fast or that the small stitches had to be even smaller. But it was a different Daisy who hovered over Olivia Jean these days. Daisy pressed Olivia Jean's shoulders when she finished explaining what was wrong with the sewing, and sometimes she put a hand on her daughter's belly and rubbed as the baby moved. Once, as Olivia Jean bent her head back to her sewing, she felt lips on the side of her head.

Birdie had not changed. She continued to make sure Olivia

Jean was eating healthy and feeling all right. There was always a bowl of cabbage or string beans with a big piece of salted bacon or even a bowl of collard greens with corn bread with her midday meal. Daisy said Olivia Jean's face was round and not all pinched from skinniness. Even her nose changed, and that caused Olivia Jean some distress. She thought that it was flatter and fuller, covering half of her face. When she mentioned it to Birdie, the old woman shrugged. "You jus' lucky your skin ain't got so bad an' you still got all your teeth. Sometimes a baby do strange things to your body. Havin' a big nose ain't so a sin. Look at mine." Birdie turned sideways as if she were modeling her nose, and then she did just about everything else in the world to make Olivia Jean laugh, including getting on the floor and turning a cartwheel in the kitchen that ended in Birdie landing so hard on her bottom that the pot on the stove shifted like it was going to fall off the edge.

Birdie got off the floor rubbing her hip. "Guess I shoud'nt a done that move."

"Grandma Birdie, you have to be careful. You coulda hurt yourself." Olivia Jean had been mixing the dough for the biscuits they were having for dinner. She had dropped the rolling pin. The thought of Birdie hurt scared Olivia Jean.

"Don't you fuss none. Stay still or you gonna get that baby in an uproar, too. Just hold still now."

Birdie stroked her hair as Olivia Jean hugged her around the waist. Birdie let her cry for a while, and then she took her apron and dabbed at Olivia Jean's face. "Girl, you look like you been playin' in that there flour 'stead of making up them biscuits. Now get on back to work. I ain't gonna be turning no more flips today. Tomorrow neither. Learned my lesson." She continued to rub her hips as Olivia Jean shaped the biscuits with a jelly-jar and got them ready for the oven. From then on when Olivia Jean thought she was tired of being in the family way or any other little thing she might think to complain of, she thought of Grandma Birdie and her turning a flip in the kitchen just for laughs.

*I*n the New Year the weather had finally changed, and the three women plus Lupe, when he came courting, sat in front of the fire most nights and told stories or swapped recipes. Birdie was telling them about Queenie Monroe, the greatest healer in Colbert County, Alabama, when Olivia Jean gave a soft gasp.

"Grandma Birdie, you know how you told me that when the baby get ready to come, I'm gonna wet myself?" Birdie nodded absently, but Daisy half rose out of her chair. "Well, it done happened already. I wet myself."

"Hold on; we gonna get you to the car. Daisy, hurrup an' find them keys," said Birdie.

"Okay, okay, honey, we goin' to the hospital. We goin' over to Coffee Memorial. They takes colored folks." Daisy started combing the room for the keys to Birdie's old pickup. "Mama, I don't think she gonna make it. Lookit her. Them pains comin' too close. Olivia Jean, why you ain't tell us you was hurtin'? We better get her in the bed."

"G'on. Put her in the big room. I'ma put some water on," said Birdie.

"Yes, baby, you gonna be all right," said Daisy.

"Daisy, hurrup an' git 'er down." Birdie was stern.

•   •   •

Olivia Jean was pushing, pushing, like she was about to do a number two, but nothing was coming out.

Lord, she thought, *can't I change my mind?*

Birdie gave her something to chew. She said it would help the pain go away. But it didn't.

Daisy stroked her hair. Olivia Jean told her, "Get the hell away from me."

Daisy didn't move and kept stroking. Birdie stood at the foot of the bed laughing. Olivia thought that Birdie had an evil side to her that she'd discovered.

"If you two don't get this baby out of me, I'm gonna tell. I'ma tell about that white lightning y'all done took to drinking on the back porch."

Daisy frowned. Birdie laughed and told her to be quiet and hurry up pushing the baby out.

No more closet for me. Ain't nobody gonna trick me into having no more babies.

When Olivia Jean breathed, panting, she could hear her own heart. She strained, but could not hear the baby's. She wanted to hear the baby's heartbeat, too.

There were moments when she lay back and she could rest. But Birdie propped her up and told her to keep breathing. And she had to.

Birdie hummed in her ear. One of those glory songs telling about God and what He could do. *What can God do? Didn't Jesus ask God to take the cup away from Him? If God didn't help Jesus, why would He help me? Jesus was twice as nice as me. Oh, I feel that baby coming from between my legs. She done split me apart.*

Birdie told her to keep on pushing, but she didn't have the strength.

Oh, I wish I had never opened my legs for that brown boy.

I sound like a dog. All I need is my tongue to hang out.

Oh, my God in heaven. Help me. Somebody.

Birdie said it's okay to scream. Olivia Jean screamed loud enough to wake the dead.

She breathed like Daisy told her. *It do hurt, but I ain't gonna die.*

She thought that she had one last scream left in her. It began in her toes, came past her bent knees, and soared out of her mouth without a thought for loudness.

It was done, and Olivia Jean could hear them from a distance. The baby was crying. She touched her own face. She was crying, too.

Daisy brought the bundle over, and her mother was smiling and her face was teary, too. Olivia Jean knew that her mother was sorry the birth hurt her so much. When her mother kissed her, Olivia put up her hand and stroked her mother's face.

Birdie was on the other side, laughing, holding her belly, bent over. At first Olivia Jean couldn't understand what she was saying, but as Daisy put the baby in her arms, Olivia Jean heard Birdie say, "You better have you lots of milk for this big ol' baby boy. He look like a hungry one."

Dammit, I done had me a baby boy, she thought. She pulled the blanket from his face, sniffing him, loving him already. *But that's all right. He's beautiful.*

*H*ow you like our new man?" Daisy and Birdie were sitting in the parlor late at night while Olivia Jean and the baby rested.

"Daisy, he something else. What she gonna name him?"

"She said Adam, on account of he the first boy in a long time."

"That be a good name. I like it."

"Me too, Mama Birdie."

"Let's go to the kitchen and get us a little taste," suggested Birdie. She had a sly grin on her face.

"Don't mind if I do have a swallow. She put us through hell with this one. Hope she ain't gonna have no more soon."

"Daisy, she told me she ain't never gonna do this again."

"Humph. We'll see. Where you put that jug?"

*B*irdie had never been known for being a woman who could tell what was going to happen before it happened. She didn't believe in that type of thing anyway. Queenie didn't either. She said, "A body ain't got no need to know 'bout no time but the time right now." And since Birdie believed in Queenie, though she was long gone, she believed in what she said, too. But Birdie arose this particular day with an ache. She checked all over her body but couldn't find anyplace specifically where the ache came from. It was not in her joints, not in her fingers, not even in her coochie, which felt lonely on account of no Lupe this month. But that ache was still there, all over the place, it seemed. So she dressed the ache up in purple, a royal color. She put on purple slippers and a piece of cloth she twisted into a turban, with a little feather to boot. Birdie felt like a princess in purple. A good, strong color. Made her feel like royalty, and got her to thinking about Queenie. She was sipping a cup of coffee, waiting for that great-grandson of hers to start his crying, when she heard the car pull up into the yard. She peeked out the curtains and the ache passed full over her body, from her toes up to the top of her head. Birdie knew they were in for some trouble. There was Turk, walking wide-legged and slow through her yard up to the porch. She knew nothing was right about him showing up now. She let him in.

He took off his hat before crossing the threshold.

"How do, Miss Birdie? I come to get my family."

She didn't trust herself to speak, but she gestured him into the house and over to the big sofa in the sitting room. She took a deep breath. "Can I get you something?"

He twirled his hat in his hands. "Yes, ma'am. I wanna see my wife and that grandson I got. Daisy called me up and told me that we got a boy, and I got here as soon as I could. How he doing?"

Her hands were on her hips, and it was a struggle to keep them there and not reach out to choke the living daylights out of this man.

"You wanna see Olivia Jean, too?" Birdie finally managed to ask. Her voice was deliberate but not harsh.

"Of course I want to see Olivia Jean. She family, even if she done slipped."

"Slipped on what?"

"You know, she done had this baby outta wedlock. I can't blame the baby. He innocent. And Daisy ain't know nothing about how that child was carrying on behind her back. I bet you she done slept with every boy she could find. Ain't no telling who the baby's daddy really is. No telling."

Birdie stood for a moment, indecisive, irresolute. Anyone else could tell that she was angry. But not Turk. He continued to rattle on and on about Olivia Jean's shortcomings, ending with the fact of the matter was that Olivia Jean was lazy.

"You feel that way? You really feel that way?"

"Yes, ma'am."

"You stay right here then. I'm gonna help you get things straightened out."

Birdie went into the kitchen and reached behind the stove, grasping the broom. She walked back into the parlor with Turk, stood in front of him, lifted the handle, and began to hit him over the head with it. Turk's mouth dropped, and he raised his arms as he tried to duck his beating. He stumbled a couple of times trying to make it to the door.

"You ain't comin' in my house talkin' 'bout my baby like she some type of slut. You the one that probably a slut. When the last time you done called your wife? Sent money for your family? You left them down here like you ain't got no responsibility for takin' care of 'em. You one sorry-assed Negro, and I'm sure 'shamed Daisy brought you home to me."

The screen door slammed behind him as he made his way out of the house. When he left, Birdie stayed by the door for a while to make sure he was truly leaving her property. She rested on the broom, a little short of breath, and closed her eyes.

"Lord, he don't love Daisy and he don't love Olivia Jean, not like he should. Lord, You know I ain't been a praying woman lately. But I beseech You, don't let them go home with this man. Lord, please."

*D*aisy heard him before she saw him. She had been in the backyard of the big house, hanging laundry.

"You ain't nuthin' but a crazy old woman. I don't wanna be in your house anyway. I just came to get my people and we leavin'. Not comin' back neither. None of us," Turk was yelling at Birdie as he made his way down the hill to his car.

Daisy stepped out onto the path and blocked his way.

The first thought she had was that he was bigger than she remembered and that he smelled of beer. His stomach was wide enough to jiggle when he walked, but she embraced him with a smile and felt his old charm start to work. When he released her after their kiss hello, he let his finger travel the length of her arm, and in an instant she was ready for him. She thought of the little house at the bottom of the hill.

He was aiming for the same thing, but between getting out of the house and walking down the path she felt a twinge of reluctance. She steered him to the water instead. Sunlight bounced off the water's edge, and she held her arms around her shoulders. There was an undercurrent of frost in the air. They could see their breath puffing out white against the diamond-sparkling water.

"I shoulda never let you stay down here. We shoulda never been apart." It was Turk grabbing her hand and kissing her knuckles.

"I got somethin' to tell you, Turk."

He bent to her and his lips found the base of her neck and then her right earlobe. She shuddered. "So, you still sensitive there?" His tongue darted again to her earlobe, and Daisy began to feel dizzy. She put out her hand to push him away, but he bent forward again.

"She ain't yours." As the words left her mouth, a great weight lifted and floated away somewhere, and she felt like she could breathe deeply for the first time in years. But Turk hadn't heard.

His mouth was aiming for her lips. Daisy grabbed him by the ears before he could kiss her again and stared him in the eye.

"Turk, Olivia Jean ain't your daughter."

"Woman, what you sayin'?" Turk was confused.

She took him by the old wood fence that stood on the pathway to the lake and told him everything.

"You ain't tellin' me this 'cause you wanna get together with this here preacher, are you?"

"No, he gone. Died jus' a little ways back. An' anyways, I ain't wanna be with him. I'm your wife."

Turk was silent for a while. "I think I always knowed. You just off an' went with me like you ain't had a care in the world. An' you was so beautiful. Wid all the men in the world to choose from, you picked me. A man gotta wonder sometimes."

"I picked you 'cause you saved me. You wanted to take care of me. An' when you opened your mouth up to sing, I loved you right away."

Turk groaned then, snatched her arm, and led her down the path to the little house. At the door he turned to her and said, "I can't wait no longer."

Daisy reached up and stroked his head.

"Me neither."

She had a stash of Pall Malls hidden under the sofa in the living room of the little house left over from before they moved. She dressed and went outside on the back porch, admiring the sun as it made its climb across the morning sky, shooting orange and red tinges outward as if they were small tentacles.

Turk rambled to the door, grinning. His arms slipped around

her waist, and they stood together on the porch for a while. Her hands covered his, and she had just allowed herself to relax against him.

"Glad you told me about Olivia Jean. Makes a difference, you know. Not with me and you. Never. But she ain't really mine, is she? We can leave her down here with your mama. They done got used to each other now; Birdie gonna wanna keep Olivia Jean. We can take the baby back with us. Act like he ours. Treat him like a prince. Now, don't you worry. Things gonna work out fine."

"I thought you loved her, Turk. What you sayin' now? We gonna leave Olivia Jean and take her baby?" Daisy leaned away, twisting her body around so they could be face-to-face. His grip around her waist tightened, and instead of struggling she stopped. Waiting.

"Daisy, I'm sayin' ain't no need of us takin' her back up there with us. She can have a life down here, and we can have a son and each other again. Ain't that what you wanted anyway? For her to stay down here? Now I know she ain't mine, I can stop bein' so upset. Ain't like I done lost my real baby girl, right? She wasn't never mine to begin with. An' I forgives you, Daisy, for not tellin' me. Jus' like I know you forgives me about runnin' around so much. Now it's gonna be right as rain. We gonna have us a new start. Only me and you an' our son. Just us." He pulled her tighter to him, and she felt the beat of his heart. She dropped her hands to her sides and stared out at the lake. A family of ducks glided across the water. Daisy shivered. Turk laughed.

"Let's get you back in the house. You gonna catch a chill if we stay out here."

She nodded as he released her, and took her Pall Malls back to the seat cushion.

• • •

$\mathcal{D}$aisy and Turk were sitting in the front parlor of the little house with the window open, listening to the crickets and the sound of the night. Birdie had agreed to let Turk stay as long as he slept in the little house at the bottom of the hill. Still, she would not make eye contact with him, and she barely addressed him at all.

Olivia Jean came by earlier, holding Adam proudly and pushing him into Turk's arms. At last Turk smiled and told Olivia Jean that she had done a good job, getting him this handsome grandbaby. Olivia Jean beamed. Daisy's palm itched to fly upside his head at the same time. Turk was a slick one. She wondered what Olivia Jean would say when he told her that he wanted Adam but not her.

And then there was his shifting back and forth, the way he didn't look like he wanted to stay more than a minute in the same place. If they were in New York on a Saturday with the breeze as gentle as this January breeze in Alabama, she knew he would be gone. Making tracks through the neighborhood, up the street and back several times, and perhaps to another woman. Maybe where he'd been all these months he'd stayed away.

When she sighed, he asked, "What was that big old sigh for?"

"I used to think that I would die if I lost you, if I thought I had lost your love or wasn't first with you anymore. Made me mad to even think that you loved Olivia Jean more than me. I was fighting my own baby girl over you." She looked out the window past the small dirt yard and to the horizon, watching the moon. And she thought of the journey the Earth made each day, twenty-four endless hours around the sun. And there were the things that happened on Earth, the love, the hatred, the petty jealousies, and then the peace that came after all the drama finished. The peace that God promised, the one that surpassed all understanding, and she knew that she had it. All her secrets were out in the open. That was her peace. She no longer had to hold on to any-one, man or woman. She could make it on her own, but for now it was so much more fun with Birdie, Olivia Jean, Adam, and even old man Lupe. She had her family now. She was content.

"I know better now, Turk. I'ma let you go on. And you let me go, too. You come on down to see Olivia Jean and the baby any-time you want. You always welcome. I'm not gonna tell Olivia Jean the truth, that you didn't want her no more, and I'ma ask the same of you. Tear her apart to think that you want her baby but not her. Tearin' me up inside, too. I always thought you loved her like a daddy should. Guess I was wrong.

"But I ain't goin' back up there with you. And neither is the baby. My home, our home, is with Birdie now. We gonna stay." She didn't add that things could have been different, would have been different between them if he had been good to Olivia Jean and taken her back, acted like he cared.

She watched as he moved to the window. He closed his eyes for a moment and opened them. But his Daisy had not waited. She didn't feel like waiting on him anymore. She was gone up the hill to meet her family for dinner. Mr. Shorty Long's dining room was best for dinners.

Birdie and Lupe were sitting in his living room with the door to the bedroom closed.

"Well, is we is or is we ain't?" Birdie asked.

"What, you wanna get married? Ain't we a little old for that now?"

"Man, I ain't talking 'bout getting no married. I loves things the way they is between us. You wanna change something?"

Birdie watched as Lupe rose from his rocking chair and came over to her on the sofa, looking down at her with his most serious face. She could not see anything in him that resembled Shorty Long. Not his dark face, creased with lines of worry and laughter at the same time. Not his tall, lean figure or the way he breathed hard whenever she was near.

"Yeah, I wanna change something." His voice was strong, resolute.

She waited, looking up at him as his fingers moved to the collar of his shirt and he began to unbutton the top button.

"Birdie, I'm sick and tired of always doing it in the bed. Let's have a go right here."

There was a smile on his thin face, and Birdie giggled and stood, wrapping her arms around Lupe and surrendering as his lips found hers in one satisfying, lip-locking kiss.

His mouth chased the ghost of Shorty Long from her mind.

Summer had arrived in Cold Water Springs, Alabama, and Adam was close to six months old. He was a good baby even if he did receive more than his fair share of loving. If it wasn't Olivia Jean kissing him, it was Daisy or Birdie. Even Mr. Lupe was guilty, and rocked him and held him often. But Olivia Jean was his mother, and he knew her voice.

She wouldn't let Daisy or Birdie get up in the middle of the night. That was her job. Sometimes she napped during the day, and Birdie would get Adam if he was restless. But Olivia Jean made it clear that Adam was her child and her responsibility. Daisy and Birdie had listened, nodded their heads when she made her speech, and laughed when Olivia Jean stepped out of the room. But they did as she asked.

Olivia Jean and Daisy had decided to stay down south with Birdie and Lupe. Turk had said that he'd come to visit them from time to time, but he hadn't. While she missed her father, Olivia Jean was glad things had turned out the way they did. She didn't want to leave Birdie, and she didn't want Daisy going back to being the old Daisy in New York. Things were different in Alabama. They spent more time together; they laughed and found ways to pass the time, like fishing in the lake or skimming stones across the water or reading to Adam. They found time to walk together in the evenings after dinner. Olivia Jean couldn't imagine going back to New York and not ever seeing the stars like they were used to seeing them in Alabama, framed in a velvet sky. She and Daisy were content.

So they stayed with Birdie and became a family. Maybe they didn't plan it that way from the start, but that was the way it turned out.

All the secrets were out now, except one. The one about Preston, who he was and what happened between them. She'd been whispering about it to Adam late at night while everyone else was sleeping. It was only fair that he knew some about his father. When he got big enough, she'd have to take him to New York and collect on that promise that Preston made to her, that he was going to come up to the baby and kiss him and hold him, if only for a minute. She believed Preston would be one sorry man if that was all he wanted after seeing his flesh and blood. But she didn't expect much from him. But did that mean he wouldn't try to see Adam, try to be some kind of daddy? She'd have to wait to find that out.

While they were sitting on the porch that night, she was going to ask Mr. Lupe to watch the baby, and she was going to take a walk with Birdie and Daisy and tell them about Preston and the closet. It was only fair, now that she knew about Mr. Shorty Long and Reverend Percy Walker. They were going to stretch their legs by the lake in front of the house, and she was going to dare Daisy to skim some stones across the surface. And Birdie would join in, because she liked to do things just for the joy of doing. So they'd skim stones and Olivia Jean would share her secret.

She got Adam ready, washing his skin—the color of Alabama earth after a hard rain—and he laughed, one dimple rising in his cheek like his daddy. She couldn't resist. She bent down and tasted his skin. He was the flavor of her love and the peppermint soap she used in his bath. She never thought things would come to this—that she would hold joy in her hands and know that there was such a thing as happily ever after, in the right here and right now.

ACKNOWLEDGMENTS

As always, to my family. My husband and boys have been especially understanding in the writing of this novel, and I appreciate the fact that they gave me the space I asked for, and on several occasions looked at me and told me to disappear.

Dr. Rick Bollinger and James Kemp gave me refuge, laughter, and good company when I needed it.

Gayle Sipes, Esq.—for her discerning eye and love throughout this process.

K. Sue Meyer, Esq., and Effie Accoff—for their long-standing friendship and support.

Overwhelming gratitude to Kim and Laurick Ingram, Sareeta and Harry Norton, Karen and Henry Noble, Phyllis and Ira Spieler, and TaWanna Furbush.

To my girls: L. Michelle Ligon, Esq.; Lisa M. Holt, Esq.; Gloria Chance; Sheila Griffin, Esq.; and Jacqueline Gayle-Kelly, Esq.—each one of you has it down—"Why you callin' me; shouldn't you be writing?"

To my TWB—Dr. J. Sid Davis—miss any planes lately?

Many thanks to my agent, Elizabeth Sheinkman, and her assistant, Felicity Blunt. I appreciate your work on my behalf.

Many thanks to Anika Streitfeld, who taught me so much during this whole process and who never gave up on me. That means so much to a writer.

And last, thanks to the Chustz and Williams families, too, who have loved and supported me through this journey.

Going Down South

Bonnie J. Glover

A READER'S GUIDE

A Conversation with Bonnie J. Glover

Bonnie J. Glover and Barb Kuroff first met in 1999 at the Florida Suncoast Writers' Conference in St. Petersburg, Florida, when Ms. Kuroff was a senior editor at F & W Books. They have been friends ever since.

Barb Kuroff: What was your inspiration for writing this book?

Bonnie J. Glover: A number of years ago I read *Bastard Out of Carolina* by Dorothy Allison. It is a beautiful book, masterfully written, about a woman who has to make some of the same choices Daisy Stone has to make about the man in her life and about her child. While reading *Bastard Out of Carolina*, I thought about how different women may make different decisions, depending on an infinite number of variables. I wondered what would happen if I wrote about a character with challenges similar to those of the mother in Allison's novel, but who handled things in another way. I knew that the themes of motherhood and choice were going to figure in

Going Down South, but I didn't know exactly how the novel was to come together.

BK: How important is setting in *Going Down South?* Why did you choose to move the story "down south"?

BG: Many families in the late 1950s and 1960s were faced with the same type of dilemma as the Stones faced in *Going Down South:* what to do with a pregnant child? The stigma was very real, even in the so-called liberal cities such as New York and especially in communities such as the one Olivia Jean grew up in where people know one another and looked after children in the neighborhood. In those days, families oftentimes did ship their daughters to relatives "down south" until after the baby arrived. Then the baby was "adopted" by another relative, and the actual birth mother was treated as a sibling, an aunt, or a cousin. There were also "homes" for unwed mothers, but those were often expensive and beyond the reach of black families.

So Olivia Jean is forced to leave the environment that she knows well and the likely censure of her northern community for a supposedly safer home in Cold Water Springs, Alabama. In essence, Olivia Jean moves down south because many of her contemporaries would have done the same thing if *they* had unplanned, out-of-wedlock pregnancies.

BK: *Going Down South* deals with some weighty themes, including sexism, racism, abortion, and rape. What would you say is the overall theme in *Going Down South* and why?

BG: While all of these themes are important, I believe that *Going Down South* is about the ties that bind us to our children. If we are committed parents, we make sacrifices. And a piece of paper doesn't guarantee continued love. If that were the case, couples would be scrambling to get that paper. I wanted to show how the weight of all of the problems that people experience in the real world will affect the family structure. These problems may even destroy the unit that is in place. Or the family may be resilient enough to survive, albeit in some mutated fashion.

BK: Do you have a favorite character in the novel?

BG: I like all three of my main female characters for different reasons. Olivia Jean is gutsy: She doesn't know what she'll have to face being a single mother in a very repressive society, but she's willing to take the chance. Daisy is realistic: She makes the same choice as her daughter but uses a man to bolster and take care of her. And then there is Birdie. Perhaps she makes the most difficult choice of the three women— sleeping with the enemy in plain sight—and gets punished over and over for her transgressions. So I would probably say that Birdie is my favorite character. In many ways she is the strongest, and yet she is also the most joyous.

BK: Are any of the characters in *Going Down South* based on real people? Which character do you identify with most closely?

BG: I think, in a lot of ways the characters in *Going Down South* are bits of women whom I have known over the years. I am always looking at people and how they interact, especially with their children. I have seen a lot of mothers like Daisy, who have a difficult time parenting when there are other issues intruding in their lives and perhaps even overwhelming them. People with Birdie's disposition are rarer, but I have come across some women who have a joy in their hearts that isn't mitigated by the wear and tear of life. And I have met a great many Olivia Jeans, who need guidance and friends to help them along the way.

I know I said earlier that Birdie was my favorite character, but I actually identify more closely with Daisy. Perhaps a better word for what I feel about Daisy is empathy. She lives in a world that she believes is secure and yet it isn't; it's very fragile, and she is holding on by a thread. Her husband haunts the streets; her daughter is pregnant at fifteen. She has to feel that her situation is desperate and that it is, in large part, her own fault. Her initial solution is to send Olivia Jean away and make things right with Turk. She can't see past the man she married at fifteen to a daughter who needs her guidance. I understand her in a way that perhaps I don't understand Birdie, who has not let the troubles of her life make her bitter or mean-spirited.

BK: Which character was hardest for you to write?

BG: Daisy was the hardest for me to write. She was almost a blank slate for a long time until I started to understand her motivations. I had to do a great deal of thinking about Daisy and the adversity she must have endured that shifted her mind-set to the point where she was not a very good parent to Olivia Jean. How can you be happy with anyone else if you are not happy with yourself? If you have felt abandoned at every turn in your life, how would you handle a relationship with your child?

Maybe I had to think about Daisy for so long before I was able to shape her because she was the closest to me in age; she had the husband and the teenager. We had so many things in common, and yet her approach to life was different from mine. I had to envision why this was the case. Neither Birdie's nor Olivia Jean's lives were as difficult to imagine. They were almost formed from the moment I started to write.

BK: How would you describe the relationship between Birdie and Lupe?

BG: In many ways they don't have a very complicated relationship. Despite Birdie's wild character, I think she feels at home with Lupe. And perhaps he's the type of man she needed after the turbulence of Shorty Long and their ill-fated marriage. A few years ago, Patti LaBelle had a song entitled "The Right Kinda Lover," and in it she sings, "A good old man, that's what I got." To me, that line sums up Lupe. He's a good man who loves Birdie. And because he loves her, he accepts and loves her family also.

BK: Did you have trouble envisioning a household with three women, since you don't have any sisters or daughters?

BG: Absolutely not. I have a lot of girlfriends who have sisters and daughters. I love to watch them all interact. One friend of mine, in particular, has three sisters, and while they are often playful and loving, some of the funniest times I've been privy to have been when they are in the midst of a family squabble. The scene at dinner where Birdie and Olivia Jean gang up on Daisy so that Daisy leaves the table might have come directly from my friend and her family. Sisters seem able to vanquish one another with folded arms and mean looks. My brothers would have laughed at me if I had ever tried anything like that on them.

BK: Food plays an important role in *Going Down South*. Do you have a sense of why this is so?

BG: During the 1950s and early 1960s, the dinner table was an important part of American culture, and certainly Southern culture. In *Going Down South* we see the characters progress from not sharing their meals together to mealtimes becoming a vital focus and revitalization for the family. The preparation and eating of food becomes a foundation from which the women begin to grow their family anew. When Birdie, Daisy, and Olivia Jean finally move into the big house and their meals become more formal, there is a sense that this ritual will continue and that the family will persevere.

BK: The male characters in *Going Down South* are mostly in the background. Why is this so?

BG: This is a book about women and mothers. Although men play a substantial role in their lives, the book depicts the struggle of these women to find strength in and from one another. Turk features very prominently in the lives of Daisy and Olivia Jean. Shorty Long is a tragic figure in *Going Down South*. He is a man haunted by the fact that he has to give up the love of his life because he is most interested in saving his entire family. And, of course, there is Reverend Walker, Preston, and Lupe Rawlins. So men are crucial to the novel but remain in the background so that the women protagonists may be more visible and their stories told.

BK: You've talked about identifying with Daisy and admiring Birdie. What, if anything, do you have in common with Olivia Jean?

BG: Olivia Jean and I both share the love of reading. When I was younger, there was no better thing for me to do than to put my nose in a book and imagine I was somewhere other than where I was. Now it's the same thing. I can lose myself in a good book at the drop of a hat. Growing up, the first novel I recall reading was *Little Women* by Louisa May Alcott. I progressed to Jane Austen, Mark Twain, and, finally, in my early teens, discovered the writers of the Harlem Renaissance. Langston Hughes became my favorite poet, and I spent hours reading his words aloud in a small hallway downstairs that led to the front steps of our two-story apartment building in Brooklyn, New York. I thought I wanted to be an orator, but I couldn't figure out how someone got paid to make speeches.

Now I read an eclectic mix of writers. I admire Ha Jin immensely for his ability to create a picture with very few words. I believe that Katherine Dunn is a genius; *Geek Love* is one of my favorites of all time. Zora Neale Hurston was a wonderful talent. I've been reading a great deal of Octavia Butler, a writer we lost much too soon, and some short stories of Toni Cade Bambara. I also admire Jamaica Kincaid, Louise Erdrich, and, of course, Maya Angelou.

Reading has helped me broaden my horizons and believe that anything is possible. It does the same for Olivia Jean. Reading makes the unbearable bearable, while putting a taste for a different type of life just beyond reach. It would be fair to say, at least of myself, that reading whetted my appetite for more, which in turn caused so many other wonderful things to happen in my life because I wanted to be fed.

Reading Group Questions
and Topics for Discussion

1. How does history repeat itself with the three women in *Going Down South*? What does Daisy inherit from Birdie, and Olivia Jean from Daisy and Birdie? How does this compare to the lessons and characteristics that have been passed down in your own family?

2. How would you describe Birdie and Olivia Jean's relationship? Why is their relationship so different from Daisy and Birdie's?

3. How would you describe the tension between Daisy and Olivia Jean? Daisy and Birdie? How is Olivia Jean's relationship with Birdie different from the others?

4. Why do you think Shorty Long does not try to stop Daisy from leaving Cold Water Springs?

5. Turk desperately wants a son. Do you think this has to do with the era, or, in your experience, do most men still think

they want sons? How, if at all, is Turk changed by being a grandfather? How has fatherhood changed the men in your life?

6. Olivia Jean has to make a momentous decision about whether or not to continue her pregnancy. How much of her choice is motivated by social climate in the early 1960s, and how much by her inability to appreciate the nature of the decision she was making? Do you think her decision would be different if she were a teenager today?

7. Why do Shorty Long and Birdie feel compelled to end their relationship? Can you imagine a way in which they might have stayed together?

8. How is Birdie changed by her time in jail? What do you think she learns in "the big house"?

9. How would you characterize Daisy's relationship with the men in her life?

10. Why is Turk so important to Daisy? How does their relationship evolve? Do you see their marriage as successful?

11. Were you surprised by Percy Walker's involvement in the women's lives? Why do you think he disavows Olivia Jean when she goes to visit him?

12. What role does Lupe play in each of the women's lives? Why is Daisy so wary of him?

13. Why do you believe Shorty Long insisted on having dinner with Daisy and Birdie every Sunday? Do you think he achieved what he intended to achieve? Why or why not?

14. How did your perceptions of each character change as the story progressed? Which of the women changes the most over the course of the novel?

15. Which of the three women do you relate to the most and why?

ABOUT THE AUTHOR

BONNIE J. GLOVER lives in Florida with her husband and two children where, in addition to writing, she mediates employment disputes and helps train new mediators.